THE
CAPTIVE
KINGDOM

THE ASCENDANCE SERIES
⸺ BOOK FOUR ⸺

THE
CAPTIVE
KINGDOM

JENNIFER A. NIELSEN

SCHOLASTIC PRESS • NEW YORK

Library of Congress Cataloging-in-Publication Data

Names: Nielsen, Jennifer A., author.
Title: The captive kingdom / Jennifer A. Nielsen.
Description: First edition. | New York: Scholastic Press, 2020. |
Series: The Ascendance series; 4 | Audience: Ages 8–12. |
Audience: Grades 4–6. | Summary: Ascendant King Jaron believes that his kingdom,
Carthya, is at peace, so he and his bethrothed, Imogen, are sailing home from a
trade mission when their ship is attacked by Prozarians, and Jaron and
several of his friends are taken prisoner: the Prozarian captain seems
to believe he had something to do with his parents' deaths and they also
know a great deal about Jaron's long-missing older brother, Darius, the
rightful heir to Carthya — who may be alive after all.
Identifiers: LCCN 2019047465 (print) | LCCN 2019047466 (ebook) |
ISBN 9781338551082 (hardcover) | ISBN 9781338551105 (ebk)
Subjects: LCSH: Kings and rulers — Juvenile fiction. | Pirates — Juvenile
fiction. | Inheritance and succession — Juvenile fiction. | Princes —
Juvenile fiction. | Brothers — Juvenile fiction. | Adventure stories. |
CYAC: Kings, queens, rulers, etc. — Fiction. | Pirates — Fiction. |
Inheritance and succession — Fiction. | Princes — Fiction. |
Brothers — Fiction. | Adventure and adventurers —
Fiction. | LCGFT: Action and adventure fiction.
Classification: LCC PZ7.N5672 Cap 2020 (print) |
LCC PZ7.N5672 (ebook) | DDC 813.6 [Fic] — dc23
LC record available at https://lccn.loc.gov/2019047465
LC ebook record available at https://lccn.loc.gov/2019047466

3 2021

Printed in the U.S.A.   23

First edition, October 2020
Book design by Christopher Stengel

To Robin,

because true heroes still exist

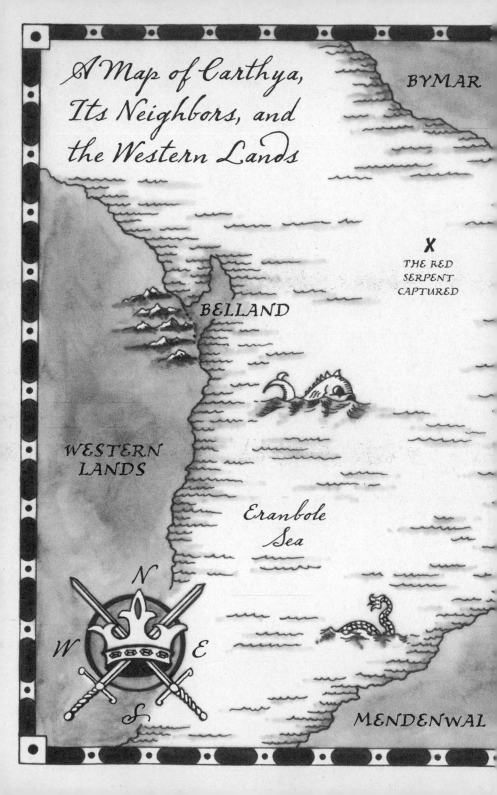

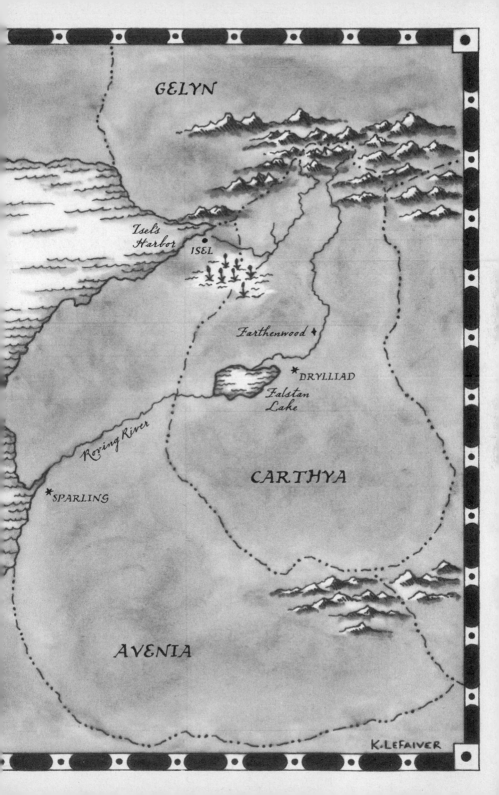

At sixteen years of age, Jaron Artolius Eckbert III claimed victory in a war launched against Carthya. A year later, he would go on to marry his great love, Imogen, but the events of this story describe some of what happened during that missing year.

· PROLOGUE ·

One may ask, how is the great King Jaron described by those who know him?

The answer rarely includes the word "great," unless the word to follow is "fool," though I have also heard "disappointment," "frustration," and "chance that he'll get us all killed."

There are other answers, of course.

"He was born to cause trouble, as if nothing else could make him happy." My nursemaid said that, before I was even four years of age. I still believe her early judgments of me were unfair. Other than occasionally climbing over the castle balconies, and a failed attempt at riding a goat, what could I have possibly done to make her say such a thing?

My childhood tutor: "Jaron has a brilliant mind, if one can

pin him down long enough to teach him anything he doesn't think he already knows. Which one rarely can."

It wasn't that I thought I already knew everything. It was that I had already learned everything I cared to know from *him*, and besides, I didn't see the importance of studying in the same way as my elder brother, Darius. He would become king. I would take a position among his advisors or assume leadership within our armies. My parents had long abandoned the idea of me becoming a priest, at the tearful request of our own priest, who once announced over the pulpit that I "belonged to the devils more than the saints."

To be fair, I had just set fire to the pulpit when he said it. Mostly by accident.

My mother loved me, and so did my father, though I frequently upset him with my inability to live up to Darius's example. That's why I had to be sent away at age ten, to save my father embarrassment while I was molded into a proper prince overseas.

I had no intention of becoming a proper anything, but I left willingly and for one reason above all others: I no longer wished to be the subject of so many conversations.

If only life were that simple.

Soon after my ship launched across the Eranbole Sea, pirates attacked and the ship was lost. I was presumed dead, which was a surprise to me since I considered myself very much alive. The second surprise came after my father found me in Avenia. Rather than bring me home, he asked that I remain missing, preserving our small country of Carthya from having to go to war.

And so I became Sage the orphan, certain no one would ever speak of me again.

Yet they did.

Mrs. Turbeldy, the mistress of the Orphanage for Disadvantaged Boys, called me a liar and a thief. I resented the insult. Lying was beneath me.

Master Bevin Conner, the man who took me from the orphanage with a plan to install an orphan boy as a false prince on the throne, called me a devil prince. That may be true enough, but what he didn't know was that I was the true prince, now to become king since Conner had killed my parents and brother, hoping to overthrow the kingdom.

Two other boys competed against me in the plot to become the false prince. Tobias believed me to be uneducated, and perhaps compared to him, I was. Roden believed himself to be a superior swordsman, and in that, he was mistaken, though I have yet to convince him of that fact.

Conner's servant, Mott, became my trusted friend and most reliable companion in battle. No doubt he had plenty to say about me, though most of his cursings against me were well deserved.

And then there was Imogen, the one person who always saw me for who I truly was. Not as a prince, or as an orphan who too often caused trouble, or even as a fool. She simply saw me. Though we're both still young, I hope to marry Imogen one day.

It took a near revolution, a defeat of the pirate king, war, more than a few near-death experiences, and one poorly conceived jump over a cliff, but eventually Carthya was at peace.

Now I am king, known as the Ascendant King of Carthya. The title is a great honor. But since I have never held on to a kind word about me for more than a few months, change is certainly coming.

And when it comes, if the worst I am called is a "great fool," I will be very relieved.

ONE

For the past several months, my country of Carthya had been at peace. Imogen and I were happier than ever, our enemies were at bay, and the closest thing I had to a mortal wound was a bruise on my thigh from when I'd bumped into my own throne last month.

In other words, I was bored.

I was also irritable, restless, and, according to Imogen, the sole reason we'd gone through eight cooks in the last month. Nine, if we counted the one who ran out crying before we'd even offered her the position. That was only half of my recent failings. I had yet to fully explain to Imogen why the Carthyan flag appeared to have been torn free from the center spire of the castle.

For those reasons, when Imogen had ducked her head into my meeting with the regents three weeks ago, suggesting we go on a trading mission to Bymar, servants had actually come running into the throne room to see what all the commotion was. There was no commotion, only me doing a literal somersault across the meeting table and frightening Mistress Kitcher so

much that she leapt away and lost her wig. Hence all the screaming. Mine, not hers.

Three days after that, to the relief of a significant percent-
age of the Carthyan population, we had set sail for Bymar, where
Amarinda was born and raised. She had been a princess there
and betrothed to the throne of Carthya, which originally meant
she was intended to marry my brother Darius. After his death,
the task fell to me, but since Amarinda would have rather married a mossy rock, we broke the arrangement. She and Tobias
were now betrothed, as were Imogen and I, and all was well.

Especially tonight.

The voyage had been an enormous success, an advantage to
all parties, and now, a little over two weeks later, we were headed
home as guests of the Avenian pirates aboard the *Red Serpent*, a
small but comfortable cog ship. It felt right to be going home,
though I already dreaded what awaited me. More meetings,
more formal suppers. More routine.

With only three days left in our journey, I was spending
the waning hours of sunlight studying Bevin Conner's old journal. I had read through it dozens of times since his death, always
searching for a better understanding of his twisted motives and
corrupted sense of heroism.

Conner had clearly specified the items that were to be
passed along to his heirs, but as he had none, the items had
stayed with me. Imogen wanted all his former possessions
destroyed. She believed they were holding me too much in the
past, but I felt there was more to be learned from them.
Particularly his journal.

I glanced up as a cheer rose from the lower deck, where nearly all the pirates were at supper. That was a good thing. If they were eating, they weren't stealing.

Over the last few days on this ship, I had often pointed out to Imogen that other than their constant attempts to steal from us, these pirates had been a pleasant crew. That was small comfort to her, but as I also had a long history of thieving, I could hardly criticize the pirates for the same behavior.

"Many of these same pirates tried to kill you once," she observed.

To be accurate, it was more than once, though I didn't feel the need to correct her. And to be perfectly accurate, I was one of "these same pirates" myself.

"Jaron, there's a ship on the starboard side," Erick called down to me. He was the pirate king, our helmsman, and a fine cook of fresh-caught fish, I'd recently discovered. But now his usually friendly voice bore a note of concern. "It's on a course aimed directly for us."

I replaced Conner's book in my shoulder bag and hurried up to the quarterdeck where he was. The ship he had observed was a caravel with a total of four mainsails; two large sails above the deck rose as high as the crow's nest, which was flanked by two smaller topsails. The crow's nest itself was accessed by a rope ladder. Above the topsail a flag hung from a mast. It was neither Avenian nor pirate, but instead a simple green flag with white trim. I did not recognize it.

A bowsprit jutted out from the front of the ship with a raised forecastle deck that would give the ship's crew an advantage in fighting. It was wide enough for two rooms to fit below the quarterdeck, wherein we had only one, the captain's quarters. Erick and I had debated multiple times about whether he or I should have that room. I had won, on the condition that I let my thirteen-year-old adopted brother, Fink, bunk there too, so he would keep fewer crewmen awake with his talking each night.

The ship angled to match our exact change in course, and this time, a shiver crawled up my spine.

"What's the firepower on our ship?" I asked Erick.

"The usual number of cannons, but they've shown us no aggression."

I disagreed. "The cannons on their deck are already manned. Can we outrun them?"

Erick shook his head and turned the wheel again to steer us away. He whistled at another pirate to take the helm, leaving him with instructions that sent my heart pounding. "Take us in any direction away from that ship. Whatever else happens, don't let it get broadside of us."

Because if it did, its cannon fire would sink us.

Erick and I raced down the stairs, with Erick shouting orders to every pirate we passed along the way. He called back to me, "I'll get our cannons loaded as well, but they're a bigger ship. Unless we get a lucky hit first, if they intend to harm us, they can do it. You'd better get your people to safety."

I nodded at him and ran into the wardroom on the main deck where Imogen, Fink, and Mott were playing cards. "There's trouble," I said. "We've got to hide as many people as we can."

Without a word, Mott stood and went belowdecks, calling for all Carthyans on board to meet him near the bunks.

Imogen looked at Fink. "Go into the galley and get as much food together as you can carry. Then report directly to Mott."

She followed me back onto the deck where it was evident the other ship was closing in. A captain stood at the forecastle with a sword aimed directly at us.

"Is this another pirate ship?" she asked. "Are we being raided?"

I shook my head. "Erick assured me this part of the Eranbole Sea belongs to the Avenian pirates. I don't think this is a raid."

"Then it's targeting us?" Her brows pressed together. "Why?"

I gave Imogen my shoulder bag and took her by the hand belowdecks where Mott was in the middle of assigning everyone a task.

"There are a few false walls in the storage areas. Take your places and the rest of us will seal you in. Stay as long as you can stand it, or until one of us pulls you out." He looked around the group. "Fink, Amarinda, Imogen —"

"No!" she said. "Mott, I want to help fight!"

I turned to her. "There will be no fight when they attack. We cannot match their strength. You must hide."

"As must you," Mott said. "Jaron, there are four spaces. The fourth is for you."

"Absolutely not!" I said. "Where's my sword?"

Roden, the captain of my guard, touched my arm. "You're the king. More than anyone else, you need to hide."

I shook my head at him, ready with a response, but there was no time for even that before someone called from up on the main deck, "Jaron, you need to see this."

I gave Imogen's hand a squeeze and said to Mott, "Begin hiding the others. I'll be back. Can someone find my sword?" Then I raced up the steps back onto the main deck.

The invaders had raised a new flag, one with painted black letters that had begun to drip with the spray of water, leaving long streaks beneath the writing itself. It read one word only: JARON.

My heart was nearly beating out of my chest as I called down to Mott. "No one comes onto this main deck until this is resolved. Those are my orders."

"Why?" Imogen replied. "What is happening up there?"

"Get everyone into hiding! Every one of you."

"What about you?" Amarinda cried. "Jaron, come down here with us!"

"Mott?" I called. "Do you have my orders?"

A long silence followed before he answered, "The king has spoken. You all know what to do."

Erick pounded up the stairs, giving me a quick glare. "I'll go anywhere I want on my ship, and I will give the order of when to fire and when to attack." Then his eye turned to the sail with my name written on it. "Oh."

"We're not going to fire on them," I said. "We've got to defeat them."

"How?"

I walked to the side of the ship as it turned broadside of us, revealing the ship's name: *Shadow Tide*. On a single whistle I heard from where I stood, its gun ports opened to reveal a dozen cannons all aimed our way.

I looked over at Erick and sighed. "Well, that's the part I haven't figured out. But it seems defeating them is the only choice we have left."

· TWO ·

Now that we were closer, I got my first real look at the captain, a tall woman of strong stature, with a square face and eyes that seemed to penetrate the distance between our ships. Her short-cropped hair was black and mostly pulled to one side, enough that I wondered if her head naturally tilted sideways to rest. She wore a long, black leather coat with a green blouse barely visible beneath it, trousers, and tall boots.

The captain called out, "In the name of our monarch, I call on you to surrender, or you will all die."

I shouted back, "All three of us? It hardly seems worth the trouble of you arming all those cannons."

"You are not a crew of three."

I looked around to be sure. "Three is all I count. In fact, if you have any spare crewmen, we could use a few extra. Unless you still intend to fire on us, in which case you'd only be drowning your own crew."

The captain had moved from the forecastle of her deck to the side of her ship directly across from me, allowing me to have a better look at her. She'd given no orders to have her crewmen fire on us yet, so I assumed she wanted to figure me out as much as I needed to understand her.

She called out again, this time adding a new threat. "Surrender your ship, or we'll sink it!"

I called back, "Go ahead and sink it. We're all very capable swimmers here."

There was a short pause as the captain looked at her other crewmen on deck. Then she shouted, "I meant that if we attack, you all will die."

"No, I don't think we will," I replied. "But if you're so concerned, you could lower your cannons and we can talk. What is it you want?"

"We want Jaron."

Her tone was icy enough to send a chill through me. I glanced over at Erick, who was staring at the *Shadow Tide* with brows furrowed tight together. One hand was on his knife, but it was still sheathed. I said to him, "How difficult would it be for them to board this ship?"

Almost as if in answer, arrows were fired from their deck to ours, each one with hooks attached. Erick yelled for his crew to come up on deck as he and I raced to detach the hooks. They were embedded deeply into the wood, so prying them out was no small matter, and before I got one out, three more had attached. Groups of eight to ten men were at the other end of the ropes now attached to us and were pulling our ship closer to theirs.

The next set of arrows to be launched were fire tipped and

these flew high, cutting through the sails and igniting them as they passed through.

"Lower the sails!" Erick cried. "Preserve what you can!"

Finally, our ships were so close that I could see the captain's piercing eyes, and she was certainly focusing on me.

"My name is Captain Jane Strick, in service of our monarch."

"Of what nationality?"

"Prozarian."

I squinted. "No, you're not. The Prozarians are extinct."

She widened her arms. "Do we look extinct?"

I scratched my jaw and looked over the great numbers of her crew. "Well, to be honest . . . a few of the people in back could pass as corpses."

If she enjoyed my joke — which was reasonably accurate — she didn't show it. "Your crew will fare no better, unless you turn over Jaron to me. Are you him?"

"Jaron will be sent over to you shortly," I said. "Truly, the crew will be glad to be rid of him. In exchange, you will agree not to cause any further damage to this ship, nor attempt to board it."

The smile remained, but something in her eyes was frozen. "In exchange, I will agree not to sink the ship. Your crewmen will be given the option to join my crew, rather than to be left out here to die a slow and miserable death."

I shrugged. "Serving on your crew is already a slow and miserable death, I'm sure. Jaron will be sent over to you, and you will depart with him immediately. No one else."

Strick gestured toward one of her men, a round-faced bulge of flesh who seemed to be built of rock embedded in mud. I immediately named him Lump. In turn, he lifted a long strip of wood with a lip on both sides to attach it to both ships.

"Prepare to be boarded," Strick said.

Erick looked at me. "I can only give you an extra second or two, but you must take it."

I started toward him. "No, don't!" But it was too late.

Erick crossed directly in front of the gangplank, raising his sword. "Not one of you is getting on this ship while there is life left in me."

Strick smiled again. "As you wish." And with a wave of her hand, another arrow was fired, striking Erick directly in the chest. Time seemed to freeze as he gasped, dropped his sword, then fell to the ground.

I felt the hit as if I had taken it myself, and pain immediately filled me. In a panic, I knelt beside him, pressing my hand to the wound. I yelled to any pirate who might hear me, "Get a rag!"

But Erick put his hands over mine and lifted them from his chest. "Forgive me," he said. "Forgive me . . . *Sage*."

"Sage?" the captain echoed.

I looked up and saw that Strick had already crossed the gangplank and was crouched above us, listening in. "Is that your name, boy? Sage?"

Without a word I stood as she jumped to the deck, ordering two of her men who had followed her across, "Toss this body overboard. It's depressing to see it."

I pushed between them, shaking my head. "He deserves a proper burial."

One of the men — a brute with a shock of red hair — shoved me aside, knocking me to the deck. "At sea, this is as proper a burial as he might get."

"Will that be enough of a burial, when I'm finished with you?" I asked, earning myself a kick.

The other man lifted Erick's body beneath the arms and began dragging him to the aft side of the deck while the captain walked forward, taking herself on a tour. I remained where I was.

"This is a pirate ship?" she asked. "Are you one of the pirates, Sage?"

"Yes."

"You must forgive me for interrupting your pleasant evening."

"I don't forgive; I stab."

"With this sword?" She snapped her fingers and a Prozarian I had not noticed before stepped forward, with my sword in his filthy hands, an insult I tolerated only because I had no other choice. "Do you claim this?"

"That's a fine sword, but this does not mean Jaron is on this ship."

"We traced him to Bymar a week ago. The port master we spoke to informed us this was the ship Prince Jaron is supposed to be on."

"I know that port master. He's older than these waters. I wouldn't trust his word."

"I trust every word given on one's deathbed."

A shudder ran through me. The port master was in good health when we left Bymar. If he was on his deathbed, it was because Captain Strick put him there.

She returned my sword to the filthy Prozarian, along with instructions to take it to her office. Then she pressed her lips together and stared at me. "You will produce Jaron on this deck in the next five seconds, or this ship will be boarded, searched, and then sunk."

I let out a slow breath and closed my eyes, trying to prepare myself for whatever might happen next. She had killed Erick without flinching, so I had no doubt she would carry out these new threats. I stood and squared myself to her. "I'm Jaron. Take me."

"No, I'm Jaron." Roden raced up the stairs, sword in hand. "Take me."

"No, I'm Jaron." Tobias followed him exactly, except his sword was held upside down. "Take me."

Strick lifted her hand, curling the fingers toward her. And one by one, Prozarians began crossing onto our ship.

THREE

A century ago, no army in the known world was more feared than the Prozarians. Their interest wasn't occupation of any territory they conquered, but rather, they bled the land of its resources and wealth before abandoning it like ashes from a spent fire. Eventually, countries began to unite for their own defense, laying aside old grudges to target a common enemy. Over time, the Prozarians themselves became the spent fire, the topic of history books and stories shared by aging soldiers in dark taverns. By the time I was a child, nobody spoke of the Prozarians anymore.

I suspected that was about to change.

These next Prozarians to board our ship were heavily armed, and each carried a length of rope. I bolted for the quarterdeck but ran straight into a fist that seemed to have appeared out of nowhere. Behind me, Roden was keeping up a fair fight until we heard a cry from Tobias and saw a knife raised against him. For his sake, we had no choice but to give in.

Little mercy was shown in the way we were thrown against the side railing and searched for weapons. Our arms were yanked behind our backs as each of our hands were tied. The man behind me must've thought he was clever for double knotting my binds. I even told him so, though my compliment also came with commentary on his rancid breath that earned me a third hit. His work wasn't so clever after all. He wasn't halfway back to the captain before I was through the first knot.

"Search below," the captain shouted, and my heart slammed into my throat.

"Where are the others?" I whispered.

"Creating a distraction," Roden said.

"No, those were not my orders."

"Imogen says since she's marrying you, she is not subject to any of your orders."

She wanted to make that an issue now? Imogen had a general resentment of the term "orders."

"What is the distraction?" I asked.

Tobias carefully looked around us before whispering, "She opened a porthole and discovered she could reach the lifeboat. She planned to release it."

"With who on it?"

Roden shrugged. "You."

A few of the Prozarians who had been belowdecks now pounded back up the steps, shouting, "Captain, the prince is escaping!"

From my position, I wasn't able to see, but Imogen must have done a decent job creating some humanlike figure in the lifeboat, for I heard a string of curses, then the captain ordering those crewmen back onto the *Shadow Tide* to prepare for pursuit.

Yet no sooner had they crossed back over the gangplank than an explosion came from the direction Captain Strick had just been looking. Not an explosion, really. It was more like a pop or a thump, unimpressive enough that the entire ship of Prozarians burst into laughter.

I angled onto one knee to see what had caused the laughter and it was well deserved. The figure that should have been me was blown onto its side, revealing it to be nothing but a bucket with an oar for a back, and clothes stuffed around it.

The captain turned to look at us, still seated on the deck. I only shrugged. "Jaron loved to experiment with explosives. So much so that everyone believed one day he'd blow himself up."

"That wasn't enough to frighten a fly," the captain said. "If that's the best they can do, we have nothing to fear." Gesturing to us, she directed her crewmen, "Take these three onto the *Shadow Tide* and find a room that locks. Despite that little game, one of them is obviously the prince. The rest of you will continue to search this ship. Find something to persuade the real Jaron to confess."

I stood, having undone my ropes. "Captain, I am Jaron."

"The pirate we killed called you Sage."

Roden and Tobias stood simultaneously, each of them still bound but claiming, "I am Jaron."

"Take them all," she said. "I'll sort them later."

One by one, we were walked over the gangplank but were made to stand on the main deck of the *Shadow Tide* while a place was prepared for us.

I looked back on our ship, watching Prozarians carry up

our bags, our weapons and food, Tobias's medicines, and any-thing else they could take. So far, I'd seen none of our people. Were they all in hiding, or had something happened to them belowdecks? I was almost ill with worry.

While quietly undoing their binds, I hissed to Roden and Tobias, "Let me identify myself as I am, or it will be worse when you're found out."

"What happens to you when it's found out?" Tobias asked.

"We're borrowing time until the three of us can figure out a plan."

Still on the *Red Serpent*, Captain Strick called out, "We intend to sink this ship. You may join my crew and serve me with loyalty, or you may go down with your ship. There are no other options."

After a pause, the pirates gradually began emerging from belowdecks. Most of them looked my way as they lined up to cross the gangplank. Some seemed apologetic, but others glared at me as if this was somehow my fault. Maybe it was, I still didn't know.

"Where's Erick?" one of them shouted, but no one answered, and by the expressions on their faces, they were already figuring out the answer for themselves. Pirates were not easily deflated, and seeing it deepened the ache in my chest.

They passed by Strick as they crossed over, muttering their required pledges of loyalty, and then seated themselves on the deck of the *Shadow Tide*, waiting for their next orders. I didn't blame any of them. Not when their only alternative was death.

"We found this one hiding behind a false wall," a Prozarian called from below. Beside me, Tobias nearly fell to his knees when Amarinda was pushed up the steps, and my heart stood still. With eyes widened by fear, she briefly glanced over at us, then gave her attention to Captain Strick, who crossed directly in front of her.

"How many of you were in hiding down there?" she asked.

Amarinda's brow creased. "I . . . I don't know. I think I was the only one."

"If anyone else is hiding, they will regret it. You, my dear, are lucky you were found." She personally escorted Amarinda across the gangplank, then shoved her into the arms of the man I had nicknamed Lump. "Take her to my office and tell Wilta to guard her. She'll be safest there."

"Amarinda!" Tobias darted forward when she pushed away from Lump, but a man swatted him from behind, sending him to all fours. Tobias's face twisted with what must have been a mighty sting across his lower back.

Captain Strick flashed a sudden smile. "Is that her name? Amarinda? That's a fine bit of luck."

"Let her go!" Tobias's voice was almost a growl.

"Prince Jaron is betrothed to a girl named Imogen. So you are not Jaron." Her stare lifted to Roden and me. "That means he is one of you two." She pointed to Tobias and ordered who-ever happened to be around her, "Kill the third."

"Captain, wait!" I said. "His name is Tobias, and he's a physician, or something close to it."

"You'll need his help on a ship of this size," Roden added.

She looked him over. "He's young."

"He's just completed the exams to begin formal training." I

knew that because at supper a day ago, Tobias had prattled on about the exams for what felt like hours.

She frowned at Tobias. "Will you pledge sole loyalty to me?"

He straightened up. "I am loyal to Jaron, king of Carthya."

"No, he is loyal to you," I said, turning to Tobias with a stern glare. "You are choosing loyalty to her."

"That is an order," Roden finished, keeping up his imitation of me.

Tobias nodded and stepped back, though he kept his eyes on me, almost as if he wanted to be ready when I found some miraculous escape. But there would be no escape. Not yet.

Tobias was told to remain on the deck with the others while Roden and I were escorted to what appeared to be an officer's quarters belowdecks. The room was cramped with a half-width bed against the far wall, and when the door locked behind us, we were completely sealed in.

I rushed to the door and put my ear against it, hoping to hear anything useful. Roden did the same by balancing on the cot and trying to listen up to the main deck.

There wasn't much I could hear from my angle, only Prozarians darting from task to task and chuckling at what a simple conquest this had been.

Roden seemed to be hearing more of value. He drew in a gasp, muttering, "They've found the crates. They've already begun bringing them on board."

The crates had been the jewel in our trading with the people of Bymar. After the recent war, Carthya's weapons supplies were massively depleted, but our last crop of food had been excellent. Since Bymar was farther north, they needed food more than weapons. And we gladly traded for their weapons, five crates full of them.

Now in the hands of the Prozarians.

Since Roden was in a better position to hear, I began searching our room. I didn't find much — a single stocking, a candle with enough wax for a few minutes of light, a mostly empty tinderbox. I pocketed the items with no particular use in mind for them, but as my only weapon was a small knife in my boot, everything I found had to be considered for its benefit.

After another fifteen minutes, we heard nothing more. The ship seemed to have gone temporarily quiet.

I looked at Roden. "Before you and Tobias came upstairs, what was the last you saw of everyone?"

He shrugged. "I don't know. Everything happened so fast. Mott sealed Amarinda in the hiding place, but once he finished, Fink said he forgot something on his bunk. Mott went to chase after him and never came back. When I last saw Imogen, she was preparing the lifeboat. Then Tobias and I ran upstairs. I don't know how things ended for any of them."

"Could they still be on the —"

My words were drowned out by the sound of cannon fire directly below us, all of it aimed in the direction the *Red Serpent* would have been. Even from within our small room, we distinctly heard the sounds of shattered wood, then the horrifying creaks of masts and beams as they fell to the deck, then silence.

Not a true silence, but the terrible shrieking of a ship

descending to its own watery grave. And I had no idea how many of my friends were going down with it.

My thoughts flew apart and I felt like screaming aloud, but I had to think. I had to concentrate. I closed my eyes and tried to imagine any possible way that Mott, Imogen, and Fink might have survived, but nothing made sense. I leaned against the bulkhead and slowly sank to the floor.

Erick was gone. And I had little reason to hope for the others.

With that thought, my body forgot how to breathe, or stopped caring to.

· FOUR ·

L ast night, Imogen had told me that the moment she knew I needed time away from the castle was when she heard Roden and me fighting in one of the reception rooms.

That day, I had somehow survived a meeting on the farming of oats, though I still wasn't sure if it had lasted several hours, or several years. After a while, it made no difference. I had tried my best to fall asleep, in hopes that when I awoke, the lecture would be over. However, it turns out that when the king sleeps, the speaker merely pauses until someone wakes him up, and then prattles on as if nothing happened.

The rest of the day was engraved in my mind. Roden had just entered the room when I told him, "Why don't you manage this? You can be my minister of oats."

Roden didn't even attempt a smile. "I'm already the captain of your guard, Jaron."

"Yes, but can you do both? I already made Tobias the minister of limiting boring people to no more than eight minutes, and you can see the task has overwhelmed him."

"I already told you that's not a real job." For most of the afternoon, Tobias had been reading at a table in the corner of the throne room. He merely rolled his eyes at Roden, then returned to his pages.

"I can't accept the position," Roden said, "and we need to talk about the second. I am resigning."

I snorted. "No, you're not."

"You may be king of Carthya, but you do not control the whole world —"

"Not yet."

"— and you do not control me." Roden faced me directly. "I will no longer be your captain."

My expression turned to stone. Without looking at anyone else, I ordered them, "Leave us."

The room emptied, except for Roden and me — and Tobias, who stayed too and was looking intently at me as a warning not to ruin everything. We all knew I probably would.

Roden began, "Just now, I was passing by the council room for my senior officers. They were discussing a concern over a report of strangers in Carthya. Did you know about this?"

"They told me yesterday."

"They didn't tell me at all. Instead, they went straight to you!"

"Well, I am king."

"And I'm their captain. They should have come to me first."

"Fine! Go tell them so."

"It wouldn't matter. In that same conversation, my officers asked one another why you chose me as captain." Roden folded his arms. "I know why. It was a bribe to get me away from the pirates. I would have killed you otherwise."

I brushed that off. "You wouldn't have killed me, Roden. We were friends. You just didn't know it yet."

"Friends?" He stepped forward. "It's simple for you to say that from where you stand, at the top of the mountain. You can look down on those of us who serve you and call us friends, but really, we are just servants."

I stood, feeling my temper warm. "You serve *me*? Do you know how many times I have nearly died for this country? How many people are still lined up, wanting my life?"

"You've become paranoid." He gestured around him. "When will you stop believing that the whole world is against you?"

"When I have evidence otherwise. Until then, I'll do what I deem is best. You have no idea what it is to be king."

He pointed to me. "And you have no idea what it is to serve a king, to serve *you*."

We paused as the doors opened and Imogen stepped into the room. Her gaze went from Roden to me, and if she sensed any tension, she simply said, "May we speak in private?"

I turned to Roden, who dipped his head to Imogen. "Can we discuss this later?" I asked.

His half-hearted shrug lacked the respect he had just shown Imogen. "We can discuss this for as long as you'd like. It won't change anything. I will no longer be your captain." Then he marched from the room and Tobias followed, promising he would try to talk to Roden.

Imogen touched my arm. "What was that about?"

After a deep breath to settle myself, I replied, "The usual foolishness. Nothing a few hours in the stocks won't cure. Do we still use those?"

Imogen frowned. "I see the servants were correct. They said that you're in a foul mood."

"Not with you."

She didn't miss a beat. "With the entire rest of the world, then?"

That was a fair question. I began counting on my fingers a review of names as they came to me. "Let me think: Roden — obviously. Mott, Tobias and Amarinda, Fink, Harlowe and Kerwyn, that man who opens the doors for me a second too late so he always bumps my shoulder." I looked over at Imogen again. "I suppose you're right. It is with the entire rest of the world."

"Well, you'll have to get over it. There's a formal supper beginning in one hour."

I took her hands in mine. "Let's cancel everything. Maybe have a quiet supper together instead. Just you and me."

"We can't cancel an hour before everyone arrives."

"We could run off somewhere and secretly marry."

"Where could a king possibly marry in secret?" She arched a brow. "Besides, you might have a good time at the supper."

"I might be struck by lightning as well. I'd prefer that, actually."

Her only reply was a soft sigh. "I heard Roden ask why you chose him as captain."

"He's asked that several times since the war."

Imogen shrugged. "Maybe you haven't given him the right answer yet." Before I could speak, she added, "Roden fights as well as you . . . almost. He has a title as grand as yours . . . almost. He is a good leader . . . but no matter how hard he tries, he is still not you. Whether you realize it or not, Jaron, you cast a long shadow. Maybe Roden is tired of living in it."

"And how do I change that? Would you have me be less than I am?"

Imogen considered that. "Roden is not you. But you are not Roden either. Help him to see that." Then her face lit up. "I have an idea, one I know you'll like."

"What is it?"

"I won't tell you until I've made arrangements, but I will give you one clue. When is the last time you snuck out of a ship's porthole?"

"When I was nearly eleven, on a trip to Bymar. But . . ." For the first time in days, my smile was genuine. I knew what her idea was and it was brilliant.

And now, three weeks later, while being held captive on the *Shadow Tide*, I suddenly sat up straight and shook Roden's arm to wake him up. "I know where Imogen is!"

Roden rubbed his eyes and tried to focus on me. "Where?"

"She must have escaped out the porthole to get on that lifeboat herself!"

"She wouldn't have exploded her own lifeboat."

"Imogen has watched me experiment with gunpowder enough to have a far better understanding of it than I do. She knew exactly how much to use to make it appear that it was a failed attempt at a real explosion. She was probably hiding directly beneath the stuffed figure, out of sight, escaping right beneath the Prozarians' noses."

Roden shrugged. "All right, so maybe she did. And maybe Fink is with her. But Mott's fist wouldn't fit through the porthole. So where is he?"

That was only one of a thousand questions still churning in my mind. I could breathe easier now about Imogen and Fink, and I hoped I was right. But I was more concerned than ever about Mott. He could not have been on that lifeboat.

"What happened to him?" I mumbled.

The door to our small room was unlocked and began to open. Roden looked over at me, his brows pressed close together. "Maybe for the next few minutes, we should worry about what might happen to us."

· FIVE ·

The man I had named Lump was the first to open our door again. When he did, I asked him about his strange name.

He squinted back at me. "My name isn't Lump."

"Are you certain?" I tilted my head and studied him. "Look at yourself. What other name could you possibly have?"

He opened his mouth to answer, then closed it. "Just call me Lump."

With a broad smile, I crossed to him and clapped a hand over his shoulder. "Now I'm curious. If you are willing to let me call you Lump, then your actual name must be so much worse. What is it?"

He pushed me away from him. "I'm here on Captain Strick's orders. She's about to give a welcome speech to the new crew. Then she wants you brought up one at a time for a public questioning and confession. To make an example of you both."

I let out a low whistle. "That sounds like torture." I glanced over at Roden. "You'd better go first."

"Seriously?" I nodded at him and he grunted. "Very well. But I can tell you right now, no torture is necessary. I am Jaron."

Lump pulled Roden out of the cabin and shut and locked the door after him. Or at least, he thought he did. I had touched his shoulder with one hand. With the other, I had inserted a small amount of candle wax into the door frame, preventing it from latching shut, even when Lump turned the lock.

I waited well over a minute to be sure they were gone, then opened the door a crack. From the sounds I heard, all crew members were on deck, just as Lump had suggested. Still, I crept out with great caution. Across from me was a room marked SICK BAY. That was probably where Tobias would be assigned.

After passing his room, I reached the center area of the ship, which was loaded with bunks, stacked three high. It was a simple thing to swipe a Prozarian coat someone had hung from a rope to dry, and then to take the rope itself. From another bunk, I stole a hat and pressed it low on my head. I was digging through another bag in search of a weapon when I heard footsteps somewhere behind me.

With nowhere to go, I froze, then heard a soft "oh" as I was spotted.

A female voice said, "I thought all crewmen were supposed to be on deck."

Without turning around, I replied, "I'll get back up there soon."

"Ah. Well, as a bit of advice, I wouldn't steal from that crewman if I were you. He's the meanest one."

I huffed and turned around, surprised to see a girl near my own age with long scarlet hair in a tangled braid that draped over one shoulder. Her natural beauty was evident, despite her dirty face and torn dress, and her eyes glistened with intelligence, though she quickly blinked that away, leaving only fear in her expression.

"You must be Wilta," I said.

Her head tilted. "How did you know —"

"Is Amarinda with you?"

"Is that her name? She hasn't spoken a word since she was brought into the captain's quarters. I snuck down here to get her something to eat."

"Is she safe there?"

Wilta tilted her head again, as if the question confused her. "Nowhere on this ship is safe."

"Are you in danger too?"

She lowered her eyes. "I'm here as a punishment for leading a rebellion. The captain won't let me die, but I cannot continue to live this way either."

"What are her plans for Amarinda?"

"I don't know. So far, Amarinda has been held in binds, but no harm has come to her."

Cautiously, I stepped forward. "Can you bring me to her? Can you help me get her off this ship?"

Her only response was the last thing I wanted to hear. "You're Jaron." Something must have flashed in my eyes, because she said, "I won't tell anyone, but the captain will have the truth figured out sooner than you think."

"What does she want with me?"

Wilta shrugged. "What does she want with any of us?"

I studied her a moment longer. She did not look like she was from any of the lands near Carthya, but she spoke the common language, so she couldn't have come from far away. "Where is your home?"

"Belland. Have you heard of it?"

I squinted, trying to remember if I'd ever heard of Belland. If my geography tutors had been more interesting, I might have stayed awake long enough to learn where it was.

When I didn't answer, she said, "Belland is a small country on the western side of the sea, though you can only reach it by water. It was formed by volcanoes hundreds of years ago."

"Is that where this ship is headed? Or somewhere else?"

Hearing a sound from above, Wilta glanced back. "I should go."

I stepped forward again, keeping my hands low so as not to appear threatening. "You're afraid, I understand that. But I have friends on this ship, and they're afraid too. Can you help us?"

Her eyes darted and she turned as if to leave, so I quickly added, "I know at one time the Prozarians were greatly feared. But I thought they went extinct years ago."

Wilta paused, confused again. "Why would you say that?"

"I battled a Prozarian boy once. He told me so."

During my time as Sage, one of the other orphans in Mrs. Turbeldy's Orphanage for Disadvantaged Boys was a Prozarian boy named Edgar. He was about the same age and build as my brother, so at first I had hoped we might become friends. But I quickly learned he was nothing like Darius in character. He had a stash of treasures he wouldn't share with anyone — rolls of gold coins, a piece of glass art, an old ring of his father's. I stole some of his coins once to buy food for the rest of us, which ended up making me his target. He began tying me up at night so that by the time I got untied in the morning, what little food there was had already been eaten. It was thanks to Edgar that I had become so quick at untying knots. And he later thanked me for making the knots tight the day I bound him in ropes and dangled him from the window. After I pulled him back in, we got along much better.

Perhaps it was an exaggeration to have called that a battle, but I had won nonetheless. The only thing that confused me now was that in one of our conversations, Edgar had told me he believed his people were extinct. Maybe he was wrong.

"Do the Prozarians have plans to invade Carthya?"

"I don't know. Though if they did, I think they simply would have invaded, not gone to the trouble of finding you."

Nor would that explain what they wanted with Amarinda. The captain had noticeably reacted to hearing her name, calling it a lucky thing to have found her.

"What is the connection between Bymar and the Prozarians?" I asked.

Wilta shrugged. "None that I know of."

Then I couldn't think of any reason that they should have cared about Amarinda's name, nor even have known it.

Up on the main deck, a voice that sounded like Lump's told everyone to quiet down and prepare to listen to the captain.

"I need information," I said. "Please help me."

She paused and straightened up, as if gathering her courage. "The Prozarians know about the war you won six months ago, which means I know a little about it too. Promise to do everything you can to free my people, and I'll give you all the information I can find."

"Agreed."

Her eyes rose to the deck. "This is the first thing I can tell you. Your friend is up there. When she discovers he is not Jaron, she will kill him."

· SIX ·

Wilta returned to the captain's cabin through what must have been a secret stairway or some passage I had not yet found. But that was hardly my biggest concern.

Dressed as a Prozarian and in the low light of hanging lanterns and a few small torches, it was a simple thing to sneak onto the deck and blend in with the others. On a casual glance, they shouldn't recognize me.

I sat in the back row of the Prozarians, which put me directly ahead of the pirates. Even dressed as I was and with my head down, when I looked back, several of the pirates gave me nods of recognition. Far to the right of the group was Tobias, who seemed to be attempting to communicate his thoughts through the intensity of his stare. I tried to return a thought as well, reminding him that he could stare at me until his eyes popped, but that still wouldn't tell me what he was thinking.

Instead of failing at mind games, I looked around for other options. Not far from me on the deck was a stack of unused torches, ones that the captain might need later in the voyage. I, however, needed one now. Scooting closer to them, I casually slid one inside my coat.

Captain Strick stood at the edge of the forecastle deck. Roden was kneeling beside her, his hands once again bound behind his back. He was staring straight forward, trying to appear unafraid, but I knew him too well to believe his act. He was terrified.

Captain Strick raised her arms to call for quiet, which wasn't necessary since it was already ghostly calm on deck. When she lowered them, she began, "Prozarians, congratulations on your conquest! We are another step closer to the greatest of rewards!"

The front half of the deck clapped and cheered for themselves. Nobody moved behind me.

Strick addressed them next. "To the crew of the *Red Serpent*, you made a valiant attempt at defending yourselves. You showed courage and strength, the same qualities we seek in our warriors. To board this ship, you already gave me your vows of loyalty, but those are only words. Now I ask for your hearts as well, that you serve me because you believe in me, and our purposes."

She waited for more applause. None came.

I would have considered applauding, but I was busy trying to casually cut a nearby rope, one that seemed to be holding an overhead beam in place. Also, I could not applaud for any speech that sent bile into my throat.

"We serve the Monarch, so you now serve the Monarch. Our leader demands absolute obedience, but will recognize

absolute loyalty." With a sharper tone than before, Strick continued, "Disobedience will result in your punishment, or execution."
Now she turned to Roden. "Lie to me, and I'll make you beg for
execution."

My knife snapped through the final threads of the rope,
which whipped up high into the air, causing the beam directly
above me to swing out wide over the sea.

Several Prozarians around me leapt to their feet, shouting
orders at one another for how to retrieve the beam. But by then,
I had already begun to climb the rope ladder. Others were
climbing ladders too so there was nothing suspicious about
what I was doing. And once I climbed high enough to be out of
range of the lantern lights below, I became relatively invisible.

I hoped.

When possible, I stayed behind posts or used the crow's
nest for cover, but I knew where I was trying to go, and so I'd
have to move slowly and stay low, and do everything possible to
not be detected.

Once the beam was retrieved and locked down again,
Strick blamed the accident on sloppy knot tying and picked up
where she had left off, with Roden.

In a voice loud enough that I could hear even at my height,
she said to Roden, "What is your country?"

"Carthya," he replied in an equally loud voice.

"What is your name?"

A pause. Then, "I am one of two people on this ship who
could be named Jaron."

Beside Strick, Lump hit Roden across the back. Roden fell

forward from his knees, nearly toppling down the stairs, but he straightened up again, with a more determined expression than before.

"Name?"

"I am one of two —"

Lump hit him again, and this time he did roll down the steps to the deck. Strick followed. I withdrew the torch from my pocket and, along with it, the tinderbox. The oil in the torch would immediately light, *if* the tinderbox still had enough life in it to create a spark.

Below me, Strick tried a different strategy.

"If you are Jaron, tell me your parents' names."

"Eckbert and Erin." He straightened up and glared at her. "I had an older brother too, Darius, but all of them are dead now."

At Strick's direction, Lump hit him again, which surprised me. There was no reason to have done it. Roden was still slumped over when Strick crouched beside him and took his right hand.

"There is no king's ring."

"I left it on the other ship."

I glanced down at my hand. I'd pocketed the king's ring when we were boarded, but I replaced it now. Then I reached into the tinderbox for a badly worn piece of flint.

But Strick smiled. "There is no evidence of a ring ever being on this hand. No discoloration of the finger, no impression on the skin." She stood tall. "You are not Prince Jaron. What is your name?"

His shoulders hunched. "I am Jaron."

"No, you are not." She put a hand on his shoulder. "You are

very brave, and what I've seen from you thus far is perhaps the most courageous act of any person on this deck. I want you to know that I sincerely regret having to kill you now."

Now she turned to address her crew. "The first show of loyalty is to carry out my orders, so, pirates, I am giving you the chance to prove yourselves. Every one of you who gave me your oath today will administer one lash to this boy, this imposter, assuming he is still alive after everyone has had their chance."

"No one will touch him!" I shouted, now standing on the lower beam. It had taken four strikes of flint to light the torch, but now it was bright in my hands. I raised it toward the nearest sail. "You will listen carefully and do everything I say, or I will turn this ship to ashes."

Strick glanced up at me and folded her arms. "Prince Jaron, welcome to the *Shadow Tide.*"

· SEVEN ·

I leaned in, certain I had not heard her address me correctly. "Pardon?"

She squinted. "I welcomed you here, Prince Jaron."

"Ah. No, I'm King Jaron. I'm a king. We even had a ceremony to make it official. Which is a problem for you. To capture a king is an act of war."

She rolled her eyes. "I'm aware of that."

"So you will release me and my friends, or —"

"We are not at war, Jaron." She threw out a hand. "Could we discuss this in a more private place? I feel like I'm shouting to the entire sea."

"None of us are going anywhere until we agree on terms. First, you will provide a lifeboat to Roden, Tobias, and Amarinda, well stocked with food, and get them safely off this ship."

Strick frowned. "The *Shadow Tide* has only one lifeboat, and I won't give it up for three people whose lives do not concern me. But I will guarantee their lives here at least until we reach our destination. Under two conditions. First is they obey my every command. Second is that Roden will give the same vow of loyalty that Tobias and everyone else on this ship did."

Roden's head turned sharply back toward her. "Only me, not Amarinda?"

"Her vow will be willingly given." Strick turned back to me. "Your threats mean nothing, Jaron. You won't set fire to a ship with three of your friends on board, unless . . ." She pointed at Roden. ". . . unless winning means more to you than their lives. Because this boy will pledge loyalty to me, or he will die here."

I lowered the torch in my hands, calling back, "I will win before this is over, Captain. But Roden may do as he'd like now. He was never particularly loyal to me anyway."

Strick smiled and said to Roden, "Well?"

Roden looked up at me for advice, and I subtly nodded back at him. What other choice did he have? Once he made his pledge, Lump untied Roden's arms and he was ordered to sit with the rest of the men.

"I've kept my promise thus far," Strick said. "Now will you keep yours and come down?"

I forced a smile to my face. "Absolutely. And since you have so kindly invited me and my friends to join this crew, I will do you a favor as well." To the rest of those on deck, I said, "I am the Carthyan king, and with Erick's death, the title of pirate king also returns to me. You will heed my orders now. If any of you were planning a mutiny, out of fears of this being a cursed ship, you will stop with your plans at once."

Wrinkles formed between the captain's brows. "There is no curse."

"I agree. It was foolish of them to think so." I turned back to the rows of assembled pirates. "Hear me now. You've given your loyalty oaths to Captain Strick, and now we all must trust her with our lives . . . or deaths, I suppose, in Erick's case. This is especially important if you are one of the many pirates here who believe this is a cursed ship." I gave just quick applause to the captain, the applause she had waited for earlier and not received. Unfortunately, she still didn't receive it, and I felt foolish for applauding alone, so I stopped.

"Did you say this is a cursed ship?" one man near the back called.

Avoiding Strick's glare, I replied, "No, I said that many of *you* believe it is a cursed ship, and although I'm sure you have good reasons for this belief, it can't possibly be true. There simply is no evidence of it. Now, imagine that there was a scarlet-haired girl on this ship — that would be a sure sign of trouble, but none of us have seen anyone like that, which means there is nothing to fear." I looked over at Strick, whose face was rapidly twisting into knots. "There, I have reassured them and I will come down."

I continued along the beam toward the nearest ladder, but one of the pirates stood and said, "There is a scarlet-haired girl on this ship! I saw her when we boarded."

"There is no curse on this ship!" Roden climbed onto one of the crates stored on the deck. "Do your oaths mean nothing to you? Sit down and maintain order!"

Strick smiled down at him, even as she glared up at me, which couldn't have been easy to do. I had started down the ladder myself, but before I got far, Lump grabbed me by one leg and yanked me down to the deck, quickly stepping on the torch to extinguish it. When I stood, he raised a fist, growling, "We never made any agreement about your safety!"

"Stop!" Strick said. "We won't deliver him covered in bruises."

"He's no threat," I said, eyeing Lump. "With a name like his, he probably can't hit hard enough to leave any marks. What is your real name anyway? Pudding? Kitten?"

Strick grabbed Lump's fist as he raised it again. "I said no."

"You'll let him get away with what he said up there, what he tried to do?"

"No, he must be punished." She frowned at me. "Get down on your knees."

I snorted. "Absolutely not."

This time, she eyed Lump, who clubbed me in the back, forcing the air from my lungs. I hunched over, trying to draw a breath in again, then stood up straight. "I will not kneel, Captain. That is not in me, no matter your threats."

"Why not? What terrible thing would happen if you simply bent the knee to me?" She stepped closer. "What are you afraid of, Jaron?"

"Spice cake. Once I had this nightmare that one was chasing me —"

She raised a hand against me, but from behind us, Roden said, "He's afraid of heights."

Strick pointed to the beam where I had just stood. "He got up there."

"Up there is nothing." Roden pointed higher, to the crow's

nest. "It's great heights that he fears. It's a cloudy night and will probably be a cold one. If you want to punish him, put him up there."

Strick turned to me. "I don't think heights bother you a bit. But the cold will. Remove those Prozarian clothes. What you wore when we captured you should be enough."

"I'm relieved to be out of these," I said, pulling off the coat first. "The stink was rubbing off on me."

With a tighter grimace, she turned to the crew. "Who will volunteer to take this prince up to the crow's nest?"

"King," I muttered. I looked around, but apparently no one was eager to climb a rope ladder high above the ship and force me into a large bucket for the night.

"Cowards, you disappoint me," Strick said.

"Agreed." I clicked my tongue. "The last people who wanted my life showed far more courage." Now I glanced over at her. "I defeated them too."

"I can do it." Roden avoided my eyes as he spoke, which was no accident. "Let me prove my oath."

She considered his offer, then slowly smiled. "Very well. In that trunk behind you is a set of manacles. Take him up there and make sure he's chained in. I want to be sure he feels his punishment for the entire night."

I pushed a hand through my hair. "Why go to so much trouble? After ten minutes of talking with you, believe me, I've been punished."

Roden returned with a set of manacles and directed the way he wanted me to walk. Prozarian crewmen stood and backed away to make room for me, though many of them spat on my boots as I walked.

I reached the center post of the ship, with Prozarians on one side of me and pirates on the other. This was a relatively minor punishment for what had been a show of major disrespect to the captain, and I knew I should have felt lucky that it was no worse.

Yet I did not. The behavior of the Prozarians felt personal. Even now as they glared at me, I felt their hatred like fire on my flesh, and I could not understand that. There was nothing I'd done to them, nothing I *could have* done.

I looked the other way, to the pirates, and saw in them disappointment, or defeat, as if they had expected something better to come from my speech. As if they were thinking I had won a major war six months ago, so why couldn't I have found a way to free them now?

I grabbed the first rung of the ladder, then stopped and turned back to the captain. "Have I wronged you in some way?"

She frowned at me. "If you have, confess now and things may go better for you on this journey."

Tempting as her offer was, I replied, "You misunderstood me, Captain. I meant that if I have not wronged you yet, then I still have time to do it."

She pursed her lips and began to say something, but I was already climbing, with Roden directly behind me.

I rolled into the crow's nest, then held out my hands for Roden. He fastened the first chain around my wrists and in a low voice said, "I know how you will fight this. I can help you."

"She will suspect your loyalties —"

"She won't know."

"You can't take that chance. Whatever she orders, follow it the best that you can."

"And what if she orders me to come against you as hard as I can?"

I sighed. "I'll have to come back at you . . . as hard as I can." The next words were difficult to say. "If you remain on her side, in the end, you will have to lose. There is no other way."

"I know." When I held out my other hand for him to bind into the manacles, he said, "It begins here, Jaron. She may send someone to check on you, so I've got to do this right." He took the second link of chains and fastened it to the rail of the crow's nest itself, preventing me from climbing down later tonight.

I glanced at Roden, who shrugged and mouthed an apology again. I mouthed something back at him too, though it was hardly an apology.

He said, "Stay alive up here. It will be a rough night." He started down once more, then paused for the last time to say, "You are my king, Jaron. You are always my king."

The rough night ahead didn't worry me. It was the rough few days ahead that were making my stomach churn.

"You are always my friend," I echoed, though he was no longer around to hear me.

No one was around. I was completely on my own now.

It was time to get to work.

· EIGHT ·

It only took the first three minutes after Roden had left to free myself of the manacles. The most challenging part had been to slide a thin metal pin from my belt into my fingers without dropping it through the gaps in the wood. I had been placed in manacles a few times before and had determined never to be controlled by them again, so Mott had designed this pin, to be hidden within the liner of my belt. No one but he and I knew it existed, and that was how I intended for it to remain. I stuck the pin into the lock of the manacles and wiggled it until I felt something turn. Within seconds I was free.

Below, the captain had begun shouting orders, assigning one Prozarian to every pirate, with the understanding that one partner would pay for any violation committed by the other. Most were assigned to go belowdecks, where new bunks were supposed to be placed, but Roden was the exception. He would return to the officer's quarters where we had been locked earlier. I assumed he would be locked in at least for the rest of the night.

Very quickly, the deck was cleared, except for two vigils

who would take the remaining shift of the night watch. Before long, I was thoroughly irritated with them.

They stayed exactly opposite each other as they rotated in a slow circle, keeping their eyes sharp and focused on their responsibilities. I cursed under my breath. My life was already complicated enough without them doing their jobs properly.

That didn't mean I was helpless, however. There were a great number of ropes and pulleys, and sails, each with a specific function. I'd spent much of my time on the *Red Serpent* learning each of their purposes and how the draw on one rope affected another. Some were vital to keeping the ship on course and in line with the winds. Some were vital to me.

If I moved slowly enough, the dark night allowed me to pull in some of those ropes without being noticed. While I redid the knots, I listened to the men conversing below, and hoped to hear something useful. Most of it was the inane chatter of half-brained slugs, saying whatever filtered into their mouths to keep themselves awake. I cared for none of it, not the shifting direction of the wind, nor the fishing boat spotted in the distance, nor their assessment of the beautiful, scarlet-haired girl just revealed to be on board.

When they finally moved to a topic that might have caught my attention — the specific mission of the *Shadow Tide* — it turned out to be equally useless. Not even the Prozarians knew why the captain had brought them all this way, other than that I had always been the target. They didn't even mention Amarinda.

In fact, there was only one thing they both agreed on: that

I had little chance of making it to our destination alive. They were surprised I'd even lasted the first night on this ship.

So was I.

But the night wasn't over yet.

By the time the next shift began, I was shivering with cold. The instant I heard the replacement crew members come onto the deck, I began descending the rope ladder. I was blocked by the sail, furled for the night, so I didn't have to be invisible, just fast. It wouldn't take them long to exchange their report of this evening's nonevents.

I was only halfway down the ladder when one of the replacements made his first round up on the castle deck, far below me. As I had done earlier that evening, I rotated to the opposite side of the post, clinging to the ropes and trying to not sway with the ship.

"So the captain put Jaron up in the crow's nest?" the pirate asked his companion. "That's a mistake." I recognized his voice. His name was Teagut, and in true pirate fashion, he'd steal the last coin from his widowed mother's purse. Aside from that character flaw, he seemed like a decent fellow.

"Why was it a mistake?"

"What do you know about Jaron?"

I crouched lower, eager to hear the Prozarian's answer.

"I know he deserves everything that is coming to him. Captain Strick is doing the four continents a favor by ridding us of him."

Teagut chuckled. "If she can catch him. I wager ten gold coins that the crow's nest is empty."

I closed my eyes and groaned. If it were possible, I'd pay Teagut tenfold in coins to keep him from making that wager.

"Then you'd better go check."

Teagut began to climb the ladder, getting closer to me with each rung he ascended. I crouched low on the rear side of the post until he passed me, then I reached around and pulled the knife from the sheath at his waist. He felt me take it and froze on the ladder. I said, "Report that I'm in the crow's nest, then find a reason to get your companion off the deck."

"I'll lose the wager."

"Better than losing your life."

He gulped and climbed the rest of the way up to the crow's nest, peeked in, then returned to where I was and shouted down to his friend, "He's curled up tight and asleep. Right where he belongs."

Once he was back on deck, he directed his companion toward the steps to the lower compartments. "I, er, did happen to notice while I was up there that the ship seems to be off balance. We brought on all those heavy crates. Perhaps we should go check the cargo hold."

Two minutes later I landed on an empty deck, then hurried to the forecastle, where a chest for tools or spare weapons lay. I had hoped to find my sword inside, or any sword for that matter, but instead I found only carpenter's tools. I grabbed those with hooks or holes and carried them back to a rope dangling from the crow's nest overhead. I tied the tools to it, then used the rope's pulley to raise the tools up high. I waited for the next angling of the ship upon the water for the tools to tilt directly over the crow's nest, then I carefully lowered them into the basket. I finished the job by tying off the end of the rope and hoped everyone had good enough sense to leave that rope alone.

Or better sense than I'd had. During all my studying and experiments with the sails on the *Red Serpent*, I'd caused hours of work for the pirate crew, who'd had to rig their sails again, and once or twice I'd confused their systems entirely. While traveling to Bymar, I'd begun to understand the intricacies of the ship's riggings. How every beam and post had to be tied with the proper knots and lengths of rope to allow the wind to catch the sails. A carelessly placed rope might bind the entire system.

In fact, that was how I'd spent my evening thus far in the crow's nest — carelessly placing ropes, developing a system I very much hoped I wouldn't have to test, because I wasn't certain of whether it would work.

The manacles that had been around my wrists were now dangling from my belt. Careful to make no more sound than was necessary, I placed them at the base of the capstan, tucking them beneath the wheel where they wouldn't be seen and fastening one end around a large eye hook attached to the deck. The other end of the manacles was left open, ready for someone's wrist.

Hopefully, the captain's wrist, or maybe Lump's, if his wrist would fit within the clasp. I might have to settle for a finger.

With that task finished, I wanted to search Captain Strick's office, but to get her out of her room, I'd need a distraction. Fire would certainly accomplish that, but it had a terrible side effect of sinking ships, so I dismissed that idea. Stopping the ship would get her attention, but I couldn't drop the anchor on my own. It took twelve men to rotate the capstan, or I figured, it'd take one Mott.

Mott. My heart clenched.

Instinctively, I looked out over the sea and hoped he was somewhere upon it, alive. I felt certain Imogen was on the lifeboat, and surely, she would have made Fink get in there with her. But I was increasingly worried about Mott.

Worried enough that when I allowed my mind to wander into the possibilities of his death, I understood how bleak my life would be without him.

I needed his strength, and even more, I needed his counsel. If he were asked to advise me right now, I already knew what he would say. Mott would suggest something cautious, something safe. I would listen to his advice, then do what I always did: the very opposite.

With that in mind, my plan became clear. Mott would tell me to go inside the wardroom next to the captain's quarters. That was where she and those in her close circle would take their meals, but extra cloaks were always stored there in case of sudden rain. Mott would want me to bring one back up to the crow's nest, hunker down, and stay safe until we reached our destination.

"A brilliant suggestion, Mott," I whispered. I started toward the wardroom, then froze at the sound of someone climbing the stairs from belowdecks; they seemed to be avoiding making any noise. Still, out of a sense of caution, I backed into the shadows, cramming myself between the posts and bulkhead as tight as possible.

Then I waited as a figure stepped onto the deck, silhouetted in the starlight. In one hand he held a knife at the ready. I already had Teagut's knife, but I wouldn't mind a second one. Specifically, that one.

My life might depend on getting it.

His life might depend on how easily he gave it up.

· NINE ·

The figure walked toward the forecastle, eyes trained upward at the crow's nest where I was supposed to be. I followed, careful to move only when he did so that I wouldn't create any additional sounds on the wood planking. But I made sure to take longer strides, so that with each step, I was closer to him than before.

He stopped at the base of the forecastle, redoubled his grip, then suddenly swung around at me.

I was ready for him and ducked, grabbing his arm and pulling him down to the deck where I knelt with one knee on his chest.

"Tobias?"

He grunted. "I sensed someone following me. I didn't know it was you."

"You sensed me following you?" That was disappointing. If I had done it correctly, he shouldn't have suspected anyone nearby. "What gave me away?"

"What gave *me* away?" Tobias asked. "How did you know I was planning to attack?"

"You checked the hold on your knife. Also, you turn slower than an old woman, so I had plenty of warning." I helped him to his feet, then asked, "What are you doing up here so late?"

"I saw the vigils come down the steps, and wanted to check on you. I also figured you might have a use for this. I found it on a lower deck."

He set a gray rock into my hands, then beamed as if he'd just handed me a bar of gold. I looked up at him, unimpressed. "A rock? Is this a symbolic offering?"

"This is a lodestone." When I still gave no reaction, he said, "Set in a cup of water, it will orient itself to the north."

Now I grinned, understanding its importance. "But if it gets too close to another magnet, for example, the one beside the helmsman's wheel . . ."

"It would pull the compass off course."

I almost laughed out loud, and withdrew my knife on the way to the forecastle deck. The compass was set into a waist-high binnacle, which would allow the helmsman to constantly track the ship's direction. I used the knife to pry out the compass, but I'd need to carve out extra space beneath it for the lodestone.

"Keep watch for anyone coming on deck," I said, crouching low to begin working.

"Who am I watching for?"

"Everyone who doesn't look like Amarinda."

"What if it's Roden?"

I paused to look up at him. "We may eventually have a problem there. Roden's only choice right now is to do everything in his power to persuade the captain to keep him alive."

"It's no different for me," Tobias said. "She told me the only reason I'm still alive is their ship's physician died of illness a week ago. This day just gets better and better."

"He probably wasn't as strong as you."

Tobias's face fell. "I'm not strong, Jaron, not the way I wish I was. But I am clever, so I have a plan."

I looked over at him again. "Oh?"

"I put together a formula that will make a person appear very ill, yet it will feel to them like only a light flu."

"Excellent. How will that help us though?"

"I'm working on that part." Tobias gasped. "Hurry faster! The captain's light just came on in her quarters."

"Duck down."

He did, and we both froze in place behind the rails as the captain's door opened and Wilta emerged, saying, "This late? I'm sure he's asleep by now."

"If I'm awake, I can demand any member of this crew to be awake," the captain called out. "Go get him."

The door closed again and Wilta pulled a shawl around her shoulders and descended belowdecks.

As quietly as possible, I made one final carving into the binnacle, then dropped the lodestone in. Angling the compass against the nearest lantern on the deck, I watched the direction change by four degrees as soon as I replaced it.

"Four degrees," I said. "Depending on how far we have left to go, we might never reach our destination."

Tobias's smile fell. "Oh, good. That means . . . even longer that we can be on this ship."

"We're not staying here."

"We're leaving tonight?" His sigh of relief was louder than it ought to have been. "I've got to get out of that tiny sick bay."

"You will. But maybe not in the way you want." I hesitated for the next part. He wasn't going to like this. "I don't want to do this to you, but we've got to trade clothes."

Tobias's eyes widened. "What? Why?"

I'd already begun unfastening the buttons of my jerkin and motioned for him to give me his simpler gray tunic.

He began to pull it over his head, then stopped. "Why are we doing this?"

In response, my eyes flicked upward.

"Oh no, no, I won't." Tobias instantly pulled his tunic back down. "I can't climb."

"You *don't* climb. That's different."

"I'm afraid of heights."

"No, you're afraid of falling, so don't do that. If you do, fear won't be your worst problem." I stepped closer and exchanged my jerkin for his tunic. "Do this for me, Tobias. I'm running out of time and I need to get inside Strick's office."

"You'll only make things worse with her."

I grinned. "Is that a challenge? Because honestly, I can't think of a better time to irritate her, when her opinion of me is already so low."

"*That's* your reasoning?"

"Give me your boots too." He did, and I said, "My reasoning is that every answer I'm looking for has got to be in her office." I paused. "Amarinda is in there."

Tobias pressed his lips together, then finished buttoning up my jerkin. "I'll do this for her."

Even before he was fully dressed, I started pushing him toward the rope ladder. "Now hurry up there. I'll be back to trade places with you before dawn."

"What if they come up to get me and realize what we've done?"

"If anything goes wrong, I'll be there to protect you."

Tobias frowned, clearly insulted. "I'm not asking you to protect me. I just want to know what to do. I can take care of myself."

"Yes, but I also know that if not for me, you wouldn't be in this situation."

"If not for you, we'd never be in any situation. Just make sure nobody else goes up this ladder."

He started up the ladder, then felt the first gust of wind. "At least my hat might block some of the wind."

"Actually, I need that hat too." He grimaced, but he shouldn't have. I didn't *want* to take it — hat rims blocked my vision, so I rarely wore them. But now I hoped his hat would block anyone getting too good a look at me.

Tobias offered me his hat, saying, "For Amarinda."

I smiled as I pulled it on my head. "This hat would look terrible on Amarinda. I thought you knew her better, Tobias."

He barely returned the smile. "Back before dawn, you promise me?"

"I'll do everything I can to get back as soon as possible."

"Strick is keeping you alive for a purpose, Jaron. She doesn't need me alive, remember that."

His words went far deeper than simply remembering. Three of my friends were missing. The other three were in serious jeopardy. I could scarcely think of anything else. I waited until Tobias was nearly halfway up the ladder, then crept toward Strick's office. One way or another, I had to get in there, and fast.

Beside her office was her wardroom. Six empty bottles were stacked in a bin in the corner. If they mysteriously got loose, they'd roll around on the deck until the captain finally became so exasperated that she'd be forced to come out and retrieve them all. Then she'd go searching for the vigils who should have been on duty, likely call everyone to attention for their punishment, and by the time she returned to her quarters, I'd be back in the crow's nest with my answers.

I reached for the bottles, then crouched lower when I heard Roden return to the main deck in quiet conversation with Wilta.

"What could the captain possibly want with me?" he asked, his tone unmistakably nervous.

"I'm sure she only wants to speak to you. The captain is always reasonable — to those who cooperate."

Roden paused on the deck to look up toward the crow's nest and hissed my name. I didn't answer, nor did Tobias.

Getting no response, he let out a heavy breath and walked to the captain's door. Wilta knocked and said, "I've brought him, Captain, as you asked."

A minute passed, then the door was opened again. "What took so long?"

"Forgive me, Captain," Roden said. "It's crowded belowdecks."

Strick was still fully dressed despite the late hour, and she gazed up at the crow's nest, as Roden had done only seconds earlier.

After a minute of silence, she said, "Do you consider yourself a friend to Prince Jaron?"

Roden hesitated nearly as long. Then he said, "Captain, my oath is to you now."

"That wasn't my question. Are you and the prince friends?"

"Yes."

"What are your duties to him?"

"I am . . . I was . . . the captain of his guard."

"Ah, military. You are a warrior!" She looked at him carefully. "What do you mean, you *were* the captain of his guard?"

Roden sighed. "Shortly before we boarded the ship to Bymar, I was angry with Jaron. I resigned, only he wouldn't accept it."

"Why were you angry?"

This time, Roden's sigh was louder. "Jaron has a difficult time with trust." He was silent for several seconds, and then the words spilled out of him. "He makes plans without informing anyone, reveals only the few details to others that he must, even if those secrets threaten our safety, or his. He doesn't seem to care what anyone thinks about him, which means there is almost nothing any of us can do or say to make him listen to our needs or complaints. And I'm sure it's difficult for him to bear the weight of an entire kingdom on his shoulders, but if he would only trust us enough to let us help him, he wouldn't have to bear the whole weight." Roden drew in a deep breath. "So I was angry."

"You had a right to be angry, Roden. You wish to prove yourself and have not been given the chance."

"Exactly!"

"I want to give you that chance, but proving yourself will be difficult. Obey me on the small things, and I'll test you with something even greater. Perhaps one day you will obtain the status you desire. You may even become a king yourself."

His brow furrowed. "I have no royal blood."

"Nor does our monarch, but that has never been important. My people believe that the throne is for the person who takes it, not for the person with the chosen bloodline."

Even from here I saw Roden's eyes brighten. The hardest part was that I couldn't tell whether he was trying to impress Strick, or whether he truly believed what she was saying to him.

"You said there was a way Roden could prove his loyalty?" Wilta asked.

Strick's answer was ready. "It's quite simple. I want Jaron on his knees to me."

Roden drew back. "Captain, he won't . . . he never —"

"He will, or he must die. But I want you to make him do it."

"I cannot control him. No one can."

Strick gestured for Wilta to come forward. "Tell Roden why you are here."

Wilta gulped and lowered her head. "Above all others of my people, I was the most defiant. The common belief was that I could never be broken, never be brought into submission. After an attempted rebellion against the Prozarians, I was captured and sentenced to a lifetime of service. But it is no longer a punishment. I have earned her trust, Roden, and I want to serve the captain. Jaron will feel the same way, in time."

"Once I break the leaders, I command their people." Strick put a pensive finger to her lips. "I simply need to understand Jaron better. Tell me something useful about him and I will reward you. Refuse, and I will have you beaten until the right words are forced out of you."

Roden's voice wavered. "There is something I can tell you. Jaron is good at hiding his fears, but I promise you, he is afraid, and probably has no idea what he is supposed to do. So even if he does not show it, he is highly vulnerable right now."

I cursed under my breath. Roden was mistaken. Right *now*, I was far more irritated than afraid.

Strick smiled. "Thank you, Roden. As a reward, you will no longer be locked in your room. But be warned, my people will be watching you at all times. You are dismissed."

In acknowledgment, he dipped his head, and she turned to go back into her quarters. Before she did, she paused and said to him, "I must admit that I am surprised."

"Why?"

"For someone who was once the captain of the guard in Carthya, you are surprisingly weak. I knew Jaron wouldn't cooperate, but in truth, I expected you would be far more difficult to defeat."

TEN

Roden was standing close enough for me to see the hunch of his shoulders. Strick's comment would have stung him deeper than she might have known. Or maybe she did know. She returned to her office, chuckling softly.

Sensing the change in his emotions, Wilta pushed her arm through his. "Don't listen to her. She gave you no choice but to tell her something, and I expect you could have revealed far more damaging information."

"Definitely. Jaron is very —"

"Don't say it." Wilta looked back toward the captain's quarters. "I don't want to know anything that she might force me to tell her."

"So you don't serve her by choice?"

Wilta shook her head, then looked up to the crow's nest. "I know that Jaron will be the same way. But if you can't get him on his knees to her, he will never reach Belland."

Roden pushed a hand through his hair. "And what happens if he is taken to Belland?"

"That depends on him . . . and you." Wilta took Roden's hand in hers. "Jaron needs you now, whether he knows it or not. But you can do nothing for him until the captain trusts you. Believe me, I learned that lesson in the hardest possible way. I lost everyone. . . ."

That was as far as she got before she drew in a sharp breath, as though holding back tears. Using the lantern light, Roden looked closer at her arm, brushing a finger up the skin. "These scars, did the captain do that to you?"

"It's proof of the cruelty of the Monarch." She paused to collect her emotions. "These people took everything from me, everyone I ever loved. I only stay now so that I can take back from them all that is rightfully mine."

As her emotions broke, Roden pulled her into an embrace. At the same time, Tobias hurled one of my boots over the side of the crow's nest. In a surprisingly good aim, it nearly hit Roden, who had to push away from Wilta to avoid it.

He chuckled, though it sounded forced and tense. "Jaron holds grudges. It's not a big problem."

Yes, I did. And if he continued to pour out my secrets to Wilta, he should consider it a major problem.

Wilta led Roden over to the rail to look up at the crow's nest. "He seems angry with you."

Roden sighed. "It's like I told the captain before. Nothing I do is ever good enough for him. He always believes he can do it better, or smarter, or bolder."

"You must make him see you as you truly are."

"Jaron will never change, no matter what I say or do.

Besides, if I want to live, then I can't think about him anymore, only the captain. I need her to trust me."

Wilta placed her hand on his cheek. "If there's a way to gain her trust, we will find it together."

"Thank you, Wilta."

He continued staring at her, and her hand was still on his cheek, and I was getting increasingly annoyed with all of it when Wilta finally stepped back. "Someone's coming."

The vigil who had been with Teagut walked partway up the stairs. "Is Tobias up here? He's needed down in the sick bay."

Roden glanced around. "No one's up here but us."

"I know he came up, not thirty minutes ago. He is here, somewhere."

With tension thick in his voice, Roden said, "I'll go look starboard." Wilta followed him and I immediately darted out of the wardroom, with Tobias's hat pulled low over my face.

"Never mind, I found him," the vigil called.

"Hush, or you'll be next in the sick bay." I pushed past him to start down the stairs just in time to hear Roden's feet pounding across the deck.

"Tobias!" he called, but I didn't look up. Obviously.

Instead, the vigil followed me down the steps and I hurried forward, trying to keep a few steps ahead of him. I didn't know how well he knew Tobias's face, or mine, but I hoped any differences would become blurred in the low light belowdecks.

I called behind me, "What's the problem?" If the patient required my use of needles or a surgeon's knife, he would have serious regrets for being ill tonight.

"It's Teagut. We were on deck keeping watch for the night. He went up to check on the prisoner we put up there, and he's been acting strange since we came down. Says he's too ill to return to the deck. I doubt he's really sick though. When the captain finds out nobody's been keeping watch on the deck, she'll have our heads."

"You'd better get up there and hope she doesn't notice," I agreed. "I'll tend to the pirate."

The door of the sick bay had a sign to indicate when some-one was being treated. I turned the sign, which read DO NOT ENTER, then shut the door tight behind me.

The sick bay was a square room with a small bed and wash basin for Tobias in one half and a narrow exam table on the sec-ond half, surrounded by shelves and cabinets and trays. Teagut was on the table, seated with his back to me, his head hung low.

"I know you're not a real physician yet," Teagut began, "but that's all right because I already know what's wrong with me."

"What's wrong is that you abandoned your post, and if the captain finds out, you'll be in trouble."

"I — wait!" Teagut twisted around as I raised my head and grinned. He did not. "You!" His eyes narrowed. "You're the solution to my problem. The captain will forget that I aban-doned my post. All I have to do is turn you in."

"Turn me in for what? As far as anyone knows, I am up in that crow's nest. And you are trapped in here, under my treat-ment, with everything I think I know about medicine."

"Then you've got to help me," Teagut said. "It's your fault I'm in this situation."

"Well, to start, are you really ill or do you need an excuse for the captain?"

He gulped. "Which answer gets me away from you?"

"The second."

"Then that's my answer." He lowered his voice. "I came here because there's a rumor about a medicine Tobias made. One that . . . makes you sick."

We hadn't even been on this ship a full day, but Tobias had made this formula, spread the word about it, and found a lodestone. That was impressive. In that same time, I'd only attempted a mutiny, and it hadn't even succeeded.

Teagut pointed to a small shelf behind me. I reached for the bottle he was pointing at and gave it a shake. Liquid sloshed inside.

A knock came to the door and I heard Roden's voice on the other side. "Tobias?"

"Tell him I'm busy," I whispered.

Teagut repeated my message and Roden responded, "May I come in?"

"Absolutely not," I hissed.

"No," Teagut said. "I'm, uh . . . spurting blood at the moment."

I rolled my eyes. That was the best he could do?

But it seemed to work. Roden said, "Maybe you heard a few things while on the deck. You and I need to talk."

"Ask him what he wants to talk about," I whispered again.

Teagut did, and after a moment, Roden responded, "I just . . . I thought you might remember back to Farthenwood, to Conner's contest for the false prince. Only one of us was supposed to survive that, remember? But for a while, you and I had an alliance, and that kept us alive. I'm asking you to hold to that again. Stay with me, Tobias, for your own sake."

Again, my temper bristled. Not only because Roden had made me think of a time that still bundled me in knots, but because he was speaking of it inaccurately. Their alliance had not saved anyone's lives. I did that. All that their alliance had done was to . . .

"Almost get me killed," I mumbled.

Teagut looked up at me, alarmed. "You're going to get me killed?"

"No! Well . . . probably not. Hush and let me think."

Had I really understood Roden correctly? Strick told him to get me on my knees — that had been Conner's plan too, in his own way. Now it appeared that Roden was asking Tobias to help him achieve that goal, so that both of them might have a chance to live.

I heard Roden's footsteps as he left, but I still had Teagut to contend with. He said, "The only oath the pirates care about earned them the same branding on their forearms that you have. Is it true that Erick is dead?" I nodded and he added, "Then you are our king again, Jaron. What do you want from us?"

"Until I say otherwise, I want you all to stay alive. Which means for now, you will have to follow the captain's orders."

Teagut tilted his head. "We are pirates! Not dainty servants laying out tea towels and seating ourselves on a filthy deck for hours. Now, I know you won't ask all of them out there to risk their lives for you, but let me help. The Prozarian vigil with me is a talkative fellow, and maybe I have information for you."

"What is it?"

Teagut sucked in a breath, feeling quite proud of himself now. "I told you, Jaron, I am a pirate. If you want the information, a few coins in my pocket might help me remember it."

"I have your knife in my pocket. It also might help you remember."

He frowned. "We're headed to a place called Belland. The Prozarians attacked Belland a month ago."

"I know about that."

"But what you don't know is that just before returning to sea, the captain brought several things with her, all of it inside a green trunk that was so heavy, she almost couldn't push it up the gangplank. The Prozarian with me rushed over to help her and about got himself run through with a sword for the favor."

"Why should this trunk matter to me?"

"He saw her packing its contents into a closet behind her desk before she slammed her door shut and the room has been kept locked ever since, whether she's in or out of it. No one is allowed to see what's in that closet." Teagut shrugged. "I figured anything she protects so carefully might be interesting to you."

"It is. So how do I get into her office?"

He held out his hand. "That information was free. I'll expect payment for anything more."

"Fair enough. But I don't have the coins yet."

"Try to pay me before Belland," he said. "Nobody believes you'll make it to land."

It probably wasn't a joke, but it made me smile anyway. "I'll do my best."

I put the bottle Teagut had showed me inside my jacket and reached for a long rag instead.

"If you fake an illness, she may decide you're not worth the risk of keeping you on board. I have a different idea, but I'll give you a choice. Either way, I will send you out of here with physician's orders that you are not to be on vigil duty for the remainder of the voyage. Your first choice is that I can break your wrist and then bind it for you — that I will do out of the goodness of my heart. Or I can simply bind the wrist and let you pretend that it's injured, but if you choose that option, there are terms."

He swallowed hard. "What are the terms?"

"At some point in the near future, I will ask a favor of you. You must do what I ask, in the moment that I ask it. Then all will be equal between us."

"What is the favor?"

I rolled my eyes. "Well, I don't know that yet, or I would've asked you now. But no worries, it won't be anything I'm not willing to do myself, and at no point will you be required to sing from the bow of the ship. I cannot guarantee where else your singing talents might be required."

He frowned. "Why would I —?"

"The point is that we can help each other, or not. Promise to help me, and I will keep you out of trouble with the captain and get you out of any future vigil duty, which means you will avoid all the trouble I will certainly cause before this trip is over. You don't want any part of that, do you?"

"No."

"Then shall I bind your wrist now, or break it first?"

He frowned up at me. "Bind the wrist now. Your terms are fair."

They may have seemed fair in that moment, but he didn't know me very well. If he had, he would have chosen the broken wrist.

· ELEVEN ·

I couldn't get back on the main deck again until the next
shift change when the new vigils would be busy receiving
orders from the previous watch. So after sending Teagut
away, I had some time inside the sick bay. I leaned into the corner, hoping for a little sleep, but that was impossible. Directly
overhead, I soon heard the captain yelling at someone.

"How dare you abandon your watch, even for an injury!"

Ah, Teagut and his fellow vigil had been caught.

They mumbled their apologies, then Strick informed them
they would go without meals for the day.

The captain's quarters went quiet again, but my mind had
already begun to turn. I had a way inside that cabin . . . more
or less.

If the layout was similar to other caraval ships I'd seen,
then Strick's locked closet would be directly above the cabinet
where Tobias kept his medicines and other supplies. Digging
through them, I found a bone saw, which would be used only in
the case of gangrene or a crushed limb, or another serious injury.
Or if I needed a way into that closet.

I had planned to rest until the next shift change, but no sooner had I lain on Tobias's bed than one of the pirates strode across the deck shouting that everyone had ten minutes to report to the captain on the main deck for the morning assignments.

I groaned. That gave me only eight minutes to sleep, and two minutes to figure out what to do once I got on deck.

When the time came, I pulled Tobias's hat low, wrapped a cloak around my shoulders to avoid anyone comparing his build to mine, then crowded in alongside the other crewmen up to the deck. Even as they grumbled to one another about being pulled from their beds so early in the morning, I kept my head down and my hand on the knife I had stolen the night before. Most of the crewmen had been asleep when we were called, so I was fortunate enough to be surrounded by half-opened eyes and men who were more concerned with the chill in the air than looking my way. Once on deck, I lined up with the others and tried not to glare at Roden, who was near the front. I was desperate to know what he had wanted to speak to Tobias about, what his plans were that made him think back to their alliance at Farthenwood.

Wilta was standing on the deck behind him, her head down and arms wrapped around herself as protection from the cold. I felt sorry for her, but there was nothing I could do to help without revealing myself.

Amarinda was not here, notably, and that worried me. Wilta didn't appear to be treated well here; could Amarinda be faring any better?

Strick called Teagut and his companion forward, explained their offense and punishment, then said, "The only reason their punishment is not worse is because I am merciful enough to believe their reasons were just. But the next time a vigil abandons his post, regardless of the reasons, he had better be prepared for the worst I can do. Am I understood?"

"Yes, Captain," the crewmen echoed around me.

"Where is our physician? Where is Tobias?" Strick called out.

From my place near the back, I raised my hand. Strick said, "Get up into that crow's nest and check on Jaron. He hasn't responded to anyone this morning, and I want to know if he's still alive."

"Yes, Captain," I replied, in my best Tobias imitation. Roden was the only one who'd know our voices well enough to tell the difference, but if he knew, he said nothing as I stepped forward, angling my body away from him and the captain to climb.

I slid into the crow's nest to find Tobias shivering with cold and clearly upset with me.

"Y-y-you s-s-said you'd be back."

"As soon as I could get here. This was as soon as I could get here, Tobias." I withdrew my cloak and wrapped it around him, then returned his hat. "Now, look over the side of the nest where they can all see you and tell them I'm sick."

Tobias's eyes widened. "I-I'm the one who's sick."

"No, you're cold. If you become sick, I will feel terrible guilt, and honestly, I don't have time for that, so as a favor to me, don't get sick. But I want them to believe I am sick. Tell them so."

Tobias groaned, then did as I'd asked, shouting down, "Jaron is sick."

"Nobody gets sick from one night out in the cold," Strick called back.

With a glare at me, Tobias replied, "I'm the physician on this ship, and I can promise you, he's sick." He rolled back to me, angry again. "We're the ones who are sick, to stand beside you from one misadventure to the next."

"We? You and Roden?"

"Me and Roden and Amarinda — everyone who has ever known you."

I stared back at him as if I'd been slapped, but there was nothing to say. Tobias had just said exactly what he meant, what Roden had meant when he tried to resign as captain of my guard. Maybe Imogen would eventually speak those same words.

"Did you at least see Amarinda?" he asked. "Is she safe? Is she still alive?"

"I didn't get in."

He grunted with irritation. "Then what was all this for? You should have stayed here, where you belonged, and I could have gotten into the office."

"I tried, Tobias."

"What good did trying do for her?"

After too long a silence, I patted the pocket in Tobias's tunic. "I have your mixture that imitates an illness. How much does it take to bring on symptoms?"

"Where did you . . . it takes a while for symptoms to show. That won't help you here."

Wilta called up, "The captain orders you to bring Jaron down. She'll determine for herself if he's truly sick."

I pulled Tobias's tunic over my head and kicked off my boots, and he did the same.

"How much do I take?"

Tobias shrugged. "A gulp should be enough."

While he finished dressing, I pulled the cork from the bottle, then drank some, trying not to spit it out all over Tobias. Licking the bottom of my boot would have tasted better.

"That was a long gulp," he said. "I just told you a gulp."

I frowned at him. "Maybe you should have explained the difference between a long gulp and a regular gulp."

"If I had intended for anything but a regular gulp, I would have said so." We fell silent again while we each dressed, then he said, "I threw one of your boots over the crow's nest last night."

"You almost hit Roden."

For the first time since he'd come up here, Tobias smiled. "Did I?"

"I couldn't have aimed better myself."

"And why are these carpenter tools up here?"

"Obviously, I'm thinking of building a birdhouse."

"That's not even close to obvious."

"Put them up on the rail of the nest."

Tobias finished buttoning his tunic, then slipped on his boots. "Why?"

"Just do it!"

"Fine." Tobias did as I asked, then peered down at the deck far below. "You go first."

"No, you go first. I need time for your formula to work."

Tobias climbed out of the crow's nest and after he was

down, I followed. I was definitely tired from the long night, but that wouldn't pass for illness.

I was halfway down the ladder when the captain said, "If you come down, you will immediately fall directly to your knees before me. If you won't kneel, then climb back up there."

I paused on the ladder, not because I was thinking over her offer, but because the first wave of a fever struck me. It hit my flesh like opening the curtains in a darkened room to full sun, and the sudden heat in my body was scalding.

That first wave settled in my gut, and I started back down again.

"So you agree to obey my orders?" Strick called to me.

"I need to go to the sick bay." It was becoming harder to keep my grip on each rung as I descended. Not only was I weaker, but my vision was beginning to blur. It was inevitable that eventually I would reach for a rung that wasn't really there.

Then I did.

And I fell.

· TWELVE ·

I must've landed on or near some crewmen who broke my fall, though I ached so much, I truly didn't know whether the fall made anything worse for me than it already was. I was sure things were much worse for the people trapped beneath me.

"Stand aside!" Tobias pushed his way forward and pressed a hand to my forehead. "He's burning up with fever, and that fall did him no favors." He called out, "I need two men to carry him down to the sick bay."

"Wait!" Roden entered my field of vision and placed one hand on my head, then looked at Tobias in a panic. "He really is sick?"

I sat up, trying to make myself heard by as many crewmen as possible. "It's this cursed ship. I wonder who this illness will strike next."

At those few words, most of the nearby crewmen backed away, leaving Roden alone near me. He leaned in closer. "Is this real?"

"Make a different bargain with her. I will not kneel, not even for you."

"How did you —" He cut himself off there, then added, "I think I'm getting closer to —"

"Take him to the sick bay," Strick said. "Tobias, you will report to me within the hour. I want to know what's wrong with him."

"Yes, Captain."

Two crewmen lifted me and headed toward the lower deck. Tobias followed, but Roden stepped in front of him. "We've got to talk."

Tobias glanced at me. "Not now."

Roden began to reply, but Tobias quickly pushed past him. As they followed me down, Roden said, "Have you been telling us the truth all this time, Jaron? If you have any secrets that we should know about, there isn't much time left to tell us."

"Then don't waste my time with questions that make no sense." What time I had left. I felt awful.

Tobias had me placed on a table in the sick bay, then hung out his sign and locked the door. I curled up in a ball to take the edge off the pain, and Tobias began rummaging through his supplies.

"*I'm* the one who's actually sick," he muttered. "*I'm* the one you abandoned in that horrid crow's nest, but somehow *you're* the one in need of care."

"Am I even still alive?" I asked him. "What was in that bottle?"

"Nothing that should have produced these effects." He

hesitated, then pulled another bottle off his shelf. "Jaron, what bottle did you grab? This is the one that gives symptoms of illness."

I fumbled for the bottle in my jacket and showed it to him.

Tobias groaned, and I thought I heard him curse, which he rarely did. "You took a medication for pain."

I looked back at him, certain I had not heard him correctly. "Why do you have a medication that *causes* pain?"

"It stops pain, unless you take too much of it. We'll have to watch you and see what happens."

I forced myself into a sitting position, or what appeared to be a sitting position, though I was certain the room was angling. "Here's what will happen. You're going to discover that I injured myself in that fall, and it will require a painful surgery."

Tobias raised his hands, firmly shaking his head as he backed away from me. "I am *not* doing a surgery on you, Jaron. I've never done a surgery on anyone!"

"Hush! I'll scream a lot, and you've got to make as much noise as you can to scream back. Now, hand me that bone saw."

Tobias stepped away. "Absolutely not."

I crouched low on his table and held out my hand for it, then looked upward. Finally, Tobias understood and gave me the saw.

At the exact moment of my first cut into the wood overhead, I let out a bloodcurdling scream. Only seconds later, someone was pounding on the door. "What is happening in there?"

Tobias said, "I'm setting a bone. It's not as bad as it sounds."

"It's worse than it sounds," I called out.

"I'll get the captain."

Good. I needed her out of her quarters, but it also meant we had to hurry. I cut deeper into the wood along its natural lines, every cut accompanied by a scream that made my head want to explode. When I couldn't stand the pain any longer, Tobias took over while I continued to cry out for mercy, or death. Whichever came first.

Only a few minutes later, someone else pounded on the door. Roden.

"Let me in!"

"Not until this is over," Tobias said.

We were close to being finished. A few more screams and we'd be through, but I didn't dare attempt them with Roden on the other side of the door, especially if Strick had accompanied him.

"If you don't open this door, the captain has given orders to break it down," Roden said.

At my direction, Tobias stashed the saw, swept the wood dust under the table, then quickly wrapped my right arm.

"Open this door now!"

Just as Tobias finished the final knot in my dressing, I realized our mistake. When I had fallen from the ladder, I'd landed on my left side. My right arm should've been fine.

"Lie down. Look sick," Tobias hissed.

Neither was a problem for me. The worst of the fever had passed, but I still felt horrible, and I was in no mood, nor in any condition, for another confrontation with Roden.

Yet here it was.

Tobias opened the door and Roden was instantly by my side.

"Why are you sweating?"

"I might be dying. Can't I be allowed to sweat while I'm on my possible deathbed?"

Roden pointed to my arm. "Is it broken?"

Tobias shrugged. "We'll have to wait a few days to know for sure."

"I'm sure you wish it was broken," I muttered. "Then you'd be responsible for the second broken bone in my body."

"You said we have to talk." Tobias cut between us. "So let's talk."

Roden made a silent gesture with his head, signaling that someone was within listening range.

Wilta stepped forward. I hadn't expected that.

"One prisoner to keep another prisoner company?" she asked.

I shook my head, and I knew Tobias saw it, but he still said to her, "We're going to take a walk. Keep an eye on him."

Silently, I muttered a few choice words intended for Tobias. He should have found a way to keep Roden in this room, where I could hear them. Tobias would know that's what I'd want. So this was obviously a deliberate conversation without me, and about me.

And here I was, with Wilta standing near the doorway of the room, watching me. I desperately wanted to close my eyes and sleep off the pain that was forcing its way through every vein in my body, but all it would take to ruin my plan was for her eyes to flick up to the corner of the ceiling. The piece that we had cut was in its proper place, but if she looked carefully, she might see the cut lines.

So I turned, forcing her into an angle of the room where it would feel unnatural to look up.

"A night in the crow's nest shouldn't have made you like this," she said in a soft voice.

As best as I could, I shrugged, though I kept one hand on the table to hold myself upright. "This is what happens to people on cursed ships."

She glanced up at me. "Do you really believe in curses?"

"At the moment, I'm certain of it. Am I on fire right now? I mean, can you see any actual flames?"

"No."

"Well, that's good."

"Amarinda finally began speaking to me this morning. She said that if anyone could save my people, it's you."

"Right now, I'm not sure if I can save myself, but I promise that if there is any way to help, I will."

A tear rolled onto her cheek. "Then let me help you first, for you are in greater danger than you know. Early this morning, the captain told a few of the crew members that if you are not more cooperative today, you will not go on to Belland. She believes your defiance creates a bad example for the pirates."

I couldn't help but smile. I'd been called a bad example more times than I could count, but this was the first time I considered it a compliment.

"I can handle myself against the captain."

That didn't seem to satisfy her. "It will not be that simple. The Prozarians came through the plague not so many years ago. Those who survived it are stronger than any generation of their history."

I closed my eyes, trying to breathe as a particularly fierce flame passed through my chest. When it had finished, I said, "How is Amarinda?"

"She's strong too. Just confused. Like you, she wonders why she was targeted by the captain."

"Do you know?" I asked. Wilta shook her head, and I said, "If it's because they believe she's a princess, that's no longer her title. She has no power in Carthya."

"She told the captain that this morning, but the captain only laughed and said it was not true. I'll try to learn more, but I think the captain is becoming suspicious of me." Wilta drew in a sharp breath. "If I'm found out, it will go worse for me than even for you, because she trusts me a little."

I curled over and tried to ignore the shooting pains down my legs and up my arms. I needed to remain focused on what Wilta said.

She stood and put a hand on my back. "Are you all right?"

"Is my head upside down right now?"

"Yes."

"Then I'm not as bad as I thought." I sat up again. "Late last night, a fishing boat was spotted in the distance. I saw it again this morning from the crow's nest."

"We've seen it too. It's just a thin old man with a fishing net he can barely drag half-full onto his deck. He's no threat to this ship." Wilta sighed. "I won't defend the captain, Jaron. I've suffered more than most because of her. But she isn't wholly evil. She won't harm that fishing boat without cause."

I hoped not. Because a plan was forming in my mind, and my only choice might be begging help from a thin old man.

Wilta took my hand. "Are you feeling any better?"

I pulled my hand free to help balance my head. I tried to answer her, but my words were blurring and finally I gave up. She couldn't understand me, and I was unable to hold two thoughts together long enough to decipher her questions. Time continued to drag by until the door opened again and Tobias walked in.

Wilta quickly stood, eager for an excuse to leave. "I should go and let you rest."

Once she was gone and the door was closed, I lay down, still curled into a ball. "What did Roden have to say?"

Tobias frowned. "The captain called Roden to the deck at first light, before anyone else was called. She asked him a question that he couldn't answer. So he wants me to ask you."

"If the question is whether Wilta likes him back, the answer is, who cares?"

Tobias sighed. "The captain asked him whether you cried at your family's funeral."

I opened my eyes, squinting at him to be sure I'd heard him correctly. "How is that relevant to anything happening now?"

"She seemed to think it was relevant, but Roden couldn't answer because he wasn't there."

"He wasn't there because he was attempting to assassinate me, if you recall."

"Of course I recall. But the question spooked Roden enough that he wants me to get you off this ship. There's only one lifeboat on this ship and he wants you on it tonight." Tobias hesitated. "I told him I would make sure you are."

I made myself sit up again and dizziness overtook me, forcing me to lie down. "You don't get to make plans for me — that is not your place. Nor is it Roden's. I will decide when to leave this ship."

"Unless the captain has you killed first — don't you think she is considering that now? Maybe she originally planned to bring you all the way to Belland, but I don't think she cares about that anymore. In fact, I think the only reason you're still here is because she doesn't want to risk a revolt from the pirates."

"The pirates would shift loyalties from me for a single gold coin."

Tobias sighed. "Then what should we do?"

My eyes turned upward. We had completed a cut into the ceiling, but in our hurry, we had made the opening too small for either of us to fit through. Nor could we widen it. As far as everyone knew, my surgery was over. Any use of the bone saw now ran too high a risk of discovery.

Besides that, I desperately needed to rest. If I'd slept at all last night, it could be measured in minutes, not hours, and I was still aching fiercely from the formula I'd swallowed. I lay on the table and closed my eyes, and in a chair beside me, Tobias did the same.

The last thing he asked before he fell asleep was, "But did you cry at their funeral?"

No, I hadn't.

· THIRTEEN ·

It couldn't have been much later before a knock came at the door, summoning Tobias out of the sick bay. My ears perked up when I recognized the voice as belonging to Captain Strick, who said, "Were you not ordered to give me a report in one hour?"

I peeked through half-opened eyes enough to see Tobias leap to his feet. He glanced back, assuring himself I was still asleep, then hurried out the door.

I felt better enough that this time when I sat up, I didn't feel like losing the entire contents of my stomach. I crept over to the door and pressed my ear to it.

"Jaron was missing from the kingdom for a while," Strick said to Tobias. "How did he come to the throne?"

"He was living on his own as a boy named Sage. A regent named Bevin Conner captured Roden, Sage, and me with the intent of making one of us look and act enough like Jaron that he could fool the entire kingdom. Turns out that Jaron was one of the boys he captured."

"Until Conner captured him, did Jaron have any idea of his family's deaths?"

"No, I don't think so. Why does it —"

"You don't *think* so? Is it possible he did?" Tobias hesitated and she added, "You gave me a loyalty oath. Answer my question."

"He kept a lot of secrets from us, so it is possible that he knew. Why do you ask?"

"If Jaron took the throne from his family, justice demands that it be taken from him."

I tilted my head, curious about her choice of words. Tobias's tone of voice suggested he was equally curious. "You misunderstood me, Captain. Jaron inherited the throne *after* his family's deaths."

Strick said, "For four years, Jaron was forced to live on his own, struggling for every minute of life. Don't you think he resented his father for that, resented his brother for living in luxury as a crown prince while Jaron fought for every crust of moldy bread, or for the corner of a filthy blanket on a cold night?"

Tobias faltered. "I don't . . . I . . . perhaps he did. But you don't think he —"

"Carthya deserves to know the truth. Jaron killed his parents so that he could take the throne."

I almost shouted out in protest, and might have done so if I could speak at all. But I remained where I was, frozen in shock at the accusation.

Tobias asked, "Is there any evidence?"

"We have all the evidence we need."

Her words stopped my heart in its place. What evidence could she possibly have to prove something that was not only untrue, but that horrified me to my very core?

Strick continued, "All I want to know is whether I can count on you, as part of this crew, to tell the truth about Jaron when the time comes."

Tobias stumbled again through finding his words. "The truth? Yes, I can do that much. Thank you for talking with me."

"Come and join us upstairs, Tobias. Amarinda has been asking to see you, and I see no reason to refuse her."

"Er . . . yes, of course."

"What is Jaron's condition? Is he still sick?"

Tobias paused a moment, then said, "I wouldn't rule out the plague."

A longer pause followed from her. "He must stay in there until you are certain. My people came through the plague only after great devastation, and I won't risk another outbreak here. We'll leave someone here to watch his door and make sure he stays put."

The instant I was sure they had gone, I pounded a fist against the bulkhead, absolutely furious for any number of reasons. This wasn't only about my parents; it was about Tobias's willingness to consider something that he knew was not true. I also wondered how he could fail to see that the captain was leading him along the very same path that Roden was on: a path that led away from loyalty to me and ever closer to being a Prozarian servant.

Soon after, the bell rang for the midday meal, and Tobias still hadn't returned. A rush of men followed from all parts of the ship into the galley, where their far inferior meal would be served. It'd likely be little more than old eggs and crusty bread, and if they offered me a single bite, I'd gratefully accept. I hadn't eaten since yesterday, and I was beginning to feel it.

The bell must have also prompted a change in vigils at my door. There was a soft knock and I opened the door to see Teagut standing there. He said, "Do you have my coins?"

"Where would I have gotten any coins? I've been trapped in here all day."

"If you had time out of the sick bay, maybe you could find me some coins." I started forward but he raised an arm, adding, "Of course, if I allow that, there will be an additional price."

"Oh?"

"Other than me, this deck is empty. But if anyone were to ask why you are no longer in the sick bay, for thirty coins, I might claim you overpowered me and when I awoke, you had escaped."

"For zero coins, I might just overpower you and escape."

"Yes, but for thirty coins, I'll save you the effort. And, because I think we make a great team, I might clear the way for you to get down to the gunpowder magazine. That's where they put most of the things they stole off our ship. There's something down there you might want to see."

"What?"

"You'll figure it out."

That bit of information might easily be worth thirty coins.

I smiled at him, saying, "When I fight, I don't generally leave any marks. You might look just the same as you do now."

"It's a pleasure to have been defeated by you. Come back with a few coins, and I'll see that this deck is cleared when you return."

I crept past him toward the open hatch and silently descended into the lowest point on the ship, the cargo hold. It was dark down there, and a favorite place on a ship for rats. I hated rats.

Packed into the bulk of this deck were the usual supplies: barrels of water, crates of grain and crackers and dried meat. But the far end of the ship contained a gunpowder magazine. This was a copper-lined area strictly forbidden to any sailors who had not been trained in the safe handling and storage of gunpowder. A single spark could sink the entire ship, and for that reason, most ships banned any use of open flames on the deck, but especially anywhere near the magazine.

However, I felt fairly comfortable in entering, mostly because after accidentally exploding plenty of things in Carthya, I'd learned how to handle gunpowder. Once, during a regents' meeting, I had noticed that other than Harlowe, my chief regent, the entire assembled group was seated in the corner farthest away from me.

"I have bathed," I told them, though apparently, that wasn't the problem.

Mistress Kitcher spoke for the rest of the group, explaining that they didn't feel safe in the same room as me, ever since I had begun — in her own words — exploding pieces of Carthya into thin air, one statue at a time. I thought that was unfair criticism. I'd only exploded one statue, and it was entirely by accident. The other targets of my experiments may have been fountains, monuments, and the occasional empty building. But there had only been one statue.

However, I had no desire to explode anything on this ship, at least not while people I cared about were still on it. So I entered carefully to look around. On the bulkhead to my left, three shelves contained rows of sealed tubes of gunpowder. In the center of the magazine was the prize of our trade with Bymar, the five crates of weapons. Regardless of why the captain wanted me or Amarinda, her possession of these weapons was highly dangerous to Carthya, to Belland, and to any country she might target next. I could not allow her to have them.

Nor could I destroy them here without sinking this ship. But I pried the crates open one by one, staring at them until at last I figured out a way to turn the theft of these weapons to my advantage. I reached for the extra stocking that I had found yesterday in the room that Roden now occupied, removed my boots, and pulled off my own stockings with a plan in mind. But opening the fourth crate shifted my attention.

The others had been entirely full — that was the agreement with Bymar. But this crate had a small gap in one corner. I couldn't imagine that Bymar would have cheated us, and maybe the Prozarians had removed a few weapons to test them, but there was another possibility. The gap in those weapons had just enough room to . . .

"Fink!" I hissed the name louder than I should have, but I already knew he was here. "Fink, show yourself now!"

A full ten seconds passed before I heard a rustling sound outside the magazine. I left the room in time to see Fink emerge from behind two barrels and a stack of extra blankets.

He looked terrified, and when I started toward him, he began backing up. "Don't be angry. I needed a place to hide. You would have done the same thing."

I grabbed him and held him by the shoulders. "Do you know how dangerous this room is?" Then I pulled him to me and wrapped my arms around him, digging my fingers into his back. Until now, I hadn't realized how afraid I had been for him. "Why are you here? I'd hoped you were on the boat that Imogen escaped with —"

"What boat?"

I stood back from him. "The lifeboat that escaped the *Red Serpent*. There was a figure inside made to look like me."

"I heard them talking about it. Imogen planned to release the lifeboat, then Mott was supposed to hide her within the walls, just like Amarinda." His brows pressed together. "I know they brought Amarinda here, I've heard them talk about her. But where is Imogen?"

I pushed a hand through my hair. "I don't know. Are you sure she didn't get on that lifeboat?"

"I don't know what happened, to either her or to Mott. I was busy looking for my own place to hide."

"You were supposed to hide in the walls too!"

He frowned. "And if I had and they sank the ship, where would I be?"

I must have had a visible reaction to his words, because he quickly apologized, adding, "Imogen wouldn't have stayed hidden once the ship took cannon fire. She would have escaped. Mott too." He paused while I collected my thoughts, then added, "I chose the crates because I knew they'd bring them here. I figured at some point, you'd need my help." He pointed to my wrist, still wrapped in the bandages. "I could have helped prevent that."

I pulled my wrist behind me. "Do you think having you here helps me, that it helps anything? I'm having trouble keeping myself safe — how am I supposed to do that for you?"

"I've stayed safe this entire trip. I've found food on my own, or at least, I did at first. Tobias will help me now."

I stopped to stare at him. "Tobias knows you're here?"

"Shortly after we boarded, I snuck into the sick bay for food. He caught me there."

"How did you get into the sick bay?"

Fink pointed out the window. "It was simple. I crawled out and grabbed a rope that was hanging low and used it to climb into the lifeboat, then pulled myself up to the nearest porthole to his room and snuck in. Like I said, simple." He drew in a quick breath. "Tobias caught me a few minutes before he went to the deck to bring you the lodestone. I found that, by the way, down here. I just didn't know what it was. So I suppose I helped you in that way too, huh?"

"*Tobias* knew you were here and failed to say anything to me?" I still couldn't believe my own words.

"He hasn't said anything to Roden either, not even when they both came down here a while ago. I —"

"Stop." I stepped toward him. "What did they say?"

Fink stared at me. "Roden said you're not king anymore, that the throne belongs to someone else."

"There is no one else."

"Roden told Tobias to get you off this ship, but said he's got to stay and see this through."

"See what through? Whatever Roden has heard, he's wrong. No one else could possibly be —" I stopped there, my heart suddenly racing. I looked at Fink. "Come with me."

"Where?"

"I need your help."

He threw a fist into the air. "I knew you would! Where are we going?"

Despite what Fink had said, I had to believe that Imogen was on that lifeboat, and Mott too, though I knew it wasn't possible. Swallowing those worries, I pointed to the porthole. "Get back into the lifeboat, and let's hope that spare rope is still there." I explained my plan to him, then practically shoved him out the porthole.

He would meet me in the sick bay when he was finished, but I needed to finish my work here and get there too. The entire future of Carthya depended on it.

· FOURTEEN ·

Despite Teagut's promise, the lower deck was far from abandoned when I climbed up to it. In fact, it was the very opposite, crowded with both pirates and Prozarians, half of them grumbling about afternoon duties when they only wanted to sleep, and the other half wanting to stay awake and gamble.

"Place your wagers," one Prozarian in the corner was calling. "Come now, pirates. You lost your ship, why not lose your coins as well?"

That set off a round of arguments and a few thrown fists, but I put my head down and walked straight through them all.

Teagut was still guarding the sick bay door and pointed out his addition to Tobias's sign, which now read, SUSPECTED PLAGUE. DO NOT ENTER. I grinned at him, promised myself again to find a way to pay him the coins he was owed, and entered.

Tobias hadn't yet returned from the midday meal, but I was anxious to speak to him. I listened at the door as a man walked up to speak to Teagut.

"Did I see that door open just now?"

"Jaron wanted to escape," Teagut replied. "I told him to go back inside and he did. He's afraid of me."

"Then you should remain as vigil. What if the plague gets loose on this ship? We'll all be dead."

A third man joined them. "Maybe this is a cursed ship after all."

Behind me, I heard a knocking sound at Tobias's porthole window. I turned and saw Fink's face, upside down, waving at me.

I rushed over to him and opened the window, then grabbed his arms to pull him through.

"Why are you upside down?" I asked.

"I pulled the wrong rope. It carried me up a little high, almost to the deck. Wouldn't that have been awful?"

He grinned. I did not.

"No one goes inside," Teagut said from outside the sick bay door. "No one."

Whoever was speaking to him was much quieter. I opened a cabinet door and told Fink, "Get inside."

"I hate hiding in dark places!"

"You got on this ship by hiding in a crate!"

"That's how I know I hate it."

"Get in." I shoved him in almost as forcefully as I'd sent him out the porthole, then closed the door in time for Tobias to enter, which he did in an unexpected good mood. Then I remembered why. He had just seen Amarinda.

"How is she?"

"Ready to escape. We all are, but only if you are there too."

"I won't leave until I have more answers."

"Amarinda has taken care of that."

"How?"

Tobias's smile fell. "She stole the captain's closet key."

"Why do you look like you've just announced a funeral?"

"What if you don't want to know what's in that closet?"

Eagerly, I held out my hand. "What if I do?"

Tobias's eyes shifted. "The key is useless down here. Amarinda will unlock the closet when it's safe."

My brows pressed together as my heart began to pound. "It will never be safe! Where does she think the captain will search first when she discovers the key is lost?"

"Is it safer to sneak you in to unlock it?"

I clenched my fists, a quieter method of expressing frustration than yelling. "What if she is caught searching inside that closet?"

"Jaron, you are not the only one who can take risks, nor the only one who can hide a secret."

"Oh, I already understand that." I opened the cupboard door and Fink popped out, breathing heavily as if he'd been holding his breath for the past ten minutes.

His first words were, "I only told Jaron so that he'd be angry with you instead of me."

Tobias slowly exhaled before looking up. "I'm sorry."

"What other secrets are you keeping from me?"

"No other secrets."

I doubted that was true, but this wasn't the time to force those secrets out of him. Nor was it that time for the next several hours as we waited within the sick bay for Amarinda's signal. I gave him every opportunity to talk to me, but he refused each time. Finally, we heard a knocking sound in our room. But it wasn't coming from the door, nor the bulkhead.

Fink had been entertaining himself by rearranging Tobias's medicines in every possible way. He accidentally knocked over a few when he pointed upward. "It's coming from the compartment overhead." Then he squinted. "Did you cut a hole in it?"

I jumped onto the medical table and steadied myself before removing the piece of wood we had cut. There was no way of knowing who would be on the other end of the hole until I saw them, but it probably didn't matter. Whoever this was obviously knew what I had done.

I wiggled the cut piece of wood until it came loose, then slowly lowered it, only to see Amarinda's face peering down at me.

"I'm sorry it took so long," she said. "Wilta's been in here until just a few moments ago. You'll want to see what I've found."

Tobias eyed me. "No, Jaron, I don't think you will."

"So there are other secrets." Disappointed, I clicked my tongue, then raised my arms to take the first item.

FIFTEEN

From below, Tobias, Fink, and I formed a line. I would take each item and pass it to Fink, who would give it to Tobias, who was standing near his bed, ready to place each item on a sheet he had laid out.

After a few breathless seconds, the first items came through, small bundles of gold coins in satin bags. They clanked louder than I wished they did, and I held them tight in my hands as I passed them all over to Fink. All of them but the last bag, which I placed inside a pocket of my jerkin. A notebook came next, presumably Captain Strick's, though I had no time to read it now.

While we worked, Tobias said, "If I have kept secrets, it's because there are things in this closet the captain will kill you for stealing. Nothing here matters as much as your life." If that was his attempt at an apology, it was pathetic.

And he was wrong. "Carthya matters more than my life."

"I know that." Tobias put his hand on my arm. "And I think it's possible that what you find in this closet might be a threat to Carthya."

Still irritated, I brushed off his hand. "All the more reason to keep going."

From above, Amarinda whispered, "I don't know what this is."

She passed down another, larger satin bag. Inside was a brass tube, no longer than my hand, with an eyepiece on one end and three slots through its middle. The workmanship was exceptional, and it bore strange markings around the rim.

A small metal box was in the same bag, and when I opened it, I saw a glass lens with etchings on it. I inserted it into the first slot and there saw an image of a large, rocky cave with a long cliff at one end that dropped into seawater. From the angle of the carving, water appeared to be passing through the cave.

"I wonder if this is Belland." I tried to pass the tube to Tobias, but he pushed it away, clearly nervous.

"That cannot be a good thing to steal!" He grabbed it and tried to hand it back to Amarinda, but I pulled his arm down and took the scope.

His eyes wide with panic, Tobias said, "Put that back, please. Don't take anything more than we must take."

"Agreed. But we must take this." I gave the items to Fink to put back into their bags, and while he did, I said, "After we've emptied that closet, Wilta knows a secret way from the captain's office down here. You've got to help Amarinda find it. Then the three of you are going to bundle up this sheet and get everything off this ship. Is the lifeboat ready for them, Fink?"

He squinted. "I suppose. Aren't you —" I glared at him and he said, "Yes, it's ready."

Tobias had understood what Fink did not say. "You said you would come with us."

"I said I would come *if* I'd found the answers I needed. I haven't found them. Now, when the time comes, I'll provide the distraction you need. Just make sure nothing remains."

Tobias raised a brow. "I know your kind of distractions." He reached for a roll of bandages and tossed them onto the sheet. "All right, but this is all we can carry."

"Jaron!" Amarinda whispered. "Is this yours? It looks similar, only larger."

She passed a crown through the hatch and immediately my heart stopped. More accurately, I felt time itself stop.

I knew this crown, but why was it here?

It was gold leaf with interwoven lacing around the rim and lined with round sapphires. Its owner used to have his servants polish it after every wearing in public, and eventually it became nearly bright as a mirror. I saw myself in the gold now. It still was that bright.

I looked up at Tobias, who eyed me with an expression of dread more than surprise. I let that soak in.

Tobias should have been surprised, or curious, or shocked, or any of a dozen possible emotions that would suggest he didn't know any better than me what was about to come through our carved hole.

But of all possibilities, it was dread. This was the secret he did not want to reveal.

"You knew about this?" I mumbled.

"From what Roden told me, I suspected there'd be something up there. I didn't know it was this. Is it real?"

I nodded, unable to take my eyes off the object in my hands. "This was my brother's crown . . . once."

When he had intended to create a false prince, Conner had taken possession of my crown. Perhaps he had taken Darius's crown too, around the time of his death. Along with my parents, Darius had been poisoned at a supper one night, a joint plan concocted by Conner and the former head of the castle guard. But why would Conner have taken this crown, and how could it have fallen into Captain Strick's hands? The Prozarians could have no connection to that plot against my family; at least, not in any way I understood.

"There's one more item," Amarinda said. "Jaron, what does this mean?"

I positioned myself directly beneath the gap. If my brother's crown had stopped my heart, then what she began lowering now made it pound so hard that I wondered how it didn't beat through my chest.

"Jaron, please put everything back," Tobias whispered.

This was a sword, one I took hold of with carefully placed fingers, noting with a quick test that it was as sharp as I remembered. "This was my brother's too." I glanced over at Tobias with tears in my eyes. "Why do they have these?"

The sapphire set into the pommel had a scratch across the center. Darius had done that when he tried to follow me up a wall of the castle years ago. He'd slipped and fallen hard enough to sprain his ankle. He never climbed again, and I'd gotten in trouble for urging him to try it.

With that confirmation, any sentimental feelings within me vanished, replaced with something beyond anger. The sudden burning in my chest was a desire for vengeance against Strick, and whoever got in my way on my path to her.

"You wanted your distraction," I said to Tobias. "Get Amarinda down here, then I want the three of you in that lifeboat immediately. This will be your only chance."

I flung open the door, wielding Darius's sword against two vigils who must have recently replaced Teagut. "Step aside or I will strike," I warned them.

They obeyed and I pushed past them, marching directly to the crewmen's bunks, where Teagut was lying on his bed. He sat up and stared at me with an open mouth. I reached into my jerkin and tossed him the sack of gold coins. "Go to the sick bay. Do whatever they ask."

Then I rounded the corner to reach the steps for the main deck. Roden stood in front of them, his eyes locking on mine. He knew I would be here. He knew *why* I'd be here. And that made me angrier than ever.

Behind me, Tobias put a hand on my shoulder. "Come back into the sick bay."

I pushed his hand away and growled, "How much of this did you two know?"

"I warned you to leave —" Roden began.

"No, I'm asking what you knew! What you still know and aren't telling me!"

A spark flickered in his eyes before he finally answered. "Earlier this morning, the captain told me she had gotten these directly from Darius. I didn't tell you because I thought she was lying —"

"She is lying. Darius is dead."

"Maybe he's not. A lot of what she claims makes sense. But I didn't want to come to you with this news until I was sure. I swear that I would have told you when I thought you'd be ready."

"You had no right to make that decision for me! You had no right to keep *this* a secret!"

"How many secrets have you kept from us? How many do you still keep?" His eyes flashed. "Tell me, right now, is there anything about this voyage that you have not shared with me?"

"Count on it."

"Well, I'm telling you everything now. Go back to the sick bay. I'll tell the captain you are having sick delusions. She might trust me enough to believe that."

"That's an interesting way of putting it, since you've done so well in losing my trust."

Roden reached for my arm, but I shook it off. "Listen to me," he said. "I am trying to help you. But you must return to the sick bay and give up this fight, at least for now."

I raised the sword. "I never give up."

"I know that." Roden's expression changed, but not to anger as I would have expected. Instead, his brows pressed low and his eyes softened to sadness. "But this one time, I wish more than anything that you would."

· SIXTEEN ·

I started toward Roden but he crossed directly in front of the steps. "You're not getting past me."

"I'll go past you or go through you, your choice." I raised my brother's sword. "Where is the captain?"

He sighed and stepped aside. "The wardroom. Don't do this, Jaron."

"The wardroom?" I arched a brow. "Good. I'm hungry." I turned back to Tobias. "Didn't I already give you other orders?"

"You're only making this worse. . . ." He brushed a hand over the nape of his neck. "Just listen to us."

"To you?" I looked from him back to Roden. "The two people on this ship who I thought were my friends have proven themselves nearly as deceitful as my enemies. Why does the captain have my brother's sword and crown?"

Roden's eyes widened. "You have the crown too? They were supposed to be her secret."

"Your secret as well, obviously." I turned to Tobias. "And

you stood face-to-face with the captain as she claimed that I killed my parents. Why didn't you defend me?"

"Weren't you asleep —?"

"Why didn't you defend me, Tobias? Conner killed my parents, you know that! He killed my whole family, Darius included. And you stood there and accepted her accusation when you know the truth!"

"Why does it matter what she thinks?"

"It matters to me. So tell me, either of you, where did the captain get these items?"

Roden shook his head. "Give me more time. I will get the answers, but until then, please stay out of this!"

"How can I stay out of my own business?" With a growl, I pushed past Roden and climbed the stairs, kicking him away when he grabbed for my leg. Minutes later, I stormed into the captain's wardroom. She had just broken some bread into her hands, where it remained. Wilta had been seated across from her but now stood, alarmed.

Finally, the captain took a bite of bread and calmly stared at me. "There you are. I wondered what was taking so long."

"Give me one reason not to use this sword," I said.

Roden burst in behind me. "Forgive me, Captain. I don't know how he got that sword."

The captain sent a glare to Wilta, who cowered beneath it. "Bring Amarinda to me. I want a word with the princess."

But when Wilta was within a few steps of me, I grabbed her arm and pulled her tight against me, raising the sword.

Wilta gasped. "Jaron, I'm innocent."

"So was my brother. Why do you have this, Captain?"

Her expression remained eerily calm. "Put down the sword, and I'll explain everything."

"Explain now. Wilta and I are fine as we are."

She lowered the bread and stood to face me. "You are wrong if you think threatening Wilta makes any difference — she means nothing to me. But I believe the owner of that sword would be ashamed to see you use it in this way."

"Its owner is dead. I'll work this out with him when I'm on the other side."

"That will come sooner than you think, if you continue on this path. I have only borrowed that sword, from the true king of Carthya. He insisted it be returned to him in the same condition as when I borrowed it."

"Who insisted?"

From behind me, Roden added, "That's what the captain is trying to explain to you, Jaron. Darius is alive."

I shook my head, angry at his lies, or his stupidity for believing her lies. Angry with all of them for using my brother's name, even his own most beloved possessions, as a tactic against me, and against all of Carthya, the country that Darius would have one day ruled.

Then I shook my head even harder, determined to stop this deception now, before it went any further.

"This sword isn't real," I said. "You've had an imitation made."

"Of course it's real," Strick said. "You know yourself that this sword wasn't at the burial."

Nor was Darius's crown. They hadn't been with my family when I came to the castle, and though I had searched for them, I'd buried my brother without either. I still regretted giving him so few honors.

Strick added, "This wasn't the way I had hoped to deliver the news to you. But you must accept the blame for that. I asked for cooperation. In exchange, you've insulted me, spread rumors around this ship, and faked a very loud episode of the plague."

"Perhaps I missed your request for cooperation when you had Erick killed. Or maybe when you captured my friends and sank my ship!"

She threw out her arms, the same way my tutors used to do when they refused to argue with me. "You make it sound like all of that is my fault. When were we ever unclear about our purpose? Had you surrendered immediately, your ship would be happily on its way by now."

I huffed but gave no response, because I had no response to give. There was too much truth in her words.

She added, "Cooperate now, and it may save those who are still alive. You care about the princess, I hope?"

"Is she safe?"

Strick gestured toward the sword. "*He* would not wish us to harm her."

I took that in, letting my eyes graze over the handle. I'd held it before, at times when Darius and I used to practice against each other. The design of a sword might be imitated, but it was highly unlikely that the weight would be so exact.

"Where did you get it?" I asked.

"As I've already tried to explain, Darius sent it with me."

I froze, finally hearing what the captain was saying.

"*Darius* sent it?"

"This is why I wanted you. This ship is headed to Belland now, as part of our agreement to bring you to him. We are in the service of the true king of Carthya. As we have served the people of Belland."

I said to Wilta, "You're here as their prisoner. Does it feel as though they've served you?"

She only squeaked out, "Right now, I feel more threatened by you than by them."

I loosened my grip on her, but that was all. She had to remain in this room until I was certain Amarinda was safely gone.

Strick said, "We offered the Bellanders a chance to join in our quest, to be part of a glorious future. They refused, and now their reward for helping is that we grant them their lives. We tried to be their friends, but we can be as harsh as is necessary until we are accepted."

"If you truly offered them friendship, harshness would never be necessary," I said. "Now, where is this brother of mine, or whoever is using his name?"

She smiled. "I told you there is an agreement between us and your brother. If anything disrupts that agreement, we will kill him and simply take what we want. So you had better start cooperating."

I'd learned to tolerate many frustrations in life: restrictive clothing, overcooked meat, the occasional threat to my existence.

But blackmail was unacceptable, particularly when it came from villains such as these.

Strick rolled her eyes. "Your cooperation begins with lowering that sword. It is impossible to have a reasonable conversation with you right now."

I had no intentions of harming Wilta, but to be fair, after all that had happened in the last day, I figured I ought to threaten someone. However, my thoughts always ended with the fact that the captain had information I desperately wanted. So I lowered the sword but kept it in my hands as I stood back.

I pointed out the nearest chair to Wilta. "Sit there." When she did, I asked, "How far away is Belland?"

"Another day at sea, if the winds remain to the west. Once we arrive, you will be greeted by your brother, who will explain his agreement with us, and your role in it. He hopes you will peacefully surrender the throne." Strick's lip curled. "Though he is prepared to take it, if you are not careful."

It was far too late for me to be careful. "How did Darius come to be on Belland?"

Strick shrugged.

"How long has he been there?"

Now she sighed. "Will there be many more questions?"

"Absolutely. Do you intend to attack Carthya?"

"Not if your brother keeps his agreements with us."

I arched a brow. "What agreements?"

"That is between me and the true king of Carthya."

I shook my head. "You may have Darius's sword but you do not have him. My brother is dead. I buried him myself."

"Did you? Or was it someone who looked very much like him? Darius has a mole on his right wrist. Did the boy you buried have that mole?"

I genuinely couldn't remember. He'd been dressed in ceremonial clothing that came past his wrists, so I easily could have missed that. And if I was honest with myself, the captain's claims weren't impossible. Once I came to the castle, enough time had passed since the deaths of my family that their bodies were nearly unrecognizable.

"There is only one way to find out the truth," Strick said. "Cooperate with me, and we'll keep you alive until we reach Belland."

My eyes narrowed. "That's another lie, Captain. You have no interest in keeping me alive, not anymore."

Her lips tightened with equal anger. "If that plan has changed, it's only because you have forced it to change."

I looked at Roden, who had remained silent in a corner of the wardroom for several minutes. "Did you know all of this?"

His shoulders fell. "No, not all."

But he had known some of it and failed to say anything to me. I wondered what else he was still holding back.

Then he added, "But if you give her that sword and agree to cooperate, she may allow you to —"

I shook my head, and addressed the captain directly. "No, this is my offer. Give me control of the ship and I'll agree to meet this person who claims to be my brother."

"Where is the advantage for us?" Strick asked.

I smiled. "A great advantage. In exchange for *your* cooperation, I will agree not to cripple the Prozarian army."

Strick smiled. "That's a kind proposal, but you should have listened to Roden."

"Roden is in your service now. He can offer nothing that I want."

Her smile became crisp and cold. "Then I will."

"Jaron, I'm sorry!"

I didn't need to turn around to know that was Fink speaking to me. My heart sank, then filled with dread. Behind me, another voice said, "We have a stowaway, Captain. What should we do with him?"

"Well, I don't know." Strick's eyes were on me. "What do you think, Jaron? Will you consider returning that sword now?"

I briefly closed my eyes, then placed the sword on the table and pushed it over to her.

Captain Strick turned to Roden next. "Do you remember what I said would get me to trust you? That time has come."

I locked eyes with Roden, casting a glare that I fully intended him to feel.

He squirmed beneath it, then said, "What will you say to the crew?"

She stood. "I will tell them that this boy must be punished for disobedience." Her eyes shifted to me. "How many rules have you broken on this ship?"

"Possibly all of them," I replied.

"If you cannot do this, Roden, if your loyalties somehow

are still attached to Jaron, then tell me now so that I can make an example of you first. Take him out to the deck and get him on his knees, either willingly or by force. Then assemble the crew for his punishment."

Now her attention returned to me. "If you resist in any way, your little stowaway friend will take the punishment for you."

I felt Roden staring at me again, but this time, I would not look back. Instead, I felt his hand wrap around my arm, and he whispered, "Tell me what to do."

Strick passed the sword over to Wilta. "Return this to its original place. Make sure that everything else is still there."

She followed Roden and me out, but when she turned away, I whispered to him, "You protect Fink, at all costs."

"I warned you to go back to the sick bay," he replied. "You should have done what I asked. I had this under control."

I stopped walking long enough to look at him. "There's a difference between us, Roden. I never fool myself into believing I have anything under control."

"I can fix this," Roden whispered.

"You can't —"

My words were cut off when Wilta screamed from inside the captain's quarters.

"You can't fix that," I said.

Wilta rushed onto the deck, the sword still in her hands. "Captain, I beg you to forgive me for having to deliver this news, but everything is gone."

"The Devil's Scope?"

"And the first lens. Everything is gone, Captain."

Roden and I locked eyes.

My options had narrowed until I'd had only one choice left. They had been warned.

Now I only had to hope my plan would work. Considering my history, it likely would not.

But I was still in a far better position than anyone else on this deck.

· SEVENTEEN ·

In the chaos that followed, Fink was able to get close to my side. I leaned over to him and whispered, "Where's Tobias?"

"He's in the lifeboat. Sorry, Jaron, I went back for something and got caught."

I was sorry too. I'd had a plan in mind for myself, but it would have to do for Fink. I whispered, "First chance you get, take the mainsail rope and tie it around your arm. Make it tight. Understand?"

"I rarely understand you. But I'll do it."

"Where are the contents of that closet?" Strick asked. Or more accurately, she yelled the question, which was unnecessary. I was an arm's length away and could hear her just fine. "I demand an answer!"

I eyed Fink, and he quietly began winding the rope around his arm.

Behind me, one of the Prozarians strode forward and belted me across the backs of my legs. I hadn't expected that and fell to my hands and knees, letting the sting pass.

"I asked you a question, Jaron."

"Touch me again and I'll have those items destroyed." I forced myself back to my feet. "Start telling me the truth and I'll consider returning the items that are yours."

"The Devil's Scope is a valuable —"

"Valuable relic, yeah, I figured it must be, and I have it. So I want answers. Where did you get my brother's sword?"

"From Darius — I've explained that! He sent me with something to convince you that he was alive."

"Well, it didn't work. I'm not convinced. If he's been alive all this time, why hasn't he returned to Carthya?"

"He's ready to return now."

"Darius is buried beside my parents. Whoever you are dealing with is a fraud."

A false prince. The words echoed in my mind.

"I've answered every question as fully as I can. Now, where are my things?" the captain asked again.

"In my control, to save or to destroy. Turn this ship over to me, or I will prove just how cursed it is."

My request was reasonable enough, but I assumed she would refuse it again. So I called out to the pirates who had already assembled on the deck, "I know what the captain carries in the cargo hold, and it's enough to sink a half-dozen ships, so imagine what might happen here. But that is not the greatest threat. The Prozarians were crippled by the plague not long ago. If you want to know whether this is a cursed ship, ask yourself if you are not already feeling some of the symptoms of the plague?"

"I am!" I looked back and saw Teagut, who winked at me, as if that favor would be free.

"I am too!" another pirate echoed, and with that, the pirates began to stir, which caused some confusion for the Prozarians, who were either becoming angry or wondering if they too felt a sudden scratch in their throats.

Captain Strick's solution was not what I had hoped for. "String him up!" she ordered Roden, pointing to me.

"Stay back, I'll do it myself." I reached up to the ropes above me and wound my hands through them, creating a slip-knot that tightened when I pulled my hands downward.

Roden came forward with the whip in his hands and reddened eyes. "Please listen to me now. You cannot win here. Return what you've stolen from the captain and maybe this will go easier for you."

That couldn't possibly be true. With an icy glare, I said, "You are still the captain of my guard. Will you protect me now?"

He shook his head. "I tried to protect you. That's all I've tried to do since the moment I agreed to be your captain. You don't know how hard you've made things for me."

If he had known how thin my temper was, he wouldn't have said that. "How hard I made *what*?"

"Everything! I spent week after week thinking of ways to protect you from yourself, knowing it wouldn't be long before you came to us with some harebrained idea that I'd have to somehow rescue you from."

"I wouldn't need a rescue now if I'd had your loyalty before."

"This is not a test of loyalty."

"It is, Roden, believe me. It is."

"I have to be loyal to Carthya now, to the true king." He glanced back at the captain. "That's my only choice."

I chuckled at that. "Are you serious? Endless weeks of planning and all you came up with was treason?"

"It's not treason if you're no longer the king!" Roden shouted. "Please, go to your knees!"

"Listen to me, Roden. Whoever is claiming to be Darius, it is not my brother."

Roden raised the whip. "Please, return what you've stolen." He stepped closer and lowered his voice. "I can still try to get you off this ship, but I can't get Fink off too. If you don't give her what she wants, she'll tell me to go after him."

I kept my eyes fixed on Roden. "Touch him and I'll cripple this ship."

His voice was louder this time. "Give her what she wants, Jaron."

"Bring me the boy." The captain's long finger pointed at Fink, but her wicked smile was sent to me.

My words to Roden had not been a threat. They were a promise. I took a step forward, then slipped my hands free from the knot, snatched the knife from Roden's belt, and in a backward motion, sliced through the taut rope nearest to my hand. It was attached to a pulley high overhead within easy reach of the carpenter's tools I'd stashed in the crow's nest the night before. Free of their rope, the tools fell to the deck, causing an adjoining rope to whisk Fink equally high into the air, his arm now suspended over his head.

Roden growled and dove forward, knocking me to the

deck, flat on my back. "You think that helped him? You make everything worse. You always make everything worse!"

I kicked back, landing my knee into his chest hard enough to force him off me, then I rolled again to get on top of him, placing that same knee over his right arm. He struggled against me with his left arm, landing a few more hits on my side than I would've liked. But it was all worthwhile when his right wrist finally maneuvered into position so that I could pull the manacles out from beneath the capstan and snap the opened manacle into place, fastening him to the deck.

He roared with anger. But the effort to get Roden into position had also distracted me, and I would pay a price for it.

Searing pain shot from the center of my thigh in all directions. I looked down and saw he had somehow gotten hold of a knife with his left hand and plunged it into my leg. Willing myself not to pass out, I focused a glare at him. "That was a big mistake."

"Jaron, I'm sorry. I never meant to —"

"What are you waiting for?" Strick cried. "Get him!"

Fink remained directly overhead, which was only half our escape. I grabbed a second rope fastened to a bolt on the deck, wound my hand around it, and held on tight.

But when I went for my knife, it had fallen out of my reach. Strick was already racing toward it, but Wilta darted between us, grabbed the knife, and set it in my hands.

"Hurry, go!" she cried.

"Come with us," I offered, but she only shook her head.

"Just go," she whispered.

"If anyone wants proof of this being a cursed ship, here it is!" I shouted.

Using the same pulley system that I'd rigged to get Fink into the air, I cut this rope and it yanked me up as high as the crow's nest. With another slash of my knife, the long sails of the *Shadow Tide* collapsed to the deck, covering everyone in the sails' fabric. The same rope that had held the sails in place also loosened the boom on which I stood, with Fink at the far end of it. I pushed off from the crow's nest, forcing Fink and the boom to swing out directly over the sea.

I lowered myself on the rope, then used my weight to swing closer to Fink. He saw me coming toward him and tried to squirm away, but as he was lighter than me, he didn't get far before I grabbed the rope holding him midair and sliced through it.

With a long cry for help, Fink fell into the water. After a few seconds, his head popped up and he began yelling my name.

A few of the crewmen who had been nearer the ends of the sails emerged and seemed to be following someone's orders to rotate the boom back toward the ship. A knife cut through the sails and Captain Strick rose up through their center.

I gave her a sharp salute goodbye and let go of my rope.

· EIGHTEEN ·

I fell deeper into the water than I had expected and returned to the surface with aching lungs and my leg shooting with pain from the salty water. Fink wasn't far away, and once he saw me, he said, "Remember that time you made us jump off a cliff? At least we were dangling over something solid!"

"Did you want to land on something solid just now?" I pointed behind him. "Swim!"

"Where?"

From what I could tell above us, the main deck was a hive of activity, with crewmen attempting to clear the sail that had fallen. Yet above all other voices, I heard Captain Strick ordering her men to get the lifeboat down to us. She would be even more furious when they told her the problem with her request: There was only one lifeboat on board this ship, and it was missing. I wondered how long it'd take them to figure out that Tobias was on it. Hopefully Amarinda was there too.

With any luck, they weren't far away. The Eranbole Sea was colder than I had expected, and my injured leg was becoming stiff.

I began to swim toward the back of the ship, where the lifeboat should have been attached by rope. When I heard a loud splash behind us, I rotated in the water and saw Wilta come to the surface. "I changed my mind," she said. "But please help me. I'm not a good swimmer."

I held out a hand and when I could reach her, she put her arm around my shoulders while I assisted her in moving toward the lifeboat. Once or twice, in her efforts to stay afloat, she kicked into my injured leg. I clenched my teeth and forced myself to keep going.

Strick's next order was shouted so loud, I heard every word. "Fire off a volley of cannonballs! They've got our lifeboat!"

"We don't see it!" someone shouted back.

"Just fire!" she replied.

"What's wrong with you?" I asked Fink, who had paused in the water to stare at Wilta. "Swim!"

The *Shadow Tide* continued sailing forward until most of the ship had passed us. Immediately behind it was the lifeboat, except Tobias was the only one in it and his eyes were red as though he'd been crying.

He extended one of the boat's oars as far as it could reach. We swam as close as we dared without putting ourselves too near the moving ship. Tobias brought in Fink first, and then Wilta.

Once I reached the side of the boat, I asked, "Where is Amarinda?"

"She couldn't find the secret escape from the captain's quarters. But she heard someone coming into the room and said she would sneak out and find you instead. She wanted me to have the boat ready to go. I had to drop it into the water once I saw Fink lifted into the air." His face fell and any hope within him seemed to dissolve. "I was sure you'd have Amarinda with you."

"That was me who Amarinda heard," Wilta said. "I was going in to replace the sword, but I never saw Amarinda."

I took an extra minute to catch my breath, then I rolled inside the boat. My emotions were still raging inside me when I turned to Tobias. "I know you're only thinking about Amarinda right now. I'm thinking about her too, but I want you to hear this. Don't you ever again make plans behind my back. Or keep a secret where Fink's life is concerned!"

Tobias responded with a sharp glare. "You're correct, Jaron. All I'm thinking about right now, all I *care* about right now, is Amarinda! And I'm thinking about how, sooner or later, you'll force us to abandon her. Whatever happens to her now is your fault!"

Tobias was only speaking through his anger and fear, but his words hit me hard. Regardless of the reasons why she wasn't here with us, eventually, I would have to give the order to leave her behind.

Almost as soon as he finished, the ports opened, and in quick succession, cannonballs were fired at various angles. Because of our proximity to the hull, none of them came anywhere close to hitting us, but we did get considerably rougher waters that nearly toppled us once or twice.

Finally, everything settled, and only then did Tobias

notice my leg. He was still so angry that he merely glared at it, then at me.

I was happy to return the glare, though I added, "Can you wrap my leg before I bleed to death?"

He glanced down at his medical bag, then tossed it into my lap. My lip curled as I considered inviting him out of the boat, but Wilta quickly leaned forward to take the bag from me. "I'll do it." She dug through the contents until she found a roll of bandages.

Tobias grunted. "No, I'll do it."

He reached for a knife to begin cutting my trousers, but I shook my head. "Absolutely not."

"I've got to get at that wound."

"How am I supposed to fight with one trouser leg flapping about in the breeze?"

"What makes you think you'll be fighting?" Tobias paused. "Oh, because you're you." He began wrapping the wound directly over my trousers. "Who did this?"

"The person I'm going to have to fight."

"I don't think Roden intended to hurt you," Wilta said. "I saw his face afterward."

"Does it matter what he intended?" Fink asked.

She turned to him. "Who are you?"

"No one," I said, motioning to Fink to keep his mouth closed.

Wilta pressed her lips together. "I will earn your trust, Jaron. You have certainly earned mine."

"It isn't personal," Fink said. "No one earns his trust."

"What about Amarinda?" Tobias asked. "We're not leaving her behind."

"We'll wait here for as long as we can," I said. Which was hardly the comfort he wanted. But it was all I could give.

"She won't know we're tethered to the ship," Tobias said. "How can you be angry with me for keeping secrets when you never bothered to tell me the details of this lifeboat?"

"I worked on the lifeboat, not Jaron." Fink pointed to the bow of the lifeboat, where a rope was knotted between the lifeboat and an eye hook in the ship's hull. It kept us in the ship's wake, so this was hardly a comfortable ride, but there was no angle from the ship at which we might be spotted.

Fink leaned back in the boat and sighed. "I have to say, that was one of the easier escapes we've ever had."

I looked at him. "We were nearly drowned, exploded, and drowned again, and Amarinda is still missing. How was that easy?"

"I didn't say it was easy. I said it was *easier*."

Tobias wasn't finished either, becoming increasingly worried for Amarinda. "They'll know she unlocked the closet! They'll ask her how all of us escaped! The punishment you should be receiving right now, Jaron, or me — what if they do that to her?"

"Strick won't harm her," Wilta said. "She will question her, yes, maybe withhold meals, but nothing more."

"What about Roden?" Fink asked. "Is he in danger?"

His question hung in the air for several seconds before Wilta said, "He stabbed Jaron's leg. Whether that signals a true shift in his loyalties or not, the captain will respect that he fought for her."

I turned to Tobias, who kept searching the waters around us, as if Amarinda might spontaneously appear there. "She'll be all right until we can get her back."

"Why do you think that? Because Wilta says so? Because you believe everything will work out for you in the end?"

"No, because she is smart and she is strong, and because she has been in difficult situations before and knows what to do."

That seemed to settle Tobias down, at least for the moment.

After a heavy silence, Wilta asked, "How long did you have this escape planned out?"

I shrugged. "This was a fairly new plan."

"Fairly new? How many escape plans were there?"

"Eleven . . . and a half, although some would have been difficult, and some required unlikely events, such as the Eranbole Sea drying up overnight. But this was the escape that best fit the situation."

She gestured to my leg. "Getting stabbed? Was that one of your planned possibilities too?"

"Well, yes. But I thought it'd be the captain to do it, and a lot sooner than it happened. At least most of my plan worked."

Tobias grunted, reminding me that the failed part of my plan was an enormous problem. But he finished working on my leg and said, "I can only wrap this wound here, but I'll need to sew it when we get off the boat, or cauterize the wound."

While Tobias tied the final knot, Fink asked, "Should we cut the rope?"

I shook my head. "Let everything settle and wait until it's dark. Do you have my bag, and the items from that closet?"

Tobias glanced over at Wilta. "Is she —"

"I already know what you stole," Wilta said. "I was the one who had to report to the captain that they were missing."

Tobias frowned, then nodded at Fink, who tugged on a blanket in the center of the lifeboat, revealing everything we had removed from the locked closet.

"How did they get your brother's crown?" Tobias asked.

"And his sword." I wished I hadn't had to leave that behind. "I don't know where they got them, but they have no right to them."

We all looked to Wilta, who only shrugged. "I knew the captain had the items, but she never told me how she got them."

"Unless what they said is true." Fink tilted his head, deep in thought. "If Darius is alive, is he my adopted brother too?"

"I buried him, Fink!" Or, I thought I had. Doubts swept over me with every memory of my brother, every detail I tried to recall as I struggled to think whether it truly had been him in that coffin. It had to be — no other explanation made sense. For Darius to be alive, there would have to be answers for how he had not only survived, but escaped Carthya when my parents had fallen victim to Conner's plot.

As the activities on the ship gradually settled, I relaxed too and began to take a closer look at the items we'd stolen from the captain. I began with the scope, running my finger over the engravings. "What do we know about this?" I asked.

One glance at Wilta's widened eyes told me that she knew exactly what this was. Before I could ask, she shook her head. "Please don't ask me anything. If she finds out I've told you —"

"She'll assume you've told me, whether you have or not." Wilta still would not speak, so I held the scope out over the water, raising all but two fingers. "Maybe it's not that important."

With a cry of alarm, Wilta darted forward, nearly throwing the boat off balance until Fink and Tobias pulled her away. Then she said, "All right, I'll tell you, if you promise to keep it safe."

I brought the scope back into the boat. Wilta's eyes fixed on it, as if looking anywhere else would put the scope at risk.

She said, "This scope is believed to be an ancient map to the greatest treasure in all the lands. At the height of the Prozarians' power, they captured it in one of their conquests. Their finest minds attempted to decipher the markings, but no one succeeded. Gradually, it was forgotten. Then, a few years ago, the plague swept through the people, killing so many Prozarians that it threatened their very existence. One day, a strange man named Levitimas came to the Prozarians with the promise of a cure, but it would not be given freely. He claimed the scope belonged to him. If the Prozarians returned it, he would heal them."

"Was that true — did it belong to him?" Tobias asked.

Wilta shrugged. "If it did, then he should have known

better than to trust the Prozarians. The agreement was made, and once the people began to heal, the Monarch, full of cruelty and ambition, cast Levitimas into a prison from which he will never return. In a search of his possessions, they found the first lens for the scope." She pointed. "Is it still in that bag?"

I nodded.

She looked up at me with the most serious possible expression. "Jaron, if you were in a bad position before, I warn you, taking this scope was the most dangerous choice you possibly could have made."

"So far." She looked confused, so I added, "That's the most dangerous choice I could have made *so far*. It'll get worse before this is over."

Wilta shook her head, perhaps trying to understand me the way that everyone else tried to understand me, and eventually failed. Everyone but Imogen, I supposed.

A lump formed in my throat when I thought of her again. I was desperate for any news of what had happened to her. She was alive — she had to be alive.

Fink asked, "Did that lens lead them to Belland?"

"Yes." Wilta's eyes filled with tears. "They came as friends, asking our help to find the second lens. When we refused to help, they became our conquerors, killing our people one by one until your brother finally confessed to having the second lens. He made some agreement with them, part of which involved them bringing you to Belland as quickly as possible."

"Why must it be so fast?"

After some thought, she said, "The Monarch is coming to

Belland soon to claim the treasure. The captain believes there are only two days this year when the sun will be at the proper angle to find the third and final lens. If the Monarch comes and the captain has not found that lens, the consequences to all of Belland will be terrible." Wilta drew in a slow breath as her eyes settled on me. "If you truly understood what you are up against, you would be just as afraid as the rest of us."

That was the problem. I knew very little of what I was up against. And I was already terrified of what was yet to come.

NINETEEN

I didn't say much to Wilta for several minutes after her
attempts to warn me away from the Prozarians. Tobias
and Fink began questioning her, but I sat back in the boat
and just listened.

I had long ago decided that if I understood the enemy, I
had nothing to fear. So all I had to do was understand Strick, as
she seemed to have an equal interest in understanding me.

And I would have to understand Wilta if I wanted to know
the truth about Darius.

Everything she had told me about the scope confirmed in
my mind that this person who claimed to be my brother was a
fraud. My family had known nothing about any scope. Darius
could not have the second lens to offer them.

Nor would my brother have negotiated for me to be brought
to Belland as a prisoner, and certainly not in exchange for the surrender of that lens. He would never have put me in so much danger,
nor would he sacrifice something so valuable into enemy hands.

I said, "Tell me more about the Prozarians."

Tobias had been studying the scope and looked up. "What

more do you need to know? These are dangerous people who are willing to kill. If you thought you were a target before, what will they do to you now?"

Wilta added, "They see the entire world as either those who will help them get the treasure, or those who are enemies. And they will destroy their enemies in the cruelest of ways. That's why Roden was supposed to get you to kneel to the captain, because she knew that single action would be harder on you than any physical pain. She instructed him to whip you because she knew that would be harder on Roden than if he took the punishment himself."

"Maybe that's why she's asked so many questions about you," Tobias said. "She can't quite figure you out, so she isn't sure how to get ahead of you."

"I can't figure me out either," I replied. "Honestly, I've given up trying."

Above us, the ship came to life again as orders were shouted for all hands to begin working on repairs to the deck.

"I thought we were supposed to be watching for that lifeboat!" someone said.

"All hands to begin repairs!" Strick shouted back.

More quietly than before, Wilta added, "Against such an enemy as Captain Strick, perhaps there is no hope for us."

"The three of us are not enough to save your people," Tobias said. "I'm very sorry."

They all turned to me, obviously wanting an assurance of victory, but I could not offer it. I only said, "How can I plan against an enemy I do not know?"

"I know something else about the Prozarians," Fink said. "Shortly after they brought the crates on board, Captain Strick came down to the cargo hold to inspect them. Without knowing I was hiding nearby, she told a crewman that her husband once violated a direct order of the Monarch and was sentenced to death. Her husband had been turned in by their son — that's how afraid he was of the Monarch."

"Yet she continues in the Monarch's service?" I asked.

"Either through loyalty or fear, they all serve the Monarch." Wilta frowned. "The captain says that although the treasure is important, far more important is their hope of returning to their former power. The Prozarians will view your possession of the scope as the greatest possible insult, not only to them, but especially to the Monarch."

Tobias leaned forward with the scope. "What will happen when the Monarch realizes this has been stolen?"

Wilta shuddered. "No one knows, but it will be awful." Her eyes filled with tears. "Keep everything else, but that scope will bring you endless trouble."

"I agree." Tobias turned to me. "We have something they want, and they have Amarinda. If it's that valuable, we can make a trade. Wilta could return to the captain and make the offer."

"No!" Wilta drew back, nearly breathless with fear. "Tobias, I will help you in any way I can, but please don't send me back to the captain. If I return to her now, it will mean my death. Maybe even worse than what she'll do to Jaron."

I hunched lower in the boat. "That will be a pleasant

question to ponder as I fall asleep." I turned to Tobias. "Wake me if anything happens."

Tobias put the scope back in its satin bag. "Let me make the trade."

"You can't do that," I said, grabbing it from him. "Right now, they don't know where we are, and it has to stay that way."

Tobias's eyes softened. "I'm scared for her."

"Me too. But we cannot help her from here. Now, please, Tobias, let me sleep."

He gave in, but he clearly wasn't happy about my decision. I passed the scope to Fink to keep safe, then closed my eyes. If I slept at all, it didn't feel any longer than a minute or two before Wilta rustled my arm, whispering, "Jaron, look!"

The night had grown dark, but in the shadows I saw the outline of the fishing boat we had seen earlier, now much closer than before. Tobias and Fink had fallen asleep too. If not for Wilta, the boat might have passed us by.

I used my knife to cut the rope connecting us to the *Shadow Tide*. As the larger ship continued to sail forward, we were slowly left behind, making the next few minutes extremely risky. If the night vigils spotted us and raised an alarm, we were utterly defenseless.

"Do you know who is on the fishing boat?" Wilta asked. "Was this one of your plans too?"

"I don't think it's a coincidence that this boat has been so near the *Shadow Tide* since we were attacked, but no, I didn't plan this." I squinted, hoping to see anyone on the deck, but was unsuccessful. It didn't matter though. No matter who appeared on the deck, we were getting on that boat.

"What will happen to me now?" Wilta asked.

"You'll be safe with us." I checked again to be sure Tobias and Fink were asleep, then in a quieter voice, added, "You know what is coming for us better than anyone else. Answer my friends' questions, give your advice. But if I ask you to keep something a secret, I must be able to trust that you will do it."

"Why keep so many secrets? If they're your friends, they'll help you."

"That's what I'm afraid of." I sighed. "The truth is, Wilta, that I can no longer trust Roden, which is a terrible blow for Carthya. And I don't know what's happening to Amarinda. I'm worried for my friends who were left behind when our ship was attacked. Fink and Tobias will want to help, but Fink is too young and Tobias can't manage a sword. I need more time to work out some details before I speak to them."

She reached for my hand and squeezed it, then we woke Tobias and Fink to help row ourselves toward the fishing boat.

It was an older craft, but large enough for a crew of ten, if they were willing to pack in close together. An open platform at the rear of the boat was for the helmsman, and behind it was a small wardroom, with sleeping quarters likely in the deck below. At the bow of the ship, a single mast carried a white sail, and notably there was no flag identifying this boat's country of origin.

Fifteen minutes later, our lifeboat intersected with the fishing vessel. Any hopes I'd had to see Mott or Imogen here immediately dissolved. Instead, a man with far more years behind him than ahead, and with less meat on his bones than the average ant, leaned over the railing and looked us up and down.

"You young folks look lost," he said.

"We'd like to come aboard," I said. "If we're welcome."

He scratched his jaw. "My name's Westler. And I've no more need of a crew. Can you get yourselves to land on your own?"

"No more need?" I squinted. "When did you acquire a crew?"

"It's not really a crew. Hold on." The man went to the center of his deck and began to climb down what appeared to be a steep ladder. A minute later, a head popped up through the same opening, and I felt almost as if for the first time in a day, I could breathe again.

With that first breath, I whispered his name. "Mott."

He climbed onto the deck, though on a night with little available light, he had to bend over the rail to see us better. His eyes gleamed when he recognized us.

In his hands was a grappling hook, which he threw over to us. Tobias caught it and linked our boats, then Mott pulled us close enough together that we could transfer to the fishing boat. I'd rarely been so happy to see someone.

Mott grabbed me when I entered and pulled me into a tight, almost desperate embrace. I gasped and pushed back, becoming aware that I may have taken on more bruises than I had earlier realized.

He helped Wilta from the lifeboat next. "She was a captive of the Prozarians," I explained, before he could ask. "Wilta has been a friend to us."

She smiled shyly as she thanked Mott for his help. "For weeks I've dreamed of escaping the Prozarians. Jaron finally made it possible. I owe him a great debt now."

"Fink and I wouldn't have made it off the ship without your help," I said. "You owe me nothing." I looked at Mott. "She needs a warm bunk. And we need to put distance between us and the *Shadow Tide*."

Mott looked at Westler, who was back at the helm. "Can you take us twenty degrees farther south?"

Westler smiled at Mott but did nothing. In a quieter voice, Mott said, "He only hears about every other word, but don't worry. Once you're settled, I'll change our course."

"I have a million questions," I said. "But I must know if Imogen is here with you."

Without answering, Mott gestured to Wilta. "If you wish, my lady, I'll take you to a place you can rest."

She nodded at him but gave a smile to me. "Thank you, Jaron. You have the gratitude of all my people."

"I haven't done anything for them yet."

"No, but if anyone can, it will be you." She leaned forward and gave me a quick kiss on one cheek, then whispered in my ear. "And I promise, I will keep your secrets."

When she pulled away, I heard footsteps hurrying up the ladder to the deck. I turned in eager anticipation, and suddenly, there stood Imogen, her eyes shifting from me back to Wilta.

Imogen's cheeks and nose were bronzed from her time at sea, and the dress she had been wearing while on the *Red Serpent* was torn and stained. Her braided hair had come loose in places from the wind, and still, I didn't think she had ever looked more beautiful.

I immediately crossed the boat, unaware of anyone who might have been between us. She began to scold me and I knew that eventually she would get her chance. But for now, I was beyond happy to see her. She was just beginning to say my name when I kissed her.

She returned the kiss, and when we parted, she seemed to have abandoned the idea of scolding me. Instead, she looked over our group and her face fell. "Where is Amarinda, and Roden?" she asked. "Why aren't they here?"

· TWENTY ·

All at once, everyone began to ask their questions, throwing them out so fast, no one had the chance to give any answers.

Finally, Westler raised his hands and said, "Enough!" When he had our attention, he said, "This is why no one gets anything done these days. Too much talking, not enough listening." He looked around at us. "Now, which one of you is some sort of king?"

"Me," I said.

He squinted and shifted his eyes from me to Tobias, the last to climb aboard. "Not him? He looks more like a king. You look like . . . a ruffian."

"We'll take things from here; thanks for your generosity, Westler," Mott said, returning to the deck, his arms loaded with biscuits and dried meats. He glanced at the food, explaining, "We're welcome to all we can eat, provided we make some needed repairs around here. He's kept me busy for two days."

"I have more work belowdecks." Westler eyed me. "And if

you're good enough to rule a country, then you're good enough to work my ship."

"Yes, sir," I replied.

Westler shrugged and returned to the helm while Mott led us all to the interior wardroom and laid out the food. I immediately stuffed one biscuit into my mouth and piled three more and an entire handful of meat in front of me, then addressed Mott and Imogen specifically. "Tell me how you both escaped."

Imogen's story was what I had expected. "The idea was to create something that would trick them, drawing their attention away from the *Red Serpent*. Then I wanted to destroy my own trick, so they would forgo any pursuit of the lifeboat. I was hiding beneath the blanket." She eyed Fink. "You were supposed to be on the lifeboat with me. What happened to you?"

He shrugged. "I ended up somewhere else."

Mott said, "I didn't know how many of us had escaped the ship and who was still there, so I went down to the bottom of the ship and found a place to hide. When I heard the first order to fire, I knew that would be the end of me. But the ship broke apart, and I was somehow still alive. Once I surfaced, I held on to some wood wreckage until this fishing boat appeared a couple of hours later. Westler picked me up and then we found Imogen. Now we're here, and it seems we came just in time. Only you could make an entire ship's crew want to kill you after only one day."

"It's closer to two days." I cocked my head. "And to be fair, it wasn't the *entire* crew."

"It nearly was," Tobias put in. "I mean, there might've been a few who —"

"Stop talking, Tobias." Mott turned back to me. "Shall we continue to follow the *Shadow Tide*?"

"No, they're headed in the wrong direction."

"The wrong direction for what?" Imogen asked.

"Belland. It's a seaside country nearly another day west of here. That's where Wilta comes from."

Mott drew back. "Never heard of it. Never heard of her. Are you sure it was a good idea to bring her on board?"

"Whether it was or not, she's here. Now, we need to get to Belland ahead of Captain Strick."

"They're already ahead of us, Jaron, and in a faster ship."

"Yes, but they're also off course by four degrees. We need to plot our course and correct for that difference."

Mott smiled. "I can do that, but you need to stop bleeding on our clean deck." He pointed to my leg. "Roden's work?"

I'd almost forgotten about my leg, but it had bled through Tobias's wrapping. "How did you know it was him?"

"It looks like his style."

After that, Tobias, Fink, and I answered their questions. About Amarinda, something Tobias clearly still blamed on me, about Fink stowing away, which Imogen also seemed to blame on me — "He must have thought you'd be proud of him if he went there." And about the state in which I had left the *Shadow Tide* upon our escape. That one actually *was* my fault.

But this led to the most difficult question, the one that I could not answer: What should we do now?

We took a break from that question long enough for Fink to go to bed, and Mott to adjust our course, leaving me alone with Tobias and Imogen.

Imogen brushed her hand over the bandage Tobias had knotted around my thigh. "I still can't believe that Roden stabbed you."

I shrugged. "He had no choice. He had to do something dramatic enough to convince the captain that he is on her side."

Tobias frowned. "Can you be sure that he isn't?"

"He's still loyal to us, Tobias."

"After what he did — after everything he's done, I don't see how you can still have any faith in him."

"Well, he is my friend."

"He's doing what he always does — switching loyalties in an attempt to work his way up the ladder."

I snorted. "Working for Captain Strick is hardly moving to a higher rung of the ladder."

"How do you know he considers you a friend?"

"Do I really have to explain this? As long as he doesn't try to kill me again, we are still friends."

"And how do you know that he won't try something?"

My shrug should have been enough of an answer. But it wasn't, so I added, "All I can say is that if he does, then he's a terrible friend."

"He stabbed you, Jaron. That's all I need to know." Imogen gestured at the items I had brought with me from the *Shadow Tide*. "When did Roden know about these?"

Tobias frowned. "I should confess that Roden told me

about the crown before Jaron found out. If you're blaming Roden for that, blame me too."

"We're leaving that behind us now." I waited to catch his eye before I continued, "Unless you have anything new to confess."

"I don't, I swear it."

"I will get Darius's sword back as soon as possible. And mine as well."

"Can we talk about Amarinda again?" Imogen asked. "You said that they chose her specifically — obviously to meet Darius. Doesn't that suggest it's really him on Belland?"

"It suggests that the captain believes it's him," I said. "Not that it *is* him."

"Strick is a known liar," Imogen said. "Whether she believes it's Darius or not is irrelevant, because either way, she's proven that she is willing to lie to you."

"But Wilta also says it's true, that Darius is there," Tobias said.

Imogen frowned. "The same Wilta who was kissing Jaron's cheek earlier? You want me to believe anything she says?"

Mott ducked into the room where we were meeting, returning to his seat as before. "I agree with Imogen. Using your brother against you is a cruel weapon, but no doubt they believed it was a powerful one."

The deck fell silent, with the only sound being soft waves lapping against the sides of the boat. Imogen placed her hand over my wrist. I met her eyes and saw fear in them. That tore at me, more than anything else possibly could.

"We can return to Carthya," Imogen whispered. "Prepare to defend it from within our borders."

I shook my head. "We must go forward, to Belland."

"If they are lying about Darius, then this is blackmail."

"That is why I must go, to stop it at its source, before the threat comes to us."

"Jaron, these people don't want money or even the throne. They want your life! If we go, then you are walking straight into their trap . . . again!"

"Yes, but what if this time Strick is walking into *my* trap? What if I can turn everything around on her? I've done it before."

"Having done something before is no guarantee of the future," Mott said. "And have you considered what it means if Darius is alive?"

"Of course."

Imogen shook her head, trying to make me understand. "Strick is probably lying to you."

"Agreed."

She flattened her hands on the table, fighting her frustration with me. "Then why would you go there?"

"It's the one word you said yourself: 'probably.' Darius is probably buried beneath the castle, this is probably a plan to pull me into danger, or to keep me away from Carthya, placing the country at risk. This is *probably* a terrible idea." I lowered my voice and stared over at her. "But what if it's not?"

"If Darius is alive, he would expect you to protect Carthya first."

"What if he is alive? Would you have me spend the next eighty years asking myself if I could have saved him, if I should have saved him? If our positions were reversed, he would have saved me."

Imogen blinked twice. With a saddened voice, she said, "No, Jaron, he wouldn't save you. . . . He *didn't* save you. Darius shared in your father's plan to strip you of your identity, knowing you could have died at any time while left out on your own. Your positions already were reversed. Your brother chose Carthya instead of you."

I stood, setting my jaw forward. "Then I am not my brother."

"You are not. And I believe you are all the more noble because of those differences. But we cannot go to Belland." Imogen stood and began to leave.

Before she did, I said, "Amarinda will be on Belland. So will Roden."

Thus, the decision was made. Imogen closed her eyes and slowly nodded, though I did not miss the tear that rolled down her cheek.

Mott stood as well. "I'll keep watch until one of you comes to relieve me in a few hours. Until then, Imogen, make sure he gets some sleep. No doubt, the hardest part is yet to come."

I'd slept for some of the day, and though more sleep might come eventually, that wasn't my plan. It was time to figure out a way to fight back.

TWENTY-ONE

I was surprised to see Wilta at the wheel when I returned to the deck the following morning. Fink was seated against the bow with a handful of biscuits and turned back only long enough to give a friendly wave.

Wilta smiled at me. "I was up early and Mott was still here. He looked so exhausted, I offered to take over for a while."

"Thank you." I walked beside her to check our position according to the compass. She was a good navigator — we were exactly where we should be.

"Mott told me you placed a lodestone by their compass. Clever."

"That was Tobias's cleverness, not mine." I sighed. "Too many details are escaping me. I don't feel particularly clever anymore."

"Because you're thinking like Jaron again." I turned to see Fink staring at us. I hadn't even realized he was listening. "I've seen you as him, and I've seen you as Sage. The Prozarians think like Sage, saying as little as possible, holding their secrets close. Keeping things unexpected." He took another bite of his biscuit and chewed it a moment before adding, "The problem is that Sage also does the unexpected. So the best possible plan would be to think like Jaron, because nobody will expect that."

Wilta chuckled. "Does his logic make everyone dizzy, or just me?"

"Most people give up hours before he finishes talking."

"'Sage' is the name the captain called you when they first brought you on board the *Shadow Tide*. Who is Sage?"

"The other half of me, I suppose. But that can be even harder to understand."

She smiled softly. "I don't think you're so hard to understand. You value loyalty and sacrifice and dedication, and you expect the same from others. But few people feel these things as intensely as you do, so few people behave with the same intensity."

I leaned against the rail and stared out across the sea. "Too often, that intensity creates a blindness in me. I expect so much from others that I fail to see them as they really are. And all the while, every flaw in me radiates for the world to see."

"The people on this boat believe in you, Jaron. They could have raced back to Carthya in fear for their lives, but they didn't. They chose to follow you because they believe you can bring them home again in victory."

I chuckled. "They came because they believe something will go wrong and that I'll need their help."

Fink put in, "That's why I stowed away. I absolutely knew something would go wrong."

Wilta laughed too. "All right, then, perhaps I am the only

one who believes in you. And you, of course. Surely you never doubt yourself."

I didn't respond, and after a moment, she noticed my leg. "You've bled through your bandage again."

I tightened up the bandage, and my thoughts inevitably returned to Roden. I wondered if I hadn't chained him to the deck, if he'd also have tried to follow me, just as Wilta did. I might have doomed him.

I worried even more about Amarinda. Despite Wilta's insistence that Amarinda would be all right, I had seen for myself how Wilta had been treated. Tobias had seen it too. It was no wonder that he was so angry with me.

Minutes later, Imogen came onto the deck. Her eyes were wary upon Wilta, then fell to my leg. "Has Tobias looked at this?"

"He's not awake yet."

Imogen glanced back to Wilta. "I can take the wheel. You probably need a rest."

She probably didn't, but Wilta took the cue and stood aside for Imogen. "That's very kind, thank you. I will go lie down now."

After we were alone, I said to Imogen, "There's nothing between Wilta and me."

"Not on your part. She may feel differently."

"There's nothing, Imogen."

Imogen met my eyes. "What you and I share is not so thin that I will react to every young woman who flirts with you, or offers you compliments, or seeks to become your favorite. I've seen it a thousand times before, and it does not bother me. But Wilta is different. She isn't looking to you for an improvement in her social status, to grant her a title, or even to be able to boast to her friends that she earned a smile from you. She's asking you to risk your life for her people."

"As she risked her life on that ship for me."

I limped over to the helm and placed one hand over Imogen's as she held the wheel. "We must be cautious around her, I agree. But right now, all I know is that I must get to Belland ahead of Captain Strick. Wilta knows where it is. I don't. We need her help if we are going to reach Belland first."

Reluctantly, she nodded, and I was sure I even saw a faint smile. "Agreed. But next time we travel, I get to choose the place."

I kissed her cheek, then said, "I will gladly agree to that."

By then, the others on the fishing boat began to join us on the deck, including Mott, who quietly resumed his navigation. Tobias took one look at my leg and said, "The bandage isn't enough. Does anyone have a needle?"

"There's no needle." Mott made a face. "Why would anyone here have a needle?"

Tobias turned to me with an apology in his eyes, but before he could speak, I shook my head. "You will not cauterize that injury! Do you know how much that would hurt?"

"It can't be worse than the wound itself."

"Well, I don't intend to find out."

"I have a needle," Wilta said, hurrying up to the deck. She lifted her skirt, where right along the edge, a small needle was stuck through the fabric.

"Do you always keep a needle there?" Imogen asked.

"All the women in Belland do. It's easy to lose them otherwise."

Imogen turned to Tobias. "If you sew up that wound, will he still have use of his leg?"

Tobias shrugged. "I'm afraid so."

Her shoulders fell with disappointment and I frowned at her. "I have to see this through, Imogen."

"I know. But I don't have to like it."

Tobias accepted the needle from Wilta, and some thread that Imogen gave to him from a loose hem in her dress. We went to the farthest end of the ship for him to sew up my leg, but even then, when he helped me limp back to the group, Fink said, "I learned some new words."

For Imogen's sake, I quickly added, "In my own defense, I've used those words before. It's not my fault that he only heard them for the first time here."

I thought that was rather funny, but Imogen did not.

"You need to get out of the morning sun," she said to Fink.

He cocked his head. "Stop treating me like a child. I'm old enough to stay for this conversation."

"But I need help below," Wilta offered, winking at Imogen as she followed a reluctant Fink down the ladder.

Which left me with Imogen, Tobias, and Mott, who led me back into the same interior wardroom where we had met last night.

I opened the conversation first with Mott. "You were awake for most of last night. Shouldn't you still be asleep?"

He quickly countered, "Did you sleep?"

"I rested."

"Did you *sleep*?"

With a sigh, I placed the scope onto the wardroom table and showed them the engravings in the brass. "This isn't a code, or at least, not one meant to be deciphered. In ancient times, all royal houses had a symbol known only to themselves. It was used in written communication much like a secret handshake might be used in person."

"Or the secret word to get inside the palace gates," Imogen said.

"Exactly!" I pointed to three symbols running along the top of the scope. At the farthest from the eyepiece was a symbol of a circle with lines dividing it into equal thirds. "This is Carthyan. It represents the original three rulers of our land, all equals. Carthya has little significance to the outside world, so I think it might be placed here on the scope for a reason, maybe for the number three, since there are three slots in the scope."

Tobias tilted his head, skeptical. "What are the other two symbols before it?"

"I don't know the first, but the middle one is Mendenwal's." It was a triangle, their depiction of strength, or of the greatness of their country. I only knew that because the king of Mendenwal had once gotten into an argument with my father over which country had the best ancient symbol. It remained to this very day the stupidest argument I'd ever heard.

Below the three symbols were many others, none of which I recognized. "I have a theory," I continued. "I think the three symbols on top are a message for how to use this scope, but the presence of all the symbols must be significant. If this leads to the greatest treasure ever known upon these lands, perhaps the message of the scope is that all countries must come together as one to find it."

Then I lifted Captain Strick's notebook onto the table. "According to this, the Prozarians haven't got the translation, but the first lens led them to Belland. They believe the second lens is there, and apparently it is." I turned a few more pages. "The person claiming to be Darius made an agreement with them in exchange for the second lens."

"Could it be him?" Imogen asked.

I turned a few more pages. "The only entry about Darius is here, like notes she made to tease out the truth of his story. I'm convinced now that my brother cannot be alive, because if it was him, he would have told her details only he and I would know. All that's here are his basic facts. And then she listed what is supposedly the official story of how he came to Belland, and it's equally sparse on details."

Mott didn't seem concerned about that. "The lack of detail is no evidence either way about your brother. Strick never intended for you to see these pages."

"It isn't only that. For Darius to still be alive, consider all the questions that must be answered." I leaned forward. "If Darius is in Belland, then he must have been at the castle up until the time that Conner put his plan into effect." I paused there, trying to rid myself of any thoughts of my parents. I still ached whenever I talked about my family's deaths. I supposed in some way, I always would. "So why did Darius leave Carthya, and why did he choose Belland as a refuge? Did he leave with the second lens for the scope, or did he acquire it in Belland? Furthermore, someone is buried in Darius's grave, someone who looked very much like him. Who is that, and where is his family? It simply does not make sense that Darius could be alive."

Mott nodded in agreement. "Darius would only have left if Conner had made that part of his planning. But I can't think of a single reason he would have done that."

"Agreed."

Imogen leaned forward. "So our plan for Belland is not to greet a brother, but to stop an imposter." She pointed at the notebook. "I'm curious. What did Strick write about Darius?"

I shrugged and opened to that page. "As I said, there isn't much: his date of birth and my father's name, and his current description, all of which could be learned by one glance at his portrait and a few questions to any passing Carthyan."

"That's all?"

"That, I believe, is where the facts end. The rest is a fine story of fiction. Most of it is the way Darius got to Belland in the first place. Strick refers to Conner only as 'the conspirator.' She claims that he wanted the older son left alive to protect the second lens. But she doesn't give any explanation for how or why he would have it."

Mott shook his head. "Conner never mentioned the scope or any lens. I certainly didn't know everything he was doing, but I'm sure I would have known about that."

Imogen pressed her lips together, then said, "Wait here." She darted out of the room and went belowdecks, then returned less than a minute later with the shoulder bag I'd had on board the *Red Serpent*.

"I rescued this on the night of the attack as well, thinking something important might be in it. You can imagine my disappointment when I only found Conner's old journal. But I've been going through it myself today. He wrote about everything — his opinion of the way your father ruled the kingdom, his plans for a false prince, and how he believed he would one day rule Carthya. But never once does he mention the scope, Darius, or anything that might have involved him."

Mott said, "If that is true, then there should be no reason to believe your brother is alive."

"Agreed," I said. There certainly was no reason to believe it, yet deep in my gut, I knew things would not be so simple once we reached Belland. They never were.

· TWENTY-TWO ·

Hours later, everyone on board had gathered to the deck, passing the long afternoon with various activities. Mott was at the helm. Tobias was reorganizing the few medical supplies he still had. Westler was teaching Fink to fish, though they had yet to catch anything large enough to eat. Imogen and Wilta sat together studying Conner's journal and comparing it with Strick's notebook. After so much time poring over the journals together, they seemed to be forming a tentative friendship.

I sat alone, staring out across the sea, thinking of Darius and how desperately I missed him, in some ways more than my parents because we used to be so close. It worried me that I might miss him so much, I would let that desire to have him back again taint my opinion of whether this person I would meet on Belland was really him.

I worried just as much that it might truly be him. Imogen's words from the previous night still echoed in my ears, that Darius had not saved me when he'd had the chance. It was true; he had sat beside my father in the fine carriages that drove right past me as I stood on the street to watch them. I wanted to believe he had never seen me. But deep inside, I knew he had.

"Land!" Fink cried.

I leapt to my feet and joined him at the bow. There was land ahead, though at this distance, we couldn't see many details.

"Is it Belland?" Tobias asked Wilta.

She stood and raised a hand to shield her eyes from the sun. "I think so. But we're still far away."

Within another hour, Wilta confirmed that this was Belland. She explained that the country existed on a narrow neck of land jutting out from the mainland and was cut off from other countries by the volcano that had once formed Belland. Steep, tree-lined slopes descended from the volcano, then gave way to lower hills, which flattened into a pebble beach with larger rocks dotting the area. We saw five large ships with Prozarian flags docked at a harbor where the greatest concentration of the population likely was. We approached from the south, where there were no Prozarian ships, nor any signs of life.

Tobias stood at the bow of the deck and stared toward the land. "How long until we arrive?"

Mott held up a hand to the wind. "It'll be a few more hours, if the breeze remains steady. I want to stay to the south and hope we're not noticed."

Despite all the excitement of seeing land, Imogen had continued studying the journals. She looked up only long enough to observe, "The interior of the country looks too dense for travel. If our movements must be kept to the beaches, we'll find it difficult to go anywhere without being noticed."

Wilta turned to her. "There are trails everywhere, connecting the beaches to the hills and even to the peak of the volcano. I can show you the most secret ways to get where you want to go."

"Will it be safe for you?" Imogen asked. "If you're found by the Prozarians, what will happen?"

Wilta's hands began to tremble. "I'll have to face them sooner or later. I won't remain in hiding here while my people are in so much danger."

"We're going to the Prozarians?" Until then, I had thought Westler was napping, but his head shot up so rapidly, I wondered if he had momentarily died and his spirit had suddenly flown back into his body. Westler dropped his fishing pole on the deck and wandered back to the navigation. "I thought they all died from the plague."

Mott joined him and gently took control of the wheel. "We're going to Belland, remember?"

"I agreed to take you there, but I will not remain anywhere that is infested with Prozarians." He shook his head. "And if the lot of you have more than feathers for brains, you will reconsider your plans."

"You've encountered them before?" Tobias asked.

He shuddered with the memory. "Almost twenty years ago. I fled to the sea and haven't returned home since. From what I hear, my former home is nothing but a wasteland now. Back then, the Prozarians were conquerors. They'd consume every resource in a territory, then move on. If the Prozarians have returned, nowhere is safe."

Wilta said, "Belland is an ancient land. Others have come

before, hearing rumors of a great treasure, but without the Devil's Scope and the first lens, they had no idea where to begin. It's different now, with the Prozarians. They will not leave until they get the second lens."

"The very reason we should not be going to Belland," Imogen said. "If Darius will give them the second lens in exchange for Jaron, that's the last place you should go."

"If I don't go, their arrangement with Darius ends, and they will kill him," I said. "Captain Strick assured me of that."

"And you promised to help us." Wilta turned to me. "You said the Prozarians took five crates of weapons off your ship. Is there any chance of getting those back and using them ourselves?"

Questions began flooding my mind. "Where do the Prozarians keep their weapons? Where do they sleep and meet together?"

"Everything happens on their ships," Wilta said. "One crate will probably be given to each ship." Her face fell. "If we could only get one crate, it would be enough, but the ships are very well guarded." Wilta closed her eyes as if lost in a memory, then seemed to shake it off. "If you could find your brother, maybe he'll know what to do."

I took a deep breath, desperate to know the answer, and afraid of what it might be. "You told me that my brother was here. Do you know him?"

"No, he keeps to himself most of the time. But he is there."

"When did he come? How did he get there?"

She shrugged. "I don't know. Didn't you say that Captain Strick had that information in her notes?"

"I hoped you'd have something more to offer."

"I'm sorry, Jaron. Usually, if he needs something, his nurse takes care of it."

Mott turned. "His nurse? Not a servant or a housekeeper?"

Beside me, Imogen pulled Strick's notebook closer to herself and turned another page.

Wilta said, "We thought that was odd too, but on the few occasions we have seen Darius, that's how he has referred to her."

"Does she have a name?" Mott asked.

Imogen looked up from the notebook. "Strick only wrote that this woman was Darius's nurse at his birth, and that she had worked as one of Conner's maids at Farthenwood." She tilted her head. "Who could that be?"

Mott didn't answer at first, and I briefly wondered if he had frozen in place. Finally, he looked down and mumbled, "As Jaron says, they are such basic notes, they're not very helpful."

Wilta shrugged. "Nor is she the one who matters to Jaron, or to any of us. Our purpose in coming here is to discover the truth about his brother." She turned to me. "And you will. I hope when you see him, you will recognize him for who he is."

"Or I will recognize him as a fraud," I said. "All you know about him is who he claims to be. If he is lying, you'd have no way to know otherwise."

"If he has lied to my people, he will find himself in greater danger from us than he ever could from you," she said. "We have treated him like a king, so he had better be one."

Gradually, our conversation faded as we stood on the deck

to watch the land grow steadily larger ahead of us. All of us except Westler, who had strangely fallen asleep with his eyes remaining half-open.

Eventually, Imogen leaned against my arm. "You haven't said much for a long time. What are you thinking about?"

"Everything."

She sighed, as if I were trying to avoid a direct answer, but that in fact was the truth. Aside from the tiredness that muddied my thoughts, my brain was full of every possible question from the last few days.

"Do you have a plan?" Tobias asked, not for the first time that afternoon.

"It's the same as when you asked me eight minutes ago," I said. "I plan to win. Need it be anything more?"

He slumped against the rail. "Well, I had hoped for a few more details."

A grin tugged at my mouth. "I can tell you that my plan is not dependent on an army of oversized turtles, though if a few were to offer their services, I would accept."

Fink and Wilta laughed the hardest, but Tobias only scrunched up his face, then asked, "Do you intend to attack?"

"With an army of six? No, Tobias, a sneeze would last longer against the Prozarians than we would."

"Then you'll try diplomacy? Or will we hide first? Or —"

"*We* aren't doing anything. You kept Fink a secret from me on the last ship, so he is your responsibility now."

Fink immediately stopped laughing. "I don't need a nanny."

"No, you need a dozen vigils who can keep an eye on you . . . just as I need you to keep watch over the items I took from the *Shadow Tide*."

"I won't play vigil, or nursemaid," Tobias said. "Amarinda will be here too, and I want to help find her."

I clamped a hand on his shoulder. "You are helping, Tobias. Please, do as I ask."

After a curt nod, he turned toward the rail, his hands clenched into fists.

"I'm going with you," Imogen said. Before I could respond, she added, "Don't you dare suggest that I should stay behind too, because I won't."

I smiled at her. "I wouldn't say that, because I know you wouldn't listen."

She smiled back. "You're finally beginning to understand me."

Mott added, "I am coming too."

"How's your shoulder?" I asked. The recent war had left its mark on him. Until those final battles, I'd never known Mott as anything but strong and willing to stay by my side no matter what trouble I might be in. Now, though he had worked as hard as anyone possibly could to recover from his injuries, he moved slower than before. That half-second delay in raising his sword was enough time for an enemy to gain the advantage over him, and I worried about bringing him to shore with me.

Mott sheathed his sword, making his intentions clear. "I am coming, Jaron." When I nodded, he leaned against the rail and folded his arms. "I know that before we left the castle,

Roden was angry with you. I heard what he said. Some of it was true; it is a hard thing to serve you."

I took a couple of breaths. "I know that, better than anyone believes."

"So make it simpler for us. We are here to help you, so tell us what you know."

Even Tobias turned around for this. Wilta and Fink sat up taller, and Mott and Imogen leaned in, all of them with expectations I could not meet. I looked from one person to another. "Do you know why Captain Strick killed Erick?"

They exchanged glances, then returned their attention to me, each of them shaking their heads.

"Because we were friends. He didn't have to protect me, I never asked him to, but he did. That very fact — our friendship — is the reason he's dead."

Imogen placed her hand over mine. "We know the risks of being close to you. We've always known them. We are prepared to fight for you, so why not trust us with the truth?"

"He doesn't trust us, that's the problem," Tobias said.

I shook my head, trying to make them understand. "You're wrong, Tobias. I do trust you. I trust every single one of you with my life, except for Westler, of course, who might not even still be alive."

His head shot up out of sleep. "Prozarian scum!"

After he fell asleep again, I sighed. "I trust all of you, but I do not trust myself, and nor should you. We all know I'll do something foolish sooner or later. I am willing to pay for the consequences of my actions, but when I let someone get too close to me, the consequences may come to them instead. I cannot allow that."

My eyes rested on Imogen as I finished. She was closer to my heart than anyone, a fact that kept me awake at night far more often than anyone realized. If I knew how to explain that, I would have, but as it was, she turned away, mumbling to herself, "Cannot allow me in too close."

Mott said, "What can you tell us? Before we reach that shoreline, is there anything in your head that you can share with us now?"

I stared back at him. My reasons for withholding secrets went far deeper than trust. Certainly he and Imogen knew some of my secrets and plans, and Tobias knew others, but no one knew everything, and that was how it had to be. If any of them were captured by the Prozarians, they needed to be able to say, with absolute sincerity, that they had no information to offer. Even what they already knew was probably too much.

But Mott was still waiting for an answer. So with absolute sincerity of my own, I said to him, "No, Mott, there is nothing that I can share with you now."

"You mean that you won't share it. You ask for help, then prevent us from giving it."

I stared back at him, and finally he sighed, then said, "We'll be at the shore of Belland by dusk. I'll prepare us some food before we arrive."

After he'd left, Imogen looked at me for an answer, but I had nothing to offer her either. She pressed her lips together, then excused herself to begin loading the stolen Prozarian items into a pack for Tobias and Fink.

"How many times can you make her angry before she gives up on you?" Tobias asked.

His question pierced me more than he knew. Eventually, everyone gave up on me; I'd learned that long ago. And I was beginning to think that Tobias's question might be answered before this voyage was over.

· TWENTY-THREE ·

A bright moon was rising when Westler found a quiet cove where we could temporarily dock. From there we transferred to the lifeboat to go ashore, and quickly began unloading the few possessions we had onto the beach.

Tobias stood aside to watch us, arms folded and his hands in fists. "What are Fink and I supposed to do while we're waiting for you to save all of us? Maybe play some Queen's Cross, or perhaps a quiet game of chess?"

"Enough!" I snapped. "I know you're angry at having to stay behind. I know you blame me for Amarinda, and maybe for every other thing that's gone wrong in your life, but I'm figuring out all of this one step at a time, and I will make mistakes! All I know is that we cannot allow what we've stolen from the captain to be stolen away from us. And I have to set foot on Belland believing that Fink will be safe. Unless I learn otherwise in the next few hours, he's the only brother I've got. So protect the things I've stolen, Tobias. And protect Fink. Please."

Tobias had frozen while I spoke, and his only response

now was to lick his lips and excuse himself to prepare for arrival. I glanced over at Imogen, hoping for a smile of support, but she turned the other way and went to help Tobias.

From behind me, Fink said, "If it helps, *I'm* not angry with you."

"You might be the only one," I muttered.

"That's because I already know you won't tell me any-thing." Hardly the comfort I wanted.

Once we reached the shore, Mott pointed out a nearby clump of trees that would offer some shelter. While the rest of the group went ahead to investigate, Wilta stayed back with me, keeping watch over everything we'd brought from the fishing boat.

"You were right to put Tobias in his place," she said. "I wouldn't have been so tolerant." I didn't respond, and finally she added, "What can I do here? I'm the only one who has not received an assignment."

I looked around the area, ensuring we were alone, then said, "There is something, but I do not want to ask."

"If I can help you, I will."

I sighed. "It's my leg. There's a reason it keeps bleeding through its bandages."

"But Tobias sewed it."

"It might be infected, and if it is, it's a serious problem. An infection will slow down my movements, muddy my thinking."

"Does Tobias have any way of treating it?"

"I don't want him to know. None of them can know."

She nodded in understanding. "There are herbs in the hills

that can help, though they are hard to find this time of year, and the Prozarians took our dried herbs for themselves." She paused a moment and said, "But I think I know where I can get some. Your brother's home is highest on the hill and the only stone-and-mortar home in the village. Meet me outside there in a few hours. If I can find any herbs, I'll bring them to you then."

"Jaron, we're ready to go."

I turned to see Imogen with Mott behind her, both of them standing on the beach.

I looked back at Wilta. "Thank you. I'll be there late tonight."

Fink followed behind Imogen, but Tobias caught up to me. "Can we talk?"

I sighed. "What now?"

He offered me his hand. "I'm sorry for how I've behaved. I know you're doing your best, for all of us. I'll do my best too, for Fink, and for you."

I shook his hand, considering the matter finished. But I did add, "If the Prozarians get too close, be prepared to move, or to keep moving."

He shifted his weight, suddenly looking nervous. "How will you know where to find us if we need to escape?"

"We're not going to escape Belland. We're going to conquer it."

His face brightened. "So there is a plan!"

"A goal more than a plan. Now, stay watchful. Fink is here. My brother's crown is here. Our only means to negotiate is left in your care."

He nodded at me and I turned to look at Fink, who only grinned. "I know, you want me to protect Tobias. Don't worry, I'll keep him safe."

I gave him a quick embrace, trying to hide how deeply worried I was. "I know you will."

Wilta left in one direction to find the herbs for my leg while Mott, Imogen, and I left in the other. But we hadn't gone far before I realized they were far angrier with me than I had realized. My whispered questions went unanswered, my warnings of uneven paths or hazards as we entered the hills were heeded without a word of thanks, and when I joked that a warrior's favorite fish could only be the swordfish, neither of them even smiled. Maybe it wasn't the greatest joke, but it should have at least earned me a groan. That's when I knew something was seriously wrong.

It didn't take us long to gain some distance from the beach, and only then did I breathe more easily. Looking back to where they had been, I saw that Fink and Tobias had cleared all our possessions away, and even erased our footprints in the sand. We were also less exposed than before, each step higher greeting us with increasingly thick fir trees and white-barked alders. At our first safe clearing, I turned to the others.

"I don't know what to expect from here. I don't think Captain Strick has arrived yet, but other Prozarians will be here. Their reputation is hardly one of gentleness and mercy, so do not get in their way. I don't know anything about the Bellanders, other than what Wilta has told us. Maybe they are peaceful and friendly, maybe not."

In response, they only stared back at me, until finally Mott shrugged. "Nothing you just said is helpful in any way. What was the point of saying it?"

I grinned. "At least it got you speaking to me again."

"We'll stand by you, defend you, and fight with you," Imogen said. "Don't require us to speak to you also."

I kissed her cheek, even though she turned away, then said, "For now, I have three out of four, and that's not so bad." Imogen said nothing, but I did catch a hint of a smile, so I figured things between us weren't too troubled. Not yet.

Night was falling fast in our trek, and though we had good light from a bright moon and stars, we would be more visible than I wanted along the rocky trail. If anyone approached us from the opposite direction, we may not have the chance to hide.

With that caution in mind, I continued to lead the way, with Imogen directly behind me and Mott at the end. We followed an established path through the trees, so clearly this was a route that had been often traveled. It might have been wiser to forge our own trail, but the dense undergrowth discouraged that choice. The occasional sharp drop-off forbade it.

After nearly an hour, I held up a hand, hearing the voices of children ahead. I pointed for Mott to go one way and Imogen to go the other, each to keep watch, all of us to remain separate enough that if there was trouble, we wouldn't be found together.

As silently as possible, I crept forward toward the voices.

Through a dense forest patch, I hid behind a wide fir tree

to peek at a group of five children who were looking out over the sea. They were dressed in long tunics with cloth strips for belts, and most had hair as unkempt and uncut as mine had been during my orphan years. Compared to most other children I'd known, they looked far too serious.

One of the older girls finally said to the others, "I don't see it."

"I'm telling you, Lavita, a fishing boat landed here and some people got off," said a boy in front of her. He instantly reminded me of Fink. He was younger and had much darker hair, but the shape of his face and tone of his voice were similar. "If we report it, the Prozarians might reward us. Return a few of our people."

"Maybe they'll send us away too," a younger girl said with a shiver.

The boy groaned. "You all stay here and hide. I'm telling them."

With no other choice, I darted out from the bushes with my hands low and visible. "Don't be afraid. I'm here to help you."

The older girl — Lavita — exchanged a look with a boy, then her eyes narrowed. "Now I believe you. We need that reward. Get him!"

Almost before I knew it, they barreled into me, throwing me off balance. I stumbled backward, then with no chance to save myself, I fell over the cliff.

· TWENTY-FOUR ·

I fumbled against the sharp cliff rock without success, though my initial fear quickly turned to a hard lesson in embarrassment when I landed on my back on a narrow ledge, not far below. It wouldn't have been visible unless I'd been looking down directly over it, but the children seemed to know it was there.

They looked over the cliff's edge above me, studying me as if I were the enemy. The girl who had ordered my capture said to the others, "You wait here and watch him."

"Listen to me," I said. "I've come to help you and your families, but you must not say anything about me, or about the boat you saw."

Lavita asked, "How can we believe you?"

On a gut instinct, I said words that had to be forced from my mouth. "I'm a friend of . . . Darius. Is he nearby?"

Immediately their faces brightened. One of the girls pointed off to her left. "Darius always does an evening walk around the whole area, making sure everyone is safe for the night."

A bell rang from far below, drawing an immediate response from the children. "We have to go!" the girl said.

I stood up. "You all must swear not to say a word about this."

The boy crinkled his nose. "We won't say anything tonight. But if you're just someone else who came here with lies, we will report you tomorrow."

After they ran away, I brushed myself off and began to climb. My injured leg protested the work, but I'd certainly faced worse situations and scaled greater distances than this. In less than a minute, I rolled back onto the ledge, then hurried along the trail in the direction the girl had pointed.

A woman entered the path ahead of me and would have seen me had she not been turned away, speaking to someone else. I immediately ducked behind a tree and crouched low to better hide myself beneath a thicket of wide-leaf bushes.

"I think those children were the last to be up here," the woman said to whomever was behind her. "Should we keep looking?"

"The bell rang, so everyone should be headed down." From that first spoken word of reply, my breath caught in my throat, locking in tighter until I scarcely could think. "We should go down ourselves, or we'll be the ones in trouble."

I recognized this voice. It was so familiar that I knew it down to my bones.

During the earliest years of my life, he had been my most constant companion. For most of those years, we had shared a room, because my parents felt someone needed to keep an eye on me. Later, in my final two years in the castle, our father had separated us in order to preserve Darius's reputation. How I had hated that, and I often snuck into his room at night to sleep.

We were tutored together, took meals together, trained together in horsemanship, sword fighting, history, and languages. Even above those of my own parents, I would know the voice of my brother.

This was Darius.

The thought itself set my heart racing and turned my limbs to lead. How easy it had been to deny the truth about Darius when I was on the ship, when logic and reason muted my every instinct to trust in Strick's words.

Darius was alive, and not a stone's throw away from me now.

Of that I was certain. What I did not know was what to do about it.

"I thought I heard someone back there." Darius took a step in my direction. "If everyone is not on the beach, you know the consequences."

The woman said, "They only care if you are not there. The Prozarians don't like it when you are away too long."

"We're cut off from the mainland, and they've taken control of our ships. Where could I possibly go?"

"I know that, but Captain Strick is expected to arrive tonight. She will want you there to greet the ship."

His sigh was heavy. "I'm dreading her arrival, Trea."

Her voice became even more tender and kind. "I was there at your birth, Darius, and have seen you in every kind of circumstance and challenge since. But never once in all your years have I seen you as anxious as you are today."

For the first time, I took the risk of peeking around the tree, desperate to see him again. The woman — Trea — was blocking my view. She appeared to be somewhere in her thirties, and she was a beautiful woman. She was dressed in clothing much simpler than the fashions of Carthya. I did not know her.

Then she moved, and suddenly, there was Darius facing in my direction. I couldn't believe my eyes, for he looked almost exactly as I remembered him from six years earlier. Older, certainly — Darius would be twenty now. But his hair was the same shade of brown, and his perfectly straight posture the same, just as Father had always required of him.

From somewhere in the distance, another bell rang. Trea immediately started forward. "The moment has come. She's here."

Trea took four steps down the trail before she looked back and stopped, realizing Darius wasn't following.

Instead, his gaze had caught in the exact area where I now stood. The instant I realized it, I pulled back into the shadows, my heart pounding like a drum. He shouldn't have been able to see me, not with only moonlight and a few stars.

But he had seen me, I knew it. I expected he would call my name, or at least draw Trea's attention to the fact that someone had been watching him.

When Trea insisted that they needed to leave, he only picked up a bag near his feet and said to her, "Do you know why I've dreaded this day?"

"Why?"

"Because Jaron is supposed to be on that ship, and I don't know which will be worse. Is it having to face Jaron, knowing what he's done? Or will it be watching Jaron face what the Prozarians have planned for him?" Darius glanced in my direction again, and this time I could almost swear that our eyes met. "Either way, I sincerely hope that he never sets foot on this soil."

"If he doesn't come, you have no agreement with the Prozarians, and then what will we do?" Trea paused. "And what if she has come with him? Are you prepared for that?"

Something changed in Darius's eyes, a softening perhaps. And I realized Trea was talking about someone else. Not Captain Strick, but a different *she*. Trea was asking Darius if he was prepared to meet Amarinda again.

Darius didn't answer any of Trea's questions, but I felt the weight of his eyes continuing to stare in the direction where I had just stood. Trea said, "Let's go, or they will come looking for you, and that never goes well."

Footsteps padded away from me, fading, and then the sound disappeared entirely.

When I was sure they had gone, I slumped to the ground, covering my mouth with one hand. I genuinely had no idea what I should do next.

· TWENTY-FIVE ·

Imogen was the first to find me and must have sensed my despair, for she merely sat at my side and wrapped her arm around my shoulders.

Finally, in a voice as gentle as her touch, she said, "I waited until it was quiet, but then you didn't return. I was worried."

"I saw Darius. He's alive, Imogen. It's him."

She froze for a beat. "How did he look?"

"The same. But different. Something is different, but I can't place what it is."

"It's dark out here. Maybe your eyes played tricks on you."

I looked at her and shook my head, then felt her hand press on my shoulder, asking me to move. "Let's go."

"I think he saw me too."

Now there was tension in her touch. "You *think* he did?"

"I know he did. And he wasn't happy about it." I didn't tell her about the children. Her brow was already creased enough.

We glanced up as Mott entered the clearing. He didn't ask any questions but seemed to simply know, as if the effects of having seen my brother were etched into my face.

Mott crouched in front of me, waiting until I was looking at him before asking, "What now?"

I closed my eyes and tried to collect my thoughts. "That bell you heard means Strick's ship has come in. Darius went to the beach to meet it, along with a woman named Trea. She said that she was there at his birth." Now I looked directly at Mott. "You know her, don't you?"

"The nurse that Strick described in her notebook, yes, that was Trea."

"You knew her name when we discussed this on Westler's ship. Instead of telling me then, you let me go into this blind."

Mott only replied, "I have reasons for my secrets, as you have reasons for yours."

I frowned back at him. "That is unacceptable."

After a short pause, Mott added, "Trea worked her whole life for Conner, as did I." His focus shifted to Imogen. "I knew her, but you must have known her too."

"Not well," Imogen said. "How could she have worked for Conner and been at Darius's birth?"

Mott rubbed a hand over his scalp as he considered his answer. "I'm sorry, I can't explain that." With his attention back on me, he asked again, "What shall we do now?"

"We must follow them, get a sense for what is happening at the docks. He is expecting Amarinda to arrive with the ship as well, so if we stay close to him, we may have a chance of finding her."

"Mott and I will go, but not you," Imogen said. "It's not safe."

"When have I ever cared about safety?" I asked.

"How can you not care? Jaron, your leg is still bandaged from the last time you didn't care!"

"He won't stay back," Mott said, showing a rare spark of urgency. "None of us will, so let's all go, together."

Imogen glared at him, her eyes widened in disbelief that Mott had actually sided with me. But she knew she had lost the argument, so she merely stood and marched ahead along the path. Mott and I followed.

The path took a sharp incline, which led to the top of a ridge. From here, we had a fine view of the village below, framed in moonlight and lit with torches and lanterns. The village was connected to the beach by a series of gravel paths, dotted with around fifty simple wood homes and open-air markets. Despite the late hour, the paths between them were filled with people in a bustle of activity as the *Shadow Tide* began to dock at the far end of five ships of similar size and with the same Prozarian flag on display.

Imogen suggested that if we continued along the path, it would lead us down to the beach. We followed that way, but veered off the path when we got lower, keeping to the dense patches of trees and underbrush, places where we hoped we would not readily be seen.

Although we were still some distance from the beach, we eventually reached a final patch of trees thick enough to hide us. Beyond here, the trees thinned, then disappeared into clumps of tall grasses, then even those gave way to pebbles and sand. This was as close as we dared get.

We kept tightly to the darkest places, taking advantage of

the fact that those around us were so busy, no one took notice of our shadows.

The beach was bustling with activity as the Bellanders delivered various goods to Prozarian vigils standing at posts along the beach. The Prozarians were easily recognizable by their brimmed hats and long coats in the same green-and-white colors as their flags. Those who weren't taking collections wandered among the Bellanders, whips in their hands, shouting orders and making threats.

The people themselves wore long, simple tunics, some belted with twine or strips of fabric. The men had close-cropped hair and the women banded their long hair down their backs. They seemed to outnumber the Prozarians by several times over, but rather than show any signs of resistance, they continued with their work, bringing food and quilts and weapons to the proper vigils. As they worked, they all seemed to be singing a common tune, one of mourning or defeat. No one sang loudly, but their combined voices created an almost haunted feeling.

"Faster!" a Prozarian shouted, raising a strap against an older man. I started forward to intervene, but Mott pulled me back, reminding me of our purpose in having come this far.

At first I was so angry with that Prozarian, I didn't notice Darius and Trea walking right past us, not until they were so close I could have reached out and touched them. They didn't seem to see us this time, but each of us froze in place.

"What will I say to the captain?" Darius was asking. "She will ask."

Trea licked her lips. "Let her do the talking, as much as

possible. The less you say, the better. Remember how many lives depend on this going well."

Indeed, within minutes of the *Shadow Tide* docking, a gangplank was lowered to the docks. Darius and Trea stepped forward to welcome the ship, though Darius was rocking on his heels, a nervous habit I thought our father had long ago weeded out of him. Captain Strick emerged first, escorted by two of her crewmen.

"They look miserable," I whispered. "As if escorting her is a punishment."

"They must've done something awful to deserve this," Imogen agreed.

I turned to look at Mott, who had not answered. I'd been so caught up in studying the area and events around me that I'd failed to notice Mott's shallow breaths and nervous fingers. Never before, in all our time together, had I ever seen him like this.

"What's the matter with you?"

"Hush."

"You look like you're about to pass out. If you are, I should know."

"Hush, Jaron!"

I followed his gaze forward to Trea, who was standing in our direct line of sight, then looked back at Mott, who wasn't blinking, perhaps out of fear that he might miss that fraction of a second to stare at her.

"You can't be serious," I whispered, but if he heard me, he ignored it.

Nor did he need to answer. I understood the expression on

his face far too well. Mott had withheld from me a far bigger secret than I had suspected. He didn't only know Trea. He was in love with her. The kind of love that might have made him forget how dangerous this moment was, how quickly a wrong move could get us caught once again within Strick's snares.

In his will, Conner had asked for a portion of his inheritance to go to Mott, as an apology. Maybe Conner was the reason that Trea left. Mott may not have even known what happened to her until this very moment.

Imogen met my eyes, and I knew she recognized Mott's expression too. Except I could not smile the same way she was, because this greatly complicated our problems. Until I knew more about Trea, I would not trust that Darius was safe with her.

Which meant she was a risk to me.

And based on the way Mott continued to stare at her, I understood that Mott had just become a risk to me too.

TWENTY-SIX

By the time Captain Strick reached the shore, all Bellanders were on their knees, many of them kneeling only after being threatened by a Prozarian. Even Darius knelt, which left me shaking my head in disgust. Did he not remember who he was, *what* he was?

The rest of the captain's crew members were beginning to leave the ship too, all of them with weapons visible. So far, no pirates had left.

Finally, at Trea's prompting, Darius stood and called out, "Hail, Captain Strick. Prozarians and Bellanders alike, give her your welcome!"

The Prozarians offered salutes of honor, but the Bellanders did not. Instead, they extended their arms straight down, hands in fists. All of them.

"They're protesting," Imogen mumbled.

The captain took notice of their actions but lifted her arms as if they were all cheering for her and loudly announced, "My friends, as you can see from the condition of our ship, we have suffered greatly while at sea, but we return in victory, with five crates of weapons to strengthen the Prozarian armies, one crate for each ship that has remained at watch here."

I felt Imogen's eyes on me and frowned back at her. We both understood the significance of losing those weapons, the terrible impact their loss would have upon Carthya.

Strick continued, "Very soon, some of you will receive orders to transfer the crates to each of our ships. Be cautious in your work. Without fail, the crates must not get wet — the contents are too precious; nor should they be exposed to flame. They were stored near a gunpowder magazine, and you will not want to be the person who discovers whether any dust settled on the crates themselves."

Imogen leaned close to me. "Without those weapons, what strength does Carthya still have?"

"Not much. A few dinner knives, and maybe we could throw dirt in the eyes of our invaders." Imogen half-smiled, but I hadn't been entirely joking. The recent war had been devastating to our supplies.

"Where is Darius?" Strick asked.

He briefly glanced at Trea, then took a deep breath and walked forward. Without warning, the captain slapped him, hard enough that his head turned to the side, where he left it while she yelled, "You might've done a better job of warning me about Jaron!"

Now he looked at her. "What did he do? I warned you of everything I knew."

"Then you do not know him well enough. He escaped my ship yesterday. Where is he now?"

I leaned forward, anxious for the answer. He might not know exactly where I was at the moment, but he did know I was here. If he was going to betray me, this was his opportunity.

But Darius only said, "Give me tonight to think about where he might have gone. I will have answers for you in the morning, I swear it."

"Why should I believe your promises now?" Strick withdrew her sword and advanced on him until he had returned to his knees. "Maybe I'll just kill you here and take the lens for myself."

"I told you before; if you kill me, you will never find the lens. Now, please, give me tonight to think of a way to mend our agreement."

"Our agreement was based on us having more time with the second lens. Your brother caused damage to the ship, which delayed our arrival."

Darius's head shot up. "Whatever Jaron did, that isn't my fault!"

"But you will bear the consequences of it. We are returning to our original agreement, including the second lens."

Darius closed his eyes. "That is too much."

"After what your brother put us through, it is more than fair." She raised her sword. "Accept now, if you wish to live."

I looked back at Imogen and saw the same alarm in her eyes that surely was in mine. With a hand on my knife, I started forward, but before I could, Trea ran between them, shouting, "Captain Strick, there is no cause for this. Darius told you everything he knew, but it has been many years since he has seen his brother. Surely Jaron has changed since then. Darius could not predict that."

The captain slowly lowered her arm, then a sly smile stretched across her face. "Our original terms are fair. Agree to them now." She looked toward the Bellanders. "Or our negotiations will begin again."

She marched forward, grabbing the arm of a girl who was kneeling in the front row. She cried out with fear and I immediately recognized her as Lavita, the older girl I'd seen with the other children.

"This one volunteers to make the next jump into the cave," Strick said. "Shall I choose another?"

"Release her. I agree to your terms." Darius lowered his head, though he was clearly shaken by what had just happened. "All of them."

"And Jaron?"

"I will have something for you in the morning, I promise that."

"You better go and start thinking." Strick released Lavita, then called back onto the ship. "Roden, you should be here by now!"

I gasped when I saw him. Roden's face was bruised, his shirt was torn, and he walked unevenly, as if exhausted. But he said to the captain, "How may I serve you?"

"What's happened to him?" Imogen whispered.

I shrugged, but the answer seemed obvious enough. He had paid dearly for my escape from the ship.

Strick pushed him forward, and he stumbled with his first

steps onto the sand. "Escort Darius to his home. Watch for Jaron along the way."

"Yes, Captain." He walked up to Darius. "You will come with me, please."

Trea touched Darius's arm, prompting him to move. "You go. I'll stay here until all the people are safely back in their homes."

"Thank you, Trea," he mumbled.

Roden gestured for Darius to begin walking, then trailed behind him along a dirt path headed toward the hills. As soon as they were out of hearing range, Strick turned to her Prozarians. "I want a full search of Belland, every home, beneath every rock, in every tree. Especially check the coves. If Jaron is here, he must have a boat docked somewhere. Find him!"

A chorus of "Yes, Captain" followed her orders as the Prozarians began spreading out toward the hills.

"I've got to follow Darius," I said.

Imogen gave my hand a quick squeeze. "I'll go back and warn Tobias."

Behind us, Mott began to stand. "I need to speak to Trea."

I grabbed his arm. "Right here? Out in the open?"

"Nobody here should recognize me. I'll blend in."

Mott was bigger than three Bellanders put together; he would hardly blend in. But because of his size, I also knew there was nothing I could do to stop him. Even if I had ordered him to stay, his gaze was so fixed on Trea, I knew he wouldn't hear me.

He stood and left without another word. I gave Imogen a quick kiss. "Be safe."

"No one here is after me," she said. "And I'll give you the advice that Mott would have given, if he was in his right mind. Please don't be foolish . . . or, any more foolish than usual."

I wished I could make Mott, or even Imogen, understand that foolishness wasn't a choice I made. It was simply part of me. With that thought, my shoulders fell. Foolishness wasn't a quality I claimed with pride.

Strick dismissed the rest of the Bellanders, who eagerly crowded the paths back to their homes. I swiped a fresh tunic from the front of one home and a coat from the clothesline of another and joined in with the group, listening to their quiet conversations as we walked.

"Darius saved Lavita's life," one woman said to another.

"Three villagers disappeared earlier this week," came the reply. "What did he do for them?"

"What more can he do? If the stories are true, it's his brother we need to worry about."

That gave me pause. What stories?

The women went one direction, toward simple homes of stacked logs and dried mud. I followed the bulk of the group toward homes a little higher on the hillside. My only giveaway was the slight limp of my injured leg. Darius wouldn't find that significant, but Roden would see through this disguise immediately.

I wondered if he would report me. Clearly he was being mistreated by Strick, but would that inspire his loyalty to her, or would he look toward the chance for escape? I needed to find out.

Gradually the crowd around me thinned as people returned

to their homes. My path continued uphill, which made it more difficult to follow without being detected.

Once we reached the lower hills, Darius pointed to a home significantly nicer than the rest, one made of rock and mortar rather than the wood of the huts everyone else seemed to have. I recognized Wilta's description of it as Darius's home.

He said to Roden, "There's no need to come any farther. You've fulfilled the captain's orders."

"I'm glad she sent me here because I wanted to speak to you alone." Roden shifted his weight, looking slightly uncomfortable. "Are you really Jaron's brother?"

Darius stiffened. "Is there any reason to doubt that?"

"If you become king of Carthya, then I will serve you. But I must know if I am serving a true king."

Rather than answer, Darius asked, "Do you know where Jaron is now?"

"No. Could he have made it to Belland?"

Darius considered his answer for a few seconds, then countered with a question of his own. "Do you have any reason to believe Jaron is here?"

A beat passed, then Roden said, "Jaron escaped the captain's ship yesterday. I can't understand how he could have made it here." Roden paused, frowning. "But you've known him longer than I have. So you must know that Jaron is capable of nearly anything."

Darius stared at him a moment. "That's what I'm afraid of. Good night."

Roden waited until Darius was inside his home, then

turned to walk back to the beach, only to find me standing in the middle of the path.

Startled, he froze, but he didn't look surprised to see me. Instead, his eyes drifted to my leg, still bandaged. "How bad is it?"

"It's the same leg that you broke last year. Do you have a specific grudge against this leg?"

"I didn't mean to hurt you. I was angry."

"I completely understand. Once when I was angry, I raised my voice." My glare hardened. "And that's nearly the same thing."

He widened his arms so that I could see him better. "I took your punishment for escaping the ship. Isn't that enough of an apology?"

"What did she do to you?"

"It might've been worse, but Amarinda begged for my life. And I'm the reason she is still being held on the ship. If I do anything that makes the captain question my loyalty, Amarinda will pay the price for it."

"Is she still being held in the captain's quarters?"

"You're not listening, Jaron." He looked around. "If I do *anything* disloyal, Amarinda pays." Satisfied that we were alone, he lowered his voice to nearly a whisper. "From this point forward, I won't be able to help you. So I'm begging you to get back on whatever boat brought you here, while you can."

"I have a few unfinished tasks first. People to save, invaders to conquer, maybe enjoy a nice meal while I'm here."

"Leave this place, or you will regret it."

My tone sharpened. "You know what I have to do here. If you won't help me, then stay out of my way."

He licked his lips, kicking at the ground as he considered an answer, finally mumbling, "I can't do that." Now he looked up. "But you'd be out of *my* way if you were on the *Shadow Tide* tonight. You'd be out of everyone's way since the captain gave permission for the pirates to go ashore and rest for the night. Starting tomorrow, they have to rebuild the ship you destroyed. The ship will be much busier then."

Now I smiled. "Is there anything else I need to know?"

He was farther down the trail before he turned back. "Don't stand directly beneath the door frame of the captain's office. She hid a key there. I'd hate for it to fall and hit you."

I arched a brow. "Perhaps you've heard that Carthya needs a new captain of the guard. When you're finished here, maybe you would consider that position."

He stopped walking, and the light dimmed in his eyes. "I cannot be the captain of your guard anymore. When this is over, Darius will be my king."

Coming from Roden, these words left a sting in my chest that I had not expected. I would no longer be king. Instead, I'd return to the person I always was before: Jaron, the troublemaker, the embarrassment, the fool.

With heavy thoughts, I began walking down a different path. Roden called after me, "Everything you plan to do here, I have to be there to push against it."

I only glanced back at him long enough to say, "And I will

push back. Nothing has changed from our conversation on the ship. If you serve the captain, you must be defeated alongside the captain."

He spoke so quietly after that, he may not have thought I heard his final words as I walked away. "I've got to defeat you, Jaron."

· TWENTY-SEVEN ·

While Roden might have been correct about the *Shadow Tide* being empty, the area around it was better guarded than I had anticipated. Vigils stood watch on posts in all directions, and for added security, others stood in a line that extended across the entire length of all the ships, six warships in total now. Most of the vigils on the beach appeared to be Bellanders who had been forced into service, but they were doing their job with strict observance. I wondered if those who were forced into service eventually became those who were rewarded for service, and if they then became willing servants.

Maybe Roden would eventually turn against me. He felt he'd had no other choice but to enter Strick's service, and maybe that was true. But at what point would he *choose* service to her? At what point would his loyalties to me feel foreign?

I also wanted to know if Darius considered himself a servant to her. He had been quick to go to his knees at the captain's arrival and even quicker to beg for her mercy when she threatened him. Darius wasn't a fighter, but he had never been one to

cower before an enemy either. Or maybe he was. He and I had never faced any real threats when we were younger.

I made my way through the bushes beyond the beach, keeping myself hidden and eyeing the vigils near me for any signs of weakness. If I was spotted, would I be reported? I had to assume it was possible. The Bellanders surely knew the consequences of disobedience better than I.

But I did intend to get on the *Shadow Tide*. Both my sword and Darius's were there, and if I happened to find anything useful while I was in the captain's office, I would steal it too.

With that in mind, I snuck far past the last vigil on duty and silently entered the water, then swam beneath the waves toward the *Shadow Tide*. When I reached a mooring rope that led directly onto the deck, I wrapped my arms and legs around the rope and began to climb, grateful for increasing clouds to mask the moonlight.

I peered over the rail and saw no one, but I had no sooner rolled onto the deck before a vigil came from behind me and let out a heavy groan.

I looked up to see Teagut on patrol, this time alone. He cursed at the devils. "Not you again."

I did a quick check to ensure that all my weapons were still in place, and found the one best suited for any confrontation with Teagut. "Twenty coins, my friend, to forget I'm here."

"That bag looks lighter than twenty coins."

"You'll get the rest when I'm safely off this ship."

I reached above the door frame and felt around until I

located the key to the captain's office. It was there, exactly as Roden had described. I grinned and whispered my thanks to him.

Teagut added, "For a second bag, I'll tell you where they are holding Amarinda."

Eagerly, I turned to him. "Is she here?"

"They removed her from the ship about an hour ago," Teagut said. "Give me some time and I'll find out where."

I closed my eyes and took that in as a headache began to form. "Who else is on this ship?"

"A few crewmen, down in the bunks, all pirates. They'll take the later watch tonight, so they're sleeping while they can."

I put the full bag of coins in his hands. "Return to the deck, please. Watch for any trouble."

He shut the door behind me, and I listened for a few seconds to be sure I truly was alone. Other than its slow creaking as the ship moved with the waves, everything was silent. And I went to work.

My highest priority was finding the two swords, but nothing replaced my joy more than the discovery of a different sort of treasure, the greater part of a spice cake, one that had probably been baked in anticipation of a safe arrival back here in Belland. Since I too had safely arrived, I clearly deserved to take a slice for myself. And by slice, I meant the entire thing.

While I ate, I searched the captain's desk. Most of what I found there were items that didn't seem particularly useful, but I did pocket the tinderbox that I'd found shortly after being captured. I wondered when the captain had stolen that from me. I took a small knife as well, then continued searching. Beneath the bed were a few other sacks of coins on top of a small tin box, also locked and heavier than it looked when I picked it up. After taking the coins, I sliced off a length of rope that suspended the mattress and ran it through the box's handle, then tied that over my shoulder. Whatever the captain found necessary to lock up, I found necessary to steal.

I started to look elsewhere, then realized I had caught the reflection of metal while cutting the rope, but my attention had been in the wrong place. I looked under the bed again and saw two swords between the web of ropes and the mattress over it. Mine, along with a belt and sheath, and Darius's.

I put the belt on and slipped Darius's sword into the sheath, but kept my sword ready in case its use became necessary. I sincerely hoped it would not.

Yet I had not taken three steps out of Strick's office when someone called out my name. I turned to see a different vigil on the deck, one of the younger pirates, and shakier in holding his sword than Tobias ever was, if that was possible. I raised my own sword, making my intentions clear if he tried anything against me. The stairs to go belowdecks were between us, and he was definitely eyeing them as his means of escape.

"I am the pirate king," I said. "You will not turn me in."

"Captain Strick said you'd be dead by tomorrow. She said the Monarch will rule us now."

"The Monarch doesn't have a sword within easy reach of your neck. I do."

He swallowed hard. "Then you are my king. At least until tomorrow."

"He won't be alive tomorrow," Strick said from behind me. "He won't be alive by dawn."

I paused long enough to briefly mutter a question to the devils, wondering why they spent so much time on me. Receiving no immediate answer, I slowly turned around, keeping my sword ready. Strick carried no sword tonight, but the six Prozarians flanking her did. Those weren't great odds in my favor.

She smiled and took a step forward. "Did Roden tell you where to find the key?"

I tilted my head. Had Roden sent me here as a trap?

"Why did you let him live, Captain?"

She took another step toward me, forcing me to back up by the same distance.

"He will live while he remains useful." Her eyes fell to my leg. "He bought himself extra time when he gave you that wound."

I shrugged it off. "This? I've had worse."

"It sounds as though it is already getting worse. We retrieved Wilta about an hour ago. She told us there's a problem with your leg."

"It's stronger than ever."

"Wilta said it's infected, that it's beginning to affect your strength, even your mind. You'll lose the leg if the infection is not treated. Tell me where the Devil's Scope is, and I'll give you the medicine to heal that infection."

"Tobias left a jar of medicine in the sick bay, in an unmarked brown bottle. If you could bring that to me, with one gulp, I'll be healed. Unless you want it."

"That is not the purpose of that bottle, though I will force its full contents down your throat if you want its sort of *healing*." She frowned and stepped forward again. "Do not take me for a fool."

A grin widened across my face. "I wish you'd have warned me of that earlier. I'm afraid it's too late now."

She paused to look me over, or to study me, really. "You have an answer for everything, a joke in the most serious of moments. Is that how you deal with fear?"

"Don't assume I'm afraid of you." I shifted my weight. "You're constantly trying to figure me out, like I'm an experiment for study. Why is that, Captain? Is this how you try to understand your own twisted mind?"

By now, the captain had edged me all the way to the side of the boat. The water here was too shallow for me to simply jump in. I angled my sword so that the sharper end faced away from me.

At that moment, Teagut's head popped up from the stairs. "Thanks for keeping watch for me. I had to —" Then he saw the captain. "Oh no."

She glanced down at him. "So you are the one stealing my coins?"

Teagut pointed to me. "He stole them. I just received a few here and there."

I looked at him. "Remember when I didn't break your wrist? You still owe me a favor for that."

His eyes darted uncomfortably. "This isn't a good time to discuss that."

"There won't be a better time. You know what I came here to find."

Strick nodded to the Prozarians with her. "Arrest the pirate. Kill the prince."

"King," I sighed. "I'm a king."

With that, I rolled over the ship's railing and swung my legs toward the water, then pushed off from the wood to one of the mooring ropes leading down to the beach. I gripped my sword's handle, wrapped my other hand around the blunter edge, and tried to remain balanced as I quickly scaled to land.

Tried, and failed.

I was halfway down when the sword slipped and I lost my grip and fell into the water. I was immediately hit by a wave that ripped my sword from my hand. I saw a glint of metal as it sank, carrying with it memories of my childhood, of the night I was crowned king, and of victory in war. In mere seconds, it was gone, never to be seen again. Much as I ached at having to keep swimming to shore without it, I had to keep going.

Because back on the ship, Strick was screaming out orders for the vigils on the beach to come for me. When I looked up, at least twenty-five were headed my way, with their weapons already out.

I still had Darius's sword, but it didn't feel right to use it. If it was true that I was no longer a king, then it seemed fitting to have lost my weapon, the sword that had defined me for nearly half my life.

If Strick had her way now, that half of my life was over. And there would be no second half.

· TWENTY-EIGHT ·

By the time I reached the shore, it wasn't only Prozarian vigils waiting for me. Thirty pirates stood to their left. Most of them were glaring at me, but I figured they were angrier with Captain Strick. I could've been wrong about that, however. These were harsh glares, even for pirates.

I first addressed the Prozarian vigils. "I have the Devil's Scope. Lower your weapons now or I'll melt it into a teacup." They looked at one another, and one by one their weapons dropped to the sand.

A few of the pirates advanced toward me, and I raised my forearm with their branding upon it. "Does this still work to call for help?"

"Should it?" one of them asked. "You got Erick killed. And you abandoned all of us on that ship when you sabotaged it."

"Are you servants now, *her* servants? Have you entirely forgotten who you are? Who I am?"

"You're our king," a few of them grumbled, with more than one adding, "For now."

That was good enough for me. "As your king, I ask you to

prove why Avenian pirates must be respected . . . if the fight is still in you." I gestured toward the Prozarians, who were reaching again for their weapons. "I'd be especially appreciative if you'd prove yourselves now."

With their pride now at stake, the pirates eagerly growled and crossed behind me to face the Prozarians while I ran in the opposite direction.

Ahead of me, the beach rapidly narrowed as a large outcropping of rock took its place. I recognized it immediately as the image on the first lens. The outcropping appeared to be made of the same lava rock as I'd seen elsewhere, and the hillside extending away from it was thick with trees and underbrush. I first ran toward the hillside, fully intending to get lost in it.

Yet with my eyes too much ahead, I tripped and fell flat on my face. When I looked back, spitting out small pebbles and sand, I saw a dead and fallen tree near me. My leg had become caught in one of the half-broken branches.

But perhaps the branch had done me a favor, for at this angle, I realized the hillside was far too steep. I wouldn't get far on it.

I untangled my foot and stood again, this time running to the right of the outcropping, skirting the edge of the beach. As I began to pass it, I realized this was no outcropping, but instead was an enormous cave, its only entrance from the beach being exactly where I stood. I darted inside to find myself surrounded by tall rock walls, some quite rounded, but others going straight up to a large opening overhead.

An exit.

An escape.

Directly beneath the opening was a pit made of smooth black rock that descended deeper underground than I could see. It was probably a lava tube that had been created by the volcano that formed Belland, and might have gone endlessly underground.

Careful to avoid it, I stepped to the right so that if I fell, I wouldn't be carried to the devils, or farther into the earth than I might ever escape. I brushed my hands against the wall until I found a solid beginning for my fingers, pressed my right foot into an indentation, and began to climb.

Despite the danger and the hurry and the protest in my injured leg, I couldn't help but smile. This was the kind of wall I had dreamed of when I was beginning to climb. The rock was jagged enough to give me plenty of choices for a grip, but not so jagged that it threatened my balance. I was making good time and even wished the climb were longer so that I could truly test myself.

In no time, I crawled through the cave's opening, made easier by a wooden arch that had been bolted into the rock itself. I wasn't sure what its use might have been in the past, but for now, it made rolling onto the hilltop much easier.

And I did so just in time, for the voices below me easily carried upward.

"Where is he?"

Another Prozarian said, "He must've circled around back to the beach. You'd better hope we find him or we'll be the next sacrifices."

Once they were gone, I lay beside the cave opening to rest,

staring up at the dark sky and slowly becoming aware of a great sound of running water. With the next break in the clouds, I sat up and in the moonlight saw a hearty waterfall running down from hills much higher up the mountain. I could also make out a wide channel near me where the water had once been a mighty river that ran through the cave opening, emptying directly into the sea.

But no longer. A wall of trees and rocks now held the water in, creating a deep pool. The excess water ran off in new channels away from the cliff, though it was far too dark to see where, nor did I much care.

Turning in the opposite direction, I found the hilltop provided an incredible view of the Eranbole Sea, almost black this late at night. I walked around the cave opening, closer to the edge of the overlook, and saw the beach below and a dozen shadows all searching for me.

But up here, I was alone. So I lay back in the grass with the intention of thinking over everything that had happened so far that night. Except this time when I did, I landed on top of the tin box that I had slung over my shoulder, forcing me to sit up again. My thoughts had been much more focused on the swords and on my escape, so that I had nearly forgotten about the box.

I had few hopes of it containing anything worth the trouble of carrying it all this way. It wasn't much larger than a book, but far heavier. I walked into the line of trees and opened the tinderbox I'd swiped. The charcloth was wet, but I gathered a few dried leaves and twigs into a pile and used the flint and firesteel to create a small fire. Then I picked up a rock and hammered it against the lock. After only a few hits, the clasp broke apart, and I opened it with no idea of what I might find. But the captain had seen fit to lock it, so it had to contain something of value.

Except when I opened it, I quickly decided this was not the captain's box, nor was it even Prozarian. When I angled it toward the fire to catch its light, I realized that, impossibly, this bore the Carthyan seal on the inner lid.

So whose was it?

My attention was first drawn to what had created the considerable weight of the box: rows of gold coins so tightly bundled in cloth they would not make a sound. I untied the first wrap and the coins that unfolded in my hand were also Carthyan, though they were older coins bearing the image of my grandfather. These hadn't been issued since before I was born.

Beneath the coins was a folded note on fine parchment. The words of the letter were simple: *My eternal gratitude for your gift. May this money help you find your own happiness.*

I'd have barely paid attention to the note, especially as it was not signed, but it did not need to be. My heart was already racing, already twisting in my chest. This was my mother's handwriting.

Scarcely able to breathe, I reached for the next item, a second note, this one much longer, and with handwriting I also recognized. This had come from Mott, and within the first few lines, I knew exactly what this was. Mott had written a love letter.

Which meant I knew whose box this was.

I knew it was a violation of Mott's emotions and Trea's

privacy to read the letter, but if anything could help unravel the mystery surrounding my brother, I had to understand it. I skimmed wherever possible, until I reached the line, *As soon as I can make arrangements to repay my debts to Master Conner, I will repay yours. Then I will propose marriage, and I hope you will agree.*

I set the note down, utterly confused. Whatever debts Mott might have owed to Conner, there had to be enough gold in this box to cover all of it.

So when did Trea get the coins, and why hadn't she used them? And what connection did she have to my mother? Mott said Trea had worked her whole life for Conner, so she could never have been at the castle.

Yet if she had never been at the castle, how could she have been there at Darius's birth?

Realization deepened within me, ideas I did not want to consider, suspicions I did not want to face.

Truths that I should have seen before now.

Despite what was recorded in the castle records, Darius had not been born at the castle. My parents had lied about that. They had lied in their story of what a simple birth it had been for my mother, with only a single lady-in-waiting to attend her.

Accepting that as fact unfolded answers to questions I'd never realized I'd had. They led me down a path I did not want to walk, a path I didn't know even existed. Yet here I was.

Finally understanding why my father always seemed frustrated when he asked how Darius could be so like him, while I was not.

Why, following the pirate attack on my ship, my father had

kept me away from the castle in hiding and had allowed Darius to remain at the castle, where it was far more dangerous.

Why my father was so insistent on my conforming to behaviors expected of a king, though as the younger son, I would only ever be a military leader, or manage the royal holdings, or become a priest. Never a king.

I reeled back, pushing my hand through my hair and fighting away tears for the truths I did not want to know, then finally letting them spill.

For I understood now who really was the eldest son of King Eckbert and Queen Erin.

Who was their only son.

Me.

Darius was my adopted brother.

· TWENTY-NINE ·

Once I understood the truth about my brother, I suddenly had to see him. A thousand questions were crashing through my mind, and the only way I'd ever get them settled was to talk to him and find answers.

My stomach churned as I made my way back to the rock home deep within the forest. I was careful to check the area to be sure no one was around, then stepped into the clearing. I wasn't sure where Darius would sleep, or if anyone else was inside, so I decided the best way to enter was through the door, as any normal person would.

I put my hand on the door, only to find it opened from within, but most unexpectedly by Mott.

I stood back, confused. He looked around the area, then said, "What are you doing out so late? You'd better come inside."

I followed him in and he closed the door, then locked it. We both turned to see Trea standing near the fireplace, a shawl wrapped over her shoulders and a solemn expression on her face. Mott began staring again.

"This is Jaron?" she asked Mott, and he nodded. To me,

she added, "You should not be here. Don't you know what the Prozarians have planned for you?"

"I'm here to see . . . my brother." Never before had it required effort to speak those words, but it did now.

"Your brother is part of those plans! He doesn't want to be, but they've left him no choice."

"I'm here to see Darius."

Mott frowned. "Trea and I have been talking. We don't think that's a good idea."

"I'm not asking if it's a good idea. I want to see him."

Trea's hand flew to Mott's arm, gripping it with the tips of her fingers. "Oh no. He has the box."

It was slung crossways over my shoulder, as it had been before, and now I shifted it to rest behind my back.

Not that it mattered. Desperation marked Trea's voice as she asked, "Where did you get that?"

"Captain Strick had it."

"The Prozarians raided this home shortly before they left for Carthya. That box disappeared in the raid, but I wasn't sure who took possession of it." She held out her hands for the box, then stared directly at me. "You didn't open it, did you?" I wouldn't answer at first, and she said, "Jaron, please tell me you did not open that box."

I blinked several times, hoping to push away any emotions, but my eyes welled with tears anyway. All I could do was nod.

Trea put a hand to her heart, as if my simple action of nodding caused her pain, and maybe it had. She led me to the corner near the fireplace. "I'm sure you have questions."

Questions? Did she think this would be so simple that I could ask my question, then walk away, as if my whole world hadn't just shifted from its axis? This wasn't only about Darius, it was about lies my parents had told to me, to the entire kingdom. What else had they lied about?

"Give her the box," Mott instructed.

I untied the rope around my shoulder and slipped the box loose, then placed it in her hands. She brought it to her chest, cradling the box as if it were a long-forgotten treasure. Mott put his arm around her, and when she leaned in to him, he kissed the top of her forehead, whispering that maybe this was for the best.

Finally, she sat on a bench and invited me to join her, which I did. She said, "You were never meant to see this, Jaron. No one was ever meant to see it."

"Has Darius seen it?"

"No, never."

"You said you'd answer my questions."

She frowned. "No, I said that I understood you'd have a great many questions. But I'm sorry, I cannot answer them."

"Then I'll ask elsewhere." I began to stand. "Do you want that?"

Mott crossed between me and the door. "Sit down. We're on your side."

"Do you know what is in that box, Mott?"

"I know some of it. A letter I once wrote to her."

"If she told you anything else, I want to know it now. I'm tired of being the last person to hear the truth about my life!"

Behind me, Trea sighed. "Every time Darius described you to me, do you know what word he most often used? Difficult. I didn't entirely believe him . . . until now."

I turned to her, sticking out my jaw. "I'll be as difficult as necessary until I get my answers. If not from you, then I will ask Darius directly. Is he here?" I looked back at Mott. "You know I will do this."

His shoulders fell. "You'd better answer his questions, Trea. I'll get him something to eat."

Despite the cake I'd recently eaten, I was still plenty hungry. It was enough to get me back onto the bench beside Trea while Mott went to dish me up a bowl of stew, still in a pot hanging over a dwindling fire.

Trea allowed me a few bites before she began. When she did, she started with a deep, anxious breath. "For a long time, your parents were unable to have children. It caused a great concern within the kingdom. Many people said because your mother had no royal blood, the saints would not grant her a child. Then one day, one of your mother's handmaidens came to her with a proposal. You see, this handmaiden had discovered she was with child, but she was unmarried and without any means to support herself and a child. In desperation, she offered the child to your mother. Your mother not only agreed but welcomed the offer with great enthusiasm."

I tilted my head. "You were the handmaiden's nurse?"

"Not exactly. I worked for a regent named Bevin Conner. He knew of the handmaiden's plight — in fact, he was the one who had suggested this solution to her troubles — and he offered to allow her to remain in his estate of Farthenwood until the child was born, even as Erin remained in seclusion from the public so that there could never be any speculation as to the adopted child's origins. After the birth, the plan was to allow the handmaiden proper time for recovery, then to bring her back to the castle to continue her duties, and to always be near her child." A tear fell to Trea's cheek. "But the handmaiden died during delivery, and so the child — Darius — was seamlessly welcomed as the eldest son of Eckbert and Erin, the crown prince and heir to the throne of Carthya."

"Why should it matter?" Mott asked. "With his adoption, he becomes a royal."

"But his birth family does not." I met his eyes. "Royals have adopted children before, but never an eldest child in line for the throne. If something ever happened to the reigning king and queen, the birth family might lay claim for the throne, shifting the line of succession."

"Away from you," Mott murmured.

"Jaron was a great surprise to them, for more than one reason." Trea's smile disappeared as she faced me. "When I gave Darius to your mother, she asked me to swear on my life that I would never reveal this secret to anyone. Now that you know, I ask for the same oath, out of respect for your mother's wishes. Will you honor this secret?"

To honor the secret required me to lie to my own people, and I'd never done that before. I'd have to lie to my closest friends, those I loved.

Imogen. How could I keep such a thing from Imogen?

It was bad enough when Conner had wanted me to become a false prince. Trea was now making the same request, for my mother's sake. I would no longer be king, for reasons based on lies.

But how could I refuse the sincerest wishes of my mother?

Finally, I nodded. "I will keep your secrets, Trea, to my grave."

A creak on the staircase behind us made me turn, and there was Darius, tying a robe around his nightclothes but staring at me with a deep frown. "I thought I heard voices. We should talk."

THIRTY

Hello, Darius."

It was a pitiful beginning for my own brother, someone I had loved and respected and admired my entire life. He had meant everything to me, and I had just greeted him with nothing warmer than I would offer a passerby on the street.

Making it worse, Darius answered with the same empty "Hello," and there we stood, facing each other like strangers.

"Did we wake you?" Trea asked.

"Jaron did, when he mentioned his grave." He turned to me. "That's not the kind of thing anyone should say around here these days."

"That's all you heard?" Trea asked.

"Yes, why?"

"Where can we talk?" I asked.

"There's a sitting room in the back of the house." Darius walked down the stairs with his eyes fixed on me as if he didn't know me. No, it was worse than that. He was watching me like I was the invader here.

I followed him into a room that was simply decorated but that still gave a feeling of authority. Much like Darius himself. He sat in one chair and gestured for me to sit in another chair across from him. Uncertain of what to expect from this conversation, I remained on my feet.

He took notice of my refusal to sit but said nothing. Instead, he leaned back and studied me. "You look exhausted."

Exhausted barely described the way I felt. Since the night our ship was attacked and destroyed, I'd barely slept two hours together. I wanted to sleep, yet every time I'd attempted it, something inside me had warned that if I gave in, I would miss some piece of information that I vitally needed.

There was the irony. I finally had that information and it was tearing me apart. Rather than returning to the ship to steal that tin box, I should have found a comfortable bed to lose myself in. Truly, I wished I had gone anywhere else. Roden's words echoed in my mind, that I should leave before I discovered things I did not wish to know.

"You found my sword?" Darius asked.

I withdrew it from the sheath and passed it over to him. "I have your crown as well, though it's hidden."

"Where?"

My eyes darted. "It's hidden, Darius."

Any warmth that might have been in his expression cooled. "You're the same Jaron as always. Sneaking around, making plans that you share with no one, plans that no one ever fully understands anyway. Keeping secrets."

Only one secret mattered at the moment. Trea said that

Darius had never seen the contents of that box. But it didn't mean he was ignorant of the truth about himself. I was desperate to ask, but to ask would be to reveal it.

So instead, I said, "You're not the same Darius as always."

"I'm the person I've had to become out here. You wouldn't understand what it does to a person to be on their own."

I tilted my head, unsure of what to say to him. Had he forgotten my years as Sage?

Rather than draw the conversation in that direction, I asked, "How did you come to be here?"

He shrugged. "Honestly, I'm not sure. I had supper one evening with Father and Mother, then felt sleepy so I went to my room to lie on the bed. That's the last I remember until I awoke on a ship. Trea was there and told me I had been sent away for my own protection. I asked what exactly she was protecting me from, but she only said that the regent, Bevin Conner, had ordered her to watch over me until it was safe to return home. How well did you know Bevin Conner?"

I snorted, loud enough to communicate my feelings there. "Better than I wish I did."

Darius didn't bother asking how I knew him, which was good considering that I could fill an entire book with that explanation. Instead, he added, "All I know is that we ended up here."

"Do the people here know who you are?"

"Yes. Although I have no authority here, I was given this home, rather than one of the thin wooden huts where most of the people live. Bellanders are good and kind, preferring the simple, isolated life. We've been happy here, though every day for almost two years, I've waited for news from home, permission to return. Eventually, I thought something horrible must have happened, and that it might never be safe to return."

My eyes moistened. "Something horrible did happen, Darius. Our parents —"

He cut me off with a sharper tone than before. "When I last saw Mother and Father, they were both alive and well. How were they when you last saw them?"

I hesitated, anticipating where this conversation was going. "They were already gone when I returned to the palace. In fact, I only returned because they were gone. I thought you were too."

"When the Prozarians arrived on our shores last month, they claimed to have come as friends. I welcomed them as such, and at supper one evening, I was foolish enough to ask if they had any news of Carthya. Oh, they did. Your name was well known to them."

"In what way?"

"You'd recently won a war, I understand, one that nobody had thought possible to win."

"Carthya is at peace now with the countries that surround us. And we hope to remain at peace."

"Thanks to you, that peace is now threatened. Earlier tonight, Captain Strick forced me into an agreement that I did not want to make."

My eyes narrowed. "What is the agreement?"

"Before she left to find you, we had negotiated a simple agreement: They promised to help me return to Carthya, and to regain the throne that should be mine."

"In exchange for what?"

"The second lens for something they call the Devil's Scope."

I threw out a hand. "Why would you agree to that? If you wanted to return to Carthya, just get on a boat and come home!"

"Don't you think I've wanted to do that? Conner's instructions were to wait here where it was safe, and to protect the second lens. But he's dead now, thanks to you. My negotiated agreement with the captain is broken, also thanks to you. Now I am taking control again. I will give the captain the second lens, then claim my throne, and try my best to rule under these new agreements, despite everything you've done."

"What are the terms of the new agreement?"

He sighed. "Carthya now must also pay the Prozarians a tribute each year, a tax. But we retain our freedom, our right to rule ourselves as we please."

"Absolutely not. I will not allow it."

Darius's eyes flashed with anger. "That's not your decision anymore. I am the rightful king of Carthya. You need to step down."

"There are still so many questions —"

He raised his voice. "I am the older son. You do not get to choose whether to step down; you will do it because you are not the true king. The throne is mine, and has always been mine. I was only offering you the opportunity to walk away with some dignity."

"When have I ever cared about dignity? I have questions."

"Answer my question first. Were you involved in any way with the deaths of our parents?"

My heart crashed against my chest. "What?" Even the mention of such a crime ripped through me. "You know I never could . . . never would . . ."

"I know you were angry when Father asked you to remain in Avenia, posing as an orphan boy."

"Angry? No, Darius, it hurt me, to see that he had chosen you. . . ." I stopped there, choking on my own words, recalling my thoughts that had led me here. My father had chosen me, keeping Darius at the castle where the risk was higher.

In my silence, Darius leaned forward. "Until the Prozarians came, I didn't know our parents had died. I thought I was in hiding, just as you were in hiding, with Conner as my protector. Then I heard you'd become king, and why." His tone sharpened. "Captain Strick made me an offer in exchange for the second lens. She would bring you here to answer for any crimes against our parents. Then I would return to Carthya and use the results of your trial to get the people on my side."

I began pacing, trying to work out the storm of emotions inside me. "Darius, this is a trick, an attempt to get control of Carthya, to create a wedge between us!"

"*You* did this to us! Do you think I want to believe something so horrible about my own brother, my own flesh and blood?"

"After all our history, why would you believe her and not me?"

"Because there is evidence!" Darius brushed at his eyes with the back of his hand. "I will make you this offer tonight and only tonight. If you give me the throne, confess your crime, and agree to a permanent exile from Carthya, I will try to make them understand no trial is necessary."

"Exile? Darius, how can you talk like this? This is not you, this is not how we ever were!"

With a cry, Trea darted into the back room. "There is trouble outside. Stay in here."

I rushed to the door in time to see Mott run out. Whatever the trouble was, I worried about Mott attempting to manage it on his own, so I returned to where Darius had left his sword on the table and ran out the door with it.

Mott was already standing in front of the home, his sword outstretched against five Prozarians who were equally armed. Without realizing I was there, he yelled, "You will not take Jaron!"

"There he is now." A red-haired man near the front aimed his sword at me. He was the one who had thrown Erick's body overboard, and he clearly remembered it too, for he said, "I won't be so kind with your remains."

I redoubled my grip on Darius's sword and charged directly at him. He struck with greater force than I'd expected, and I fell back a few steps. At my left, Mott began fighting two men together, but he quickly received a long cut on his forearm, and the remaining two were waiting for an opportunity to leave their mark.

I set my feet more squarely against the red-haired man ahead of me, ducking as he took a second swing, and elbowing him hard enough in the thigh to force him back. His leg folded slightly, allowing me to rotate, striking at a Prozarian raising his sword at Mott's back. In that same rotation, I was about to strike the red-haired man, when he dropped his sword and collapsed to his knees.

I angled my weapon against his neck. "End this if you want to live."

He immediately shouted to his companions, "Lower your weapons!" They hesitated, and with a sharper press of my blade at his side, he added, "Do it!"

Swords clattered to the ground. I told them, "Run away now, while you still can."

The red-haired man stood again, but his smile poked at my temper. He said, "You think defeating us means anything? We were only the distraction."

"Run," I hissed.

After they were gone, Trea ran outside and wrapped Mott's uninjured arm over her shoulder, propping him up to walk him back inside the house.

Except that she had to push past Darius, who was still standing in the doorway. I walked back to him and threw his sword at his feet.

"Why didn't you help me?" I scowled. "You were here, you saw it!"

"Why *did* you fight?" he countered. "When the captain finds out, do you know how angry she'll be?"

"I make people angry all the time. And if doing what's right makes someone angry with me, then may I cause rage and fury wherever I go."

He frowned. "Trust me, Jaron. You do."

I waved my hand around us. "How long has Belland been your home? You owe something to these people."

"No, Belland is my prison. They are prisoners here, just as I am. You want me to save them? Well, I have. Until I agreed to give the Prozarians the second lens, they were killing one person here after another. I saved these people, just as I will save Carthya!"

"Explain how enslaving anyone sets them free."

"Because they get to live — isn't that what you want? And they are not enslaved. Carthya will pay its tax to the Prozarians, and they will leave us alone."

I gestured to where the fight had just taken place. "Is that what it looks like to be left alone?"

"All they ask is that we keep our agreements and obey their rules."

I snorted. "That will never be me."

"I know that." Darius's voice had become notably sadder. "They know it too. I'm truly sorry for what's about to happen. I wish this wasn't necessary."

Then, with the snap of twigs beneath someone's foot behind me, I understood what Darius meant. The red-haired man had said they were only distractions. The five Prozarians had not come to take me; they had come to lure me out of the house. And Darius must have known it.

I turned in time to see Wilta step from behind the trees. Her eyes were wet with tears and the sleeve of her dress was ripped. "I swear I didn't tell them anything."

I nodded back at her, even as Captain Strick emerged from behind the trees with the same crewmen who had been with her on the ship, and Roden behind them all, holding a torch.

The captain said, "I let you go earlier tonight only because I knew where I'd find you again."

I looked at Wilta. "You must have told her. Nobody else knew I'd be here tonight."

"It wasn't her." The captain smiled up at Darius. "You promised to give me answers by morning, and you kept your promise. How did you know that your brother would come here?"

Darius glanced over at me. "I know him."

"Apparently better than I know you." My gut twisted in anticipation of whatever the captain might do to me next, but that was nothing compared to the wounds Darius had just inflicted. I continued to stare at him, hurt, angry, disappointed. I was flooded with so many emotions, I wished it were possible to feel nothing at all.

"This is your last chance," Darius said. "Give me the throne."

"As you are now, I will never allow you a minute upon the Carthyan throne."

"Then I already know you are guilty. You killed to take the throne, and you must die to surrender it."

Strick nodded at her soldiers. "Take him."

Roden stepped forward with the others, and our eyes locked in a steady glare as they searched me for weapons and bound my hands. Finally, I asked him, "Was that a trap, to lure me onto the ship?"

He only frowned and said, "I warned you that I would interfere with your plans. And I have."

· THIRTY-ONE ·

At first, the imprisonment hadn't been so bad. The single cell was at the far end of a larger underground room, which kept it at a manageable temperature, and a quick inspection showed no sign of rats. The worst news was that in addition to my lost sword, the few weapons I'd had before were also gone, again, and there was nothing I could do about any of it. Exhausted as I was, I had lain on the wood bunk in the corner of the cell and immediately fallen asleep.

It was light outside when I awoke, and I sat up, expecting to be greeted by someone ready to threaten me, or curse me, or with some luck, feed me. But nothing happened, no one entered, and after a while, I began to wonder if I'd been forgotten entirely.

Which meant that hours later, I was already at the edge of my temper when two men entered the cell room and walked down the carved rock steps to where I was being held. The first man who entered was tall and narrow, and I stood to prepare for whatever trouble he might bring, but was surprised to recognize the second, wider man to come through the door. "Lump! I hoped to see you again."

His forehead wrinkled, suspicious. "Why?"

"Isn't it obvious? You never told me your real name."

"We're not here for that." His thick hands curled into fists.

"Ah. The last time I saw you, the captain wouldn't let you harm me." I clicked my tongue. "May I assume those orders have changed?"

He grinned. "That is correct."

Although we were still separated by bars, I backed up. "I'm changing those orders again. You will not touch me, and you will tell me where Amarinda is being held. As a reward for your help, I'll leave you alive when I conquer Belland."

"Do you think I'm stupid?"

"I considered the possibility. Prove me wrong and help me. Please, Lump."

"Why would I help you?" His voice grew colder. "I've been waiting for this since the moment you escaped the *Shadow Tide*."

"Stand back farther from the door," the narrow man ordered.

I remained exactly where I was. I'd been through this often enough to know that things never ended well for me, whether I cooperated or not.

The narrow man unlocked my cell door, but Lump was the first to push through it. He grabbed me and speared a fist into my gut.

I remained crumpled over until I found my breath again, then straightened up, only to be on the receiving end of another swipe to my jaw that did send me to the ground, where I stayed. Lump didn't seem like the kicking type, so it seemed safer down here.

"You'd better give me a good meal after this," I said. "If not, then go away."

Now the narrow man entered the cell, almost seeming to carry his shadow with him. I immediately understood why. As physically intimidating as Lump was, this man was his very opposite: ghostly pale, thin and willowy, and controlled enough to hold his body together in a tight straight line. Round glasses distorted his long face, and not in a good way. They shrank his eyes into cold, almost lifeless, beads.

"You must be named Mercy," I said. "Were your parents great believers in irony?"

He didn't flinch, or blink, or show the slightest hint of any emotion whatsoever.

"I know this is what you do," he replied. "You believe if you can make someone angry, it will disrupt their plans. That won't work with me."

"It doesn't work with Lump either." I frowned over at him, full of pity. "Mostly because he can't understand half my insults."

It turned out Lump was a kicker, after all. I regretted not knowing that before remaining on the ground.

"We are here for answers," Mercy said. "Tell us where the Devil's Scope is."

"Personally, I think any object with such a name should be avoided. Perhaps if it were called the Dessert Scope, or the Happiness Scope —"

Lump kicked me again, harder this time, and near the injury in my leg. Once I regained my breath, I'd have to get out of reach from his boots.

Mercy continued as if I had not spoken. "Give us the scope now and make this easier on yourself."

I still hadn't fully recovered from the last kick, but I said, "Actually, you should release me and make things easier on that scope. I'm counting each hit you give to me. Will that pretty glass lens be able to take the same number of hits?"

Mercy's eyes flashed, the first sign that he had human emotions. "Refuse to give me the answers I want, and we'll move on to torture."

"Refuse to release me, and I will torture that scope."

Now his face twisted. "What does that mean, that you'll torture the scope?"

I made myself stand again, though I was certain I'd regret it. "I can do this all day. Anything you do to me, I will make sure it is done to that scope and its lens. But first, I will destroy your entire fleet, force all Prozarians to scatter from this land like the cowards you are, and ensure that whenever you even think my name in the future, you will shudder and curse my existence." I looked over at Lump. "Though in all fairness, I planned to do all of that even before you hit me."

Lump rewarded my speech with a fist to my eye, which would likely leave it bruised and a little swollen. It hurt, but it wouldn't change my threats. I could accomplish everything I wanted with only one good eye.

I staggered forward, crashing hard into Mercy and wrapping my arms around his waist to keep from falling. He brushed me off as one might an eager dog, but I somehow remained on my feet.

"It doesn't work to hurt him. He only gets meaner," Roden said, walking down the steps to enter the prison room. "If he hasn't talked yet, anything you do will make him more determined not to speak to you."

"He's speaking plenty," Lump said. "That's the problem."

"Yes, but I'm finished speaking with you two, so you're dismissed." I turned to Roden. "Get them out of here, and then you and I can talk."

"The captain wants to see you both at once," Roden said. "The pirates attacked a group of Prozarians last night, and she wants you to confine them to their ship from now on."

Mercy shook his head. "Our orders were to remain here until he gives us answers."

"I have a few questions of my own that you might be able to answer," I said. "How can Lump be so big and still hit like a kitten?"

Lump started forward but Mercy put an arm in front of him, holding him back.

"Mercy, if you tell me his name, I'll promise not to make fun of you when you're not looking."

This time, they both started forward, but Roden said, "The captain gave you new orders! I won't take the blame if she finds out you ignored them."

Mercy obeyed only after a long glare at Roden, but Lump followed him up the stairs without a word.

Roden waited until they were gone, then said, "Those are her top enforcers. You shouldn't have made them angry."

"They shouldn't have made me angry."

Roden sighed, reached into his pocket, and pulled out some bread, which he pushed through the bars toward me. I took it and mumbled a thanks.

He only shrugged. "You'll need it today." Silence followed, then he added, "I heard your leg is infected."

"If it gets worse, I won't be able to fight on it." I paused, then added, "I've seen you staring at Wilta. Do you like her?"

He shuffled his feet. "She's very pretty."

"Do you like her?" He didn't answer, so I said, "Just be careful around her."

"Fine advice coming from someone who hasn't been careful a day in his life." He gestured at my leg again. "The Prozarians took all the medicines from Belland. Maybe Tobias will have something to help."

For some reason, that irritated me. "You're worried about my leg? After what you just saw in here, why should my leg matter to you now?"

He shrugged. "Because I still have hope for you. More than for myself even. I would consider myself lucky to be on your side of the bars rather than on mine."

"If you're convinced of that, change places with me."

"I didn't mean it that way," Roden said. "I just wanted you to understand that in my own way, I'm as imprisoned as you are."

My tone softened. "Yes, I know."

"I've asked Darius if he can help me, and he promised to try. He'll be the king now."

"*I* am still your king, Roden. And maybe I wasn't always the friend you wanted, but I tried to be the king you needed."

He frowned at me. "I never should have said those things I did in your throne room. I'm sorry. I didn't mean any of it."

"Maybe you meant some of it."

"Maybe." He frowned again. "But it's too late. I cannot help you anymore. I cannot help myself. This may be all that I can do for you."

He gave a low whistle, and on cue, two Bellanders entered, leading Imogen down the stairs, her wrists tied in rope. I rushed to the bars, eager to see her but wishing we could have met anywhere else. She eyed me with pity, even as I looked at her with a growing panic. If Roden thought my spirits would be lifted by seeing the girl I loved inside a prison cell, he was deeply mistaken.

My cell door had remained open, but once Imogen was inside, Roden locked it, then said, "Remember, we're only allowing you to see him because you promised to talk him back to his senses."

Imogen straightened her spine. "You made a coward's choice, Roden. Leave us alone, or Jaron and I won't say a word."

His expression fell, and his eyes quickly shifted to me. "Listen to her, Jaron. She's the only one you ever listen to."

After everyone had left, I immediately began untying Imogen's wrists. "Did they hurt you in any way?"

"No, but the captain questioned me, mostly about you. Why is she so interested in understanding you?"

"I don't know. What answers did you give?"

"There weren't many I could give, since you share so little with me."

I finished unwinding the rope, then took her hands in mine, hoping things were not too broken between us. "That's the very reason I share so little."

Imogen let a beat pass. "No, Jaron, that's not the reason."

There was so much I wanted to tell her, the truths about me and my history, secrets that had been tucked into the deepest parts of my heart. But she was right, as always. It terrified me to think of telling her too much, of revealing something that might create a barrier between us, one she could not cross.

For now, I said, "Ask me anything."

"I have only one question. What do you need me to do?"

"Tell me everything you've learned. Is there any news of Amarinda?"

Her face fell. "I was hoping you'd have news for me."

"Not yet. But I do believe she's still alive, and safe. They'll bring her out at some point when they feel Darius needs to be controlled. Were you able to find Tobias and Fink?"

"I got there too late. They'd already been forced to separate, so I only found Fink. He was on the north end of Belland." She leaned in closer to me and whispered, "The scope and lens are in my bag, hidden not far from here. I didn't want to risk Fink being caught with it."

"Does anyone know?"

"I don't think so."

I was relieved to hear that Fink was still safe, but I was equally concerned for Tobias. Fink had spent most of his young life surviving on his own. Tobias hadn't.

Imogen touched my face, bringing my attention back to

her. "Talk to me, Jaron, please. I know you're carrying something big inside you. Don't you understand that I feel the weight of it too?"

Her words hung in the air as she continued staring at me. Finally, I broke. "Darius wants the throne."

"Oh. What did you tell him?"

"What can I tell him? He is the elder brother."

Imogen drew in a slow breath. "What if he's not?"

Based on Imogen's expression, I was certain that what she was about to say, and the secret I had promised Trea to keep, were the very same.

"He is my brother, Imogen." I'd spent half my time in this cell debating how to manage what I now knew about Darius. This was not a decision I had come to lightly, but I had made my decision.

She led me to the slab of wood where I'd slept the night before and sat beside me. "I haven't stopped thinking about Trea since we saw her last night. I told you that I knew her a little when I was at Farthenwood. Every evening at seven, I used to bring a cup of tea to Conner in his office. One evening, shortly before you came to Farthenwood, I started to enter his office, but I heard raised voices. Conner finally shouted that his orders would be obeyed or the consequences would be severe. Seconds later, Trea came from the office, crying. I had hidden around the corner so neither of them saw me, and I never did see her again until now."

"Did you hear what the orders were?"

Imogen pressed her lips together, clearly aware of how

difficult this conversation was for me. "He told her to take the boy away. That didn't mean anything to me then, but it does now. Obviously, he was talking about Darius."

"Yes, but what does it matter?"

Imogen took my hands in hers. "You know I've been reading Conner's journal. He wanted his possessions distributed among his heirs, correct?"

"Yes, but he has no heirs."

Imogen took a few measured breaths. "What if he did? Jaron, I don't know who Darius's mother was, but I do believe —"

"No!" I stood and backed away from her, horrified by her suggestion. "You are pulling these ideas from thin air. I will not discuss something that would strip Darius of his identity. He is the rightful king of Carthya!"

"Jaron, he's not! Conner said —"

"It doesn't matter! If his adoption means he is not my brother, then Fink is not my brother, and I am once again without a family! I don't care about tradition. I don't care about his origins."

"You should care! Do you know why the Prozarians brought you here? They plan to kill you today."

"Only if I'm convicted at the trial —"

"Which you will be."

"And only if I can't make Darius remember who he was before coming here! Maybe he is adopted, but none of that matters to me!"

She lowered her voice. "Would it matter if you knew who his father really is?"

A heavy silence followed, when all I could hear was my heart slamming against my chest. "Do not say it."

"Conner set his plan in motion to find a false prince because he believed war was coming. He killed your parents and then began searching for someone he could put on the throne — anyone the people would accept as you. He sent Darius here, out of harm's way. We know he planned to take control of the throne through the false prince. What if he planned to eventually dispose of the false prince, then bring Darius back to the throne?" She drew in a slow breath. "Jaron, the night that Conner sent Trea away, I only heard his last words to her: 'my son.'"

"No, Imogen."

"I believe that Darius's father is Bevin Conner."

· THIRTY-TWO ·

I sat with Imogen's suggestion for several minutes, unable to speak, or really, to fully absorb the weight of the consequences if she was right.

There were many things I owed to Conner. Because of him, I had returned to the throne and claimed my identity again. Because of him, I had Imogen in my life, and Mott and Tobias, and Roden. I was still alive thanks to him, for near the end of the war, he had sacrificed himself to save me.

Yet for all that, I could never forget the fact that he had killed my parents, and Latamer, and committed any number of other crimes in his quest for power and control. Despite the good that he had brought into my life, it was always clear in my mind that he was a villain and that his fate was what he had deserved.

Was he also Darius's father?

Imogen and I said little more about that possibility, even as the afternoon sun made our cell uncomfortably warm. I told her about my lost sword, listened to her thoughts, and asked her forgiveness once again for putting her in so much jeopardy.

Eventually, I reclined against the wall with Imogen in my arms, letting thoughts flow through my mind like drifting waves. Some crashed harder against my conscience than others, but nothing could make them stop.

I was almost grateful for the interruption when the door to our prison cell opened, long enough for one of the Prozarian vigils to call down to me, "Prepare yourself, if you can. Your trial will begin in fifteen minutes."

The instant he left, I turned to Imogen. "You need to leave."

Her head tilted. "You have a way out?"

With a sly grin, I withdrew the key to the cell door from my jerkin. That had been the reason for crashing into Mercy so clumsily. Perhaps I had sacrificed my pride to cling to him in such a pathetic way, but that's how long it had taken me to get the key from his pocket.

I pointed deeper within this underground room, which significantly narrowed beyond this cell. "Hide there, as far into the shadows as you can get."

"That's hardly an escape."

"It will be." I opened the cell door, then kissed her before nodding in the direction I wanted her to go. "Hurry, Imogen. They'll be back any moment."

"You're not coming?"

"I have to be at that trial."

She threw out her arms. "Why would you do that? You know how it will end!"

"No, I don't know. If I can still change things with Darius, I have to try."

"Didn't you hear anything I said to you?"

"I heard all of it. That's why I have to help him now, and I won't be able to do that if I escape with you. Will you try to find everyone you can, and gather them together where it's safe? I'm going to force the Prozarians to surrender, and we need everyone's help."

She bit her lip and looked as though there was something more she wanted to say, but instead she nodded and ducked into the shadows.

Just in time too, for no sooner did she slip behind an outcrop of rock than the door at the other end of the room opened again. Lump entered, pausing at the entrance as though bracing himself for my insults. When none came, he began, "It is time for —" He stopped and walked the rest of the way down the stairs. "Where's the girl?"

I looked around me. "I see no one here but you and me."

"There was a girl, I saw her."

"Oh, *her.* Yes, well, she already escaped."

"How?"

I lifted Mercy's keys. "These."

Lump advanced, his eyes increasingly narrowing with each step he took. "Give those to me."

"Where would be the fun in that?" Instead, I hurled the keys through the bars into the opposite corner of the room from where Imogen was hiding. He darted for them and I pushed open the cell door, which I'd kept unlocked, and raced for the stairs.

Lump doubled back to chase me, but I scaled the steps in

half the time he did, exited the prison room door . . . and crashed straight into Mercy. Only this time, without intending to. He grabbed one arm and I used the other to get in a punch to his gut. That forced him to release me, but I'd no sooner done that than Lump emerged and wrestled me down from behind.

"You'll pay for that," Mercy said, still half-doubled over.

"Give him to me." Roden rounded a corner. "Now!"

Lump still landed a fist against my side before leaving me on the ground. Roden crouched in front of me and said, "What was the point in attempting an escape now? Wouldn't you assume they had a dozen vigils up here waiting to escort you to the trial?"

I stared at him. "That's exactly what I assumed."

Now he took a slow breath. "I've been thinking about the trial. If you tell the captain where you've hidden the scope, you might be able to bargain for your life."

"Let me speak to Darius."

"They won't let you do that, and from what I saw last night, that's the worst thing you could do. But there is someone who wants to speak to you."

Whoever it was, if they were brought here by the Prozarians, I had no desire to see them. "I'm busy."

Roden stepped aside as Tobias came around the corner from the back of the prison house. His eyes were on me as if trying to communicate answers to the dozens of questions suddenly filling my head.

Roden seemed to know what Tobias was unable to say. "They found the camp. Tobias sent Fink in one direction and came down to the beach to meet the searchers, to delay them.

Fink's footprints disappeared once he crossed onto rock, but they know he was headed north, and they will pick up his trail again."

Which meant they might also find Imogen, who would soon be on her way back to Fink.

I glanced at Tobias, who gave me a slight, almost imperceptible nod, answering the obvious next question. Aside from the scope and lens, Fink had all the items I had stolen from the captain's office. That would be too much for him to carry.

"The Prozarians couldn't follow a trail paved in gold," I said. "They're no threat to Fink."

"This is serious!" Roden said. "Why is your only response to tell a joke?"

I lowered my eyes. I made jokes because I had long ago understood that when I did, people either laughed or became furious, and either way, it pulled them off course. I made jokes because the alternative was to scream as loudly on the outside as I was on the inside. Because I needed to laugh so that I wouldn't burn with anger at the injustices around me.

"Belland is a small place. Strick will find what she's looking for." Roden's eyes sharpened. "She will find Fink."

My stomach knotted. "She didn't find him on the *Shadow Tide*; she won't find him here. Fink will slip through her fingers like smoke."

I hoped.

Fink wasn't much like smoke. He was more like that dog that always gets caught upon a single wire in the corner of an open field. I was a little surprised he hadn't already been found.

"Fink will be fine, but can you worry about yourself for a few minutes?" Tobias stepped closer to me. "This trial will only end one way. We have to negotiate with them."

"My innocence is not up for negotiation." I stuck out my jaw. "Take me to the trial."

· THIRTY-THREE ·

Roden led me out of the village and up the trail that took us directly past Darius's home. Farther on, we came to a wide, grassy clearing with an easy view of the former volcano that had formed this land. Most of the clearing was so thick with onlookers that I wondered if guests had been brought in from neighboring countries. Surely the population of Belland, even with the Prozarian occupation, could not be so great. Even worse was that as I scanned the faces, none of them seemed friendly. The warnings I'd been given were true: I was already convicted.

I was brought to the center of the gathering and a chain was wrapped around each wrist, forcing me to hold my arms out wide, away from my body. The chain on my right arm was attached to a sturdy post in the ground, but the chain on my left was attached to a leg of a chair not far away, as if the need for a second chain had been a last-minute decision. Worse still, the chair was currently occupied by Mercy, who looked quite comfortable. The red-haired man I'd fought last night was here as well, glaring daggers at me. He and I were not finished with each other. Several other chairs were in a row beside them, slowly being filled with what I assumed were some of the higher-ranking Prozarians.

I whispered to Tobias, who stood at my side. "There's a metal clip inside the lining of my belt. Get it out and put it in my left hand. Don't let anyone see."

"How am I supposed to . . . oh, all right, but it will be embarrassing."

Loudly, Tobias said, "I just realized I might never see you again." And he closed me into a tight embrace. I felt his fingers fold back the belt, and seconds later he pulled his hand away.

"You were supposed to save me, not suffocate me," I told him.

Tobias stepped back. "You asked me to." He reached for my hand to shake it but dropped the clip. I put my foot over it and his eyes widened. "How can I get it now?"

"You can't. Honestly, Tobias, I don't ask you for much."

"That clip won't make a difference anyway. They claim to have evidence against you. Let me negotiate with them."

"No."

More people continued to fill the clearing, the Bellanders being directed toward the left, the Prozarians standing to the right where more shade was available. Mott and Trea entered the clearing ahead of me, hand in hand. Mott's injured arm was bandaged but otherwise he seemed to be all right. Trea looked terrified, but Mott's expression was like stone. We locked eyes, but it did me no good. I could not tell what he was thinking. They found places somewhere behind me, among the Bellanders.

I wished Mott would have stayed where I could more easily see him. Not because he could do anything for me, but because I was nervous. So many things could go wrong before this was over.

Darius entered the area next and stood beside the stump of a tall tree that had been smoothed and polished as a sort of podium. I stared directly at him while he took great efforts to look anywhere else. The longer I watched him, the more I saw worry lines forming across his brow and the shadows deepening beneath his eyes. He was alone here, much as I often felt in Carthya, only his situation was far worse. Trea watched over him with all the care and affection of a mother, but he had no one else. I had Imogen and Mott and Fink, and friends beyond that. For all that I had lost, he had lost so much more.

"Darius," I said, getting his attention. "You were always the better brother, the better person. You didn't deserve this."

"Tell me the truth now," he said. "Do you deserve what you will receive here?"

I hesitated to answer, which cost me the opportunity to ever answer him as I wished to. Shouts and cheers rose up from the Prozarians, who parted for Captain Strick to enter. At least forty other Prozarians followed her, but this new group was different than the others. They were not onlookers; these were vigils who took their places around the perimeter, ensuring that nobody would come or go without their permission.

Strick raised her arms high to get the crowd's attention, which was hardly necessary since everyone had already gone silent with her arrival. Then she said, "Bellanders, you all know that Darius is the rightful king of a country across the sea, a place known as Carthya. It is a land that has been illegally occupied for some time by a younger brother who obtained his throne through deception and dishonor. As part of an agreement with King Darius, we have brought this boy here, to allow the true king to claim what should be his. Darius will soon reign again beneath the hand of the Prozarian Monarch, over the tribute country of Carthya."

I coughed, loudly, and she stopped to look at me. "Forgive me," I said. "But you are pronouncing 'Carthya' incorrectly, and I can't stand it any longer. You spend far too much time on the final vowel. Is that typical of all Prozarians?"

Her face reddened, and she said, "Darius, you asked to run this trial. Do you have anything to say?"

Darius turned back to face me, the intense look in his eyes begging for the answer he wanted. "Will you give me the throne, Jaron?"

I stuck out my jaw. "Under your current arrangement with the Prozarians, no, I cannot."

His face tightened. "We've already discussed this."

"Then let's discuss how we might bring freedom to these people. If these are *your* people now, then tell them they have a chance for freedom!"

Tobias had been standing far to my right but he leaned in and whispered, "Jaron, can we focus on saving you first? Then we'll save everyone else."

"Get to his crimes!" Strick snapped at Darius.

"You will stay out of this trial!" Darius responded, a rare

show of force from him, and he quickly softened. "You swore that I would conduct this trial, and only me."

Her eyes flashed, but she gestured toward me with her arm. "Then do it."

Darius hesitated, then said, "Jaron, from what I'm told, you came to the throne less than two weeks after our parents' deaths. That cannot be a coincidence."

"It is not. Tell me, Darius, what do you know about Bevin Conner?"

Darius straightened his spine. "I know he was a great man. He sent me here, which saved my life. I have a letter from him that promises me a king's inheritance one day, and his assurances that he was a great patriot of Carthya."

Then he probably did not know that Conner was likely his father. And I'd never get him to believe that someone he clearly respected was responsible for our parents' deaths.

Unaware of the secrets I was holding in my heart, Tobias stepped forward. "Conner was no patriot. He poisoned the king and queen of Carthya."

"That's a lie!" Darius turned to face Tobias squarely. "Conner was one of my father's regents, and a loyal servant."

"And he was a murderer."

"Can you prove this?" Darius's tone felt like a warning, that if Tobias failed to prove his accusation, he would also be in trouble.

Tobias glanced back at me for support, but I shook my head. This was not how I wanted the trial to go.

Darius turned my way as well. "If Conner had committed

the murders, surely you would have followed the law and had him executed. Did you?"

I stared back at him. "I did not."

"I'm also told that he was allowed to escape. How did that happen?"

It was irrelevant how it happened. The greater problem was how the question must have sounded to the audience, as if his escape was my plan all along.

Darius continued, "And later, Conner sacrificed his life to save yours. That doesn't sound like he was ever anyone's enemy."

"He came to my side. As you were once on my side." I tried a different approach. "Do you remember when I was ten and I challenged the Duke of Mendenwal to a duel? It was in defense of our mother's name."

Darius smiled, despite himself. "Of course. You lost the duel."

"And you later told me that you regretted letting me fight that alone. Fight for me now. You know that I had nothing to do with our parents' deaths." He flinched, and I added, "Be my brother again; stand at my side the way I always tried to stand at yours. Darius, I need my brother back in my life, as before."

Captain Strick stood, holding a paper in her hands. "We have evidence — a letter from Conner himself, detailing Jaron's involvement in the crimes."

Tobias immediately darted forward, now with Conner's journal in his hands. He could only have gotten that from

Imogen, so I knew she must be hiding somewhere in the crowd. "This book was written by Conner's own hand. Compare it with the note."

Darius walked over to Strick, who rolled her eyes before giving him the paper. He laid it out flat on one half of the journal in Tobias's hands and studied one page and then the other.

"The handwriting is different," Darius mumbled. His expression seemed to soften.

"Then someone else wrote that letter for Conner," Strick said. "A trusted servant perhaps."

"I was his trusted servant, and I never wrote that letter."

My head flipped to the side to see Mott emerge from the crowd. Captain Strick shouted, "This man was involved in an attack on Prozarian officers last night! He must be arrested."

She may have believed her words would turn the crowd against Mott, but most of the Bellanders I saw began nodding at him with respect, and none of the Prozarians seemed to want to take him on unless they were specifically ordered to.

Mott stepped past her and addressed Darius directly. "Before Jaron took the throne, I served Conner every day of my life. I was there when he planned the murders, yours included, or so I thought." Now he spoke louder. "Listen carefully, all of you. Jaron knew nothing of the murders, and once he did know, his every thought was given to unmasking the conspiracy behind who had done it. Jaron is innocent."

Darius shrugged, unmoved. "From what I'm told, you are

with Jaron every time he goes into battle. Obviously you will want to protect him now."

"As I have always tried to protect you," Trea said as she joined Mott and took his hand again. "Darius, I know why you agreed to have Jaron brought here, and I know you believe you have to decide against him, but you don't. There is a plan that can save these people, but you must find Jaron innocent."

Darius glanced over at Strick before looking back at me. "And then what? If we go home together, will the people welcome me as their king, or shout me down because they prefer you?"

I locked eyes with him, as if no one else existed but him and me. "Come home, Darius. But come home without a Prozarian weight on your back. I'll help you."

He hesitated. "What about Amarinda? Can you save her as well?"

That was a far more complicated question, and he took note of it. "We will find her," I said.

"Amarinda is waiting for you," Captain Strick said. "*After* you find Jaron guilty."

"What?" If Tobias had been sitting, he would have fallen off his chair. Even on his feet, I worried at his look of alarm. I shook my head at him, warning him to stay quiet.

"I agreed to conduct the trial," Darius said. "I never agreed to the outcome."

From his seat, Mercy pulled out a book and widened it to a handwritten page, where even from here I saw Darius's signature. Mercy said, "You agreed to give us the second lens if we brought Jaron here for trial. If Jaron was found guilty, you agreed to give the Prozarians legal right to carry out his punishment. In exchange for that right, we would deliver Amarinda here to you."

With greater urgency, I turned back to Darius. "Whatever you decide, they will not send Amarinda to you. They will set new terms, new demands, and force you to give in once again."

His tone sharpened. "Amarinda is here, somewhere, and then we'll be married, as was planned from the beginning. I can't risk her life, and you can't promise it."

I drew in a breath. "We should discuss Amarinda in private."

Darius clenched both fists. "Why? She is alive, she is here. . . . Is she still the betrothed princess?" His eyes widened in realization. "She is betrothed to the throne, not the prince." His voice rose in pitch. "Jaron, you didn't . . . you haven't . . ." Angrily, he grabbed my shoulders.

Tobias pushed between us, forcing Darius back. "It's not Jaron! Amarinda is betrothed to me now. When we get back to Carthya, she and I have plans to marry."

Darius's eyes turned to ice as he looked Tobias over, then with one hand, he shoved him away. "Who are you? You're no prince. Not a drop of royal blood in you, is there?"

Tobias lowered his head. "No, I am not a prince. But I do love her."

Darius turned and pointed to Tobias. "I lived for her! I did whatever was necessary to keep myself alive, for her! You are no one, you are nothing. How dare you suggest you could ever be my equal?"

Reflecting the tension in the air, the crowd behind us seemed to be growing more agitated, with some Prozarians already calling out for Darius to pronounce me guilty. Trea rushed forward to speak to him while Mott stood protectively near my side.

Darius ignored Trea and turned his anger toward me. "This arrogant nothing who came to defend you, is he your friend?"

"He is."

"Then you have chosen him over me. You have robbed me of a throne that should have been mine, and he has robbed me of the girl I've expected to marry my entire life. Let the devils have him now. Let the devils have you both!"

He began to leave, but Lump crossed into his path, his message clear. From behind us, Strick said, "You had your trial, Darius. Give us what you promised."

"Do not give them that lens!" I shouted.

Darius lowered his head, reached into the pocket of his long red coat, and withdrew a lens from a black satin bag. He offered it to Lump, who held it up to the light for a quick examination. Similar to the first disk, this lens could easily be concealed in a person's hand, though it was thin enough that it could break if not handled carefully. Holding the lens in the palms of both hands, Lump ran it over to Captain Strick. Without a single glance back at me, Darius slinked through the crowd, then folded his arms as he leaned against a nearby tree, almost glowing with anger.

By now, the crowd was calling more openly for a decision from Darius, but he was still glaring at Tobias. To my left, Mercy had leaned back in his chair with a wide smile on his face, drawing pleasure from the discord. Ahead of me, Roden had turned his back to try to settle the growing disputes in the crowd, but no one demanded my attention more than Captain Strick. She faced me with a smug expression of total satisfaction, as though anger and a broken relationship between brothers was the perfect outcome to this trial.

I could make it worse.

I shouted, "People of Belland, we cannot allow these invaders to keep that lens. Help me, and together we will take back your homes. By tomorrow night, you will be a free people!"

A cautious cheer rose up among the Bellanders, one that grew enough that the Prozarians began to look anxious. Strick motioned to Mercy, yelling, "Stop him now!"

I had been waiting the entire trial for Mercy to have a reason to leave that chair.

The instant he moved, I yanked my left arm inward, then crouched down to retrieve the pin. The motion simultaneously pulled Mercy's chair toward me, hard enough that it swept his feet out from beneath him. With my hands still chained, I grabbed the chair and held it legs out, as a sort of weapon.

"If anyone helps that boy, you will join in his fate!" Strick shouted to the crowd. "Everyone fall to your knees or face the wrath of the Prozarians! Go to your knees now!"

There were twice the number of Prozarians as there were Bellanders, and no pirates were here. Upon the captain's command, all Prozarians in the audience withdrew their weapons, mostly swords and knives, though I saw a few bows as well. They were only waiting for the orders to move, to strike against the unarmed and defenseless up here.

Mott turned to me, also waiting for orders. "What do you want, Jaron?"

I looked around the area. The Bellanders didn't have a chance if fighting began. I had friends here in the crowd, but not enough, and I was still in chains.

I answered him, "I want you to leave, Mott. The only reason Strick hasn't had you captured yet is that I'm too much on her mind. But she will remember you." He still hesitated, and I added, "Get out of here, protect Trea. Those are my orders."

Mott dipped his head at me, though he glanced back several times as they left.

Tobias came forward and spoke in a low voice. "Please let me negotiate with the captain. You have no chance otherwise."

"You've given up already?" I frowned at him, genuinely disappointed. "When did you stop believing in me?"

His frown became more pronounced as he replied, "I think you're in too deep this time."

I placed the chair on the ground and stood on it, shouting to the Bellanders, "Do as the captain says!" The area quieted and I added, "I promised you freedom tomorrow, and I will keep that promise. But today, we must cooperate."

As ordered, the crowd fell to their knees, though their feelings of sadness, even abandonment, hung so heavy in the air that I felt the weight of them. I had promised something that I was not yet sure I could provide. If they got their freedom, it was possible I would not be there to see it.

Nearby, Tobias was in conversation with Captain Strick, who turned and motioned for me to step down from the chair, which I did. She faced the crowd and said, "Darius has failed to pass judgment on Jaron. But you just witnessed him attempting to inspire violence among your people. That is surely a crime."

"No one threw a single fist. Release me, Captain."

She stiffened her spine. "And you have stolen the Devil's Scope."

"We don't need it anymore." Mercy had taken the second lens from Strick and held it up against a thin paper with a sketch of the first lens on it. "If my drawing is correct, then the third lens will be found exactly where we thought it would be. We still have time to retrieve it, if we hurry." He eyed me. "And we no longer need Jaron."

Tobias leaned over to Strick and said something more to her. She smiled and turned to me. "Your friend just made a suggestion that might save your life." Her words were followed by a coldness in her expression that sent a chill through me. I knew what Tobias had offered, and I wanted none of it.

I stuck out my jaw. "I will not help you get that third lens."

Her eyes became focused on someone behind me. "Oh yes, you will."

I turned too late. Lump's beefy hands wrapped around my wrists like vises.

I didn't fight him. There would have been no point in it now. Instead, I twisted around until I locked eyes with Darius, still leaning against the tree, staring through me as if I weren't even here. All my life, he had defended me — to our parents, to commoners, and to staff at the castle. But I'd never had to rely on him before for my very existence.

Until now.

· THIRTY-FOUR ·

With Lump and Mercy holding each of my arms, I was half walked and half dragged to stand directly before Captain Strick, who couldn't wipe the smug anticipation off her face.

Loud enough for the crowd to hear her, she began, "We are benevolent —"

"Benevolent conquerors," I finished for her. "You don't want to kill or threaten or wound or maim anyone here, but somehow it's necessary."

"Necessary," she echoed, as if repeating that word somehow made it more important than my accusations. "You are a threat to our plans, to our quest. You are a disruption and a troublemaker."

I grinned. "Please stop, Captain, you embarrass me with so many compliments."

Her eyes became murderous. I knew that look too well. "You've seen the Great Cave, no doubt."

It must have been the cave I'd climbed in to escape last night. The one pictured on the first lens.

She continued, "Since arriving on Belland, we have believed the third lens must be in there. We also believe the lens will only be found during high tide. In the past month, we have sent over a dozen people inside to test for the best way to search the cave. Not one of them has come out alive."

I pressed my brows low. "Yesterday, you told Darius you had only two days. Is that two days to find the third lens?"

"If we read the markings on the scope correctly, then it is only two days every ten years, and only for a few precious minutes when the sun is in the proper alignment. That window opens very soon."

She gestured for Roden to come forward. He did, though his feet moved as if made of lead. "Take Jaron to the overlook."

Roden's words were as strong as I'd ever heard him speak before. "This is wrong, Captain. You've wanted to punish Jaron all along. You were always going to find a reason to do it."

She widened her hands. "Obviously."

He stepped forward, preparing to draw his sword, but I gestured for him to back away. "I don't need your rescue." My attention shifted to Darius, who had separated himself from the crowd. "I need yours."

"He can do nothing for you," Captain Strick said. "Your brother knows the consequences if he breaks our agreement again. Isn't that correct, Darius?"

He dipped his head at her, then said to me, "I know you've never been one for rules, but you must understand that here, they cannot be violated. Do you remember that time you fell from the parapet?"

I smiled at the memory. In an attempt to complete a race around the entire castle, I had tripped and fallen, but caught a flagpole on my way down. It took a few kicks to break the window beneath it, but I did get in. "Father yelled at me for hours."

However, of the many lessons I'd learned that day, the consequences of violating rules was not one of them. I'd run across that same parapet only a week later. It was an odd story for Darius to mention.

Strick looked at Darius. "You will return to your home and stay there until the evening bell, understood?"

"I just gave you the second lens. I want to see what comes of it."

She lifted her chin. "If you defy me, I won't send Jaron into that cave. Perhaps I should send a princess?"

Darius lowered his eyes, instantly defeated. "No, I'll leave. I'm sorry for this, Jaron." He frowned at me, then without another word, he retreated down the hill.

"Bring Jaron to the overlook," Strick told Roden. "And if you question my orders again, you will go into the cave with him."

Roden hesitated, but I said cheerfully, "It's perfectly fine. No visit to Belland would be complete without a visit to the overlook."

Strick arched a brow. "You're an arrogant fool of a prince."

"King," I muttered.

Then she called to those who were still part of the crowd, "The Prozarians are one step closer to the end of our quest. Follow me!"

Roden led me along with them until we caught up to

Tobias, who said, "I told her you can climb that cave. She would have killed you otherwise."

"Her plans haven't changed — you just gave her the way to do it." Roden looked around us and lowered his voice. "Let's run, all three of us."

I furrowed my brows. "I can't."

"Why not?"

"Running isn't part of my plan."

"You have no plan!"

"You don't know that."

Roden let out a heavy sigh. "All right. What's your plan?"

"I don't have one. But sometimes, not having a plan is the best possible plan."

Since this was going nowhere, Tobias tried his alternative approach of logic. "Give them the scope, and maybe they'll send someone else into the cave."

"This has nothing to do with the scope. How will it look to Darius when he comes to rescue me and I'm not even there?"

Roden's mouth practically fell open. "*That's* what this is about? Jaron, he won't come back, even if he wanted to. If he defies them, he puts Amarinda at risk, or Trea, or anyone else around here." He lowered his voice. "Wilta told me that in the first week of their occupation, Darius kept trying to organize revolts. Every time he did, three or four Bellanders would disappear . . . into that same cave where they're sending you!"

Tobias stepped closer. "If we go now, you have a chance to find Fink and, hopefully, Amarinda too. That is more important than fixing your relationship with your brother."

"No, it all fits together, can't you see that? Yes, we need to find Fink, and Amarinda . . . but neither of those matters if I don't also make things right with Darius."

Tobias said, "Darius can't be trusted. He gave up the second lens for Amarinda, he gave you up for her. He is only thinking about Amarinda!"

My glare sharpened. "Are you any different?" When he didn't answer, my expression tightened. "For the last time, I'm going to the overlook."

Roden pushed his hand through his hair, thoroughly frustrated. "Very well. Thanks to you, the devils will have us all in the end." He frowned and they escorted me up the hillside, past the waterfall with the rock wall and pool, past the place where I'd lain in the grasses and opened a tin box that had torn at my heart. And all the way to the opening of the cave where I had climbed to my freedom only last night. I would soon descend there in captivity.

The tall wooden arch I'd seen last night was still there. But now a pulley was suspended from its center with two ropes slung over it, one dyed red, the other blue. One end of each rope was knotted to the arch itself.

Why were there *two* ropes?

"Please don't send me down there!" Wilta screamed.

I turned to see two Prozarians dragging Wilta toward the arch. Her scarlet hair was tangled, her face was dirty, and the hem of her dress was torn worse than before.

Forgetting me, Roden ran forward to Captain Strick, who was speaking to Mercy and Lump near the arch.

"Why is she here?" he shouted. "She is innocent!"

Lump swatted Roden across the mouth, knocking him to his back.

Strick laughed. "She has been helping Jaron."

"So have I." Roden stood again. "If this is a punishment, then use me instead."

By then, I had reached the cave opening. I peeked down and quickly pulled back, feeling dizzy. Heights had never bothered me, but this was different. When I had entered this same cave last night, it was during low tide when there was only beach. But it was high tide now, and the entrance was entirely filled with water, in constant turbulence as it crashed against the cave walls.

Ignoring Roden, Strick stood across the opening from me. "I know your plan. If I sent you down alone, you would return, claiming to have found nothing, and later return to fetch the lens for yourself."

I clicked my tongue. "That's a terrible idea. Only a great fool would ever think of it."

Strick missed my insult, which was disappointing. Instead, she continued, "Wilta is the guarantee that you will not trick us. In twelve minutes, the sun will fall to the exact position necessary to show where the third lens is hidden. In fifteen minutes, the tide will have risen inside the cave high enough to reach Wilta. If you have the lens by then, we will pull you both out alive. In thirty minutes, the tide will be high enough that any chance to recover the lens will be lost, and your lives will be lost with it. If anything happens to that lens — a scratch, a smear of dirt — both you and Wilta will pay the price for it."

I arched a brow. "That's rather dramatic, don't you think? Why don't you send Wilta down and leave me out of it?"

"What?" Wilta's eyes widened almost more than I would have thought possible. "Jaron, this is no game."

"Of course it is." I looked over at Mercy. "Or am I wrong in thinking you were just exchanging wagers with a few people in the crowd?"

He shrugged. "Some of us believe you will find the third lens in there. Most of us think the two of you will die before either finds it."

"And you honor your wagers, I assume."

"Yes, always."

"Put me down for us both escaping the cave without anyone knowing if I've found the third lens. That is my wager against the entire total that you collect from everyone else."

He cocked an eyebrow. "You cannot wager for yourself. Where would I get my money after you die?"

I looked at Roden. "He'll pay it."

Roden cursed under his breath. I figured I deserved at least that much.

"And what if you win?" Mercy asked.

"You help me rescue Amarinda."

Mercy smiled at this new development. "There is only one way out of the cave, and that is back into our hands. You cannot win this wager."

"That's why the stakes are so high."

"Very well." Mercy recorded my wager in the book he carried, and no doubt he was pleased with the numbers he saw there.

Wilta's hands were shaking when Lump led her closer to the opening, but her expression when she looked at me was sharper than a dagger.

One end of the red rope was tied around Wilta's chest while tears streamed down her face. She folded her arms tightly around her middle, shaking her head and silently mumbling what might have been a prayer to the saints. I could almost guarantee that only the devils would listen.

Mercy led me to the opposite side of the opening, removed my jerkin — leaving me only in a white linen shirt — and tied the blue rope around my chest and beneath my arms, the same as had been done to Wilta. Both of our knots were fastened at the back, where we could not reach them.

I looked over at Strick. "Let's be serious now about what matters most. What is Lump's name?"

Mercy cinched the knot tighter. "That is not your concern. You are full of arrogance, witless humor, and flawed intelligence. No one will mourn if you do not survive."

"Then I have nothing to lose."

I turned around to see the gathered crowd, almost double the number of those who had been at the trial, since the pirates had been allowed here. The same Prozarians who had stood as vigils for my trial now created a barricade to ensure that nobody came too close to the arch. The former riverbed was empty other than Prozarians who stood between the groups, calling for any last-minute wagers.

Roden had been allowed to stand beside Wilta. He held her hands and seemed to be giving her every assurance that I would keep her safe. I wished he wouldn't have done so.

Captain Strick took another step toward me. "You thought you had the advantage by keeping the scope, but you were wrong. Thanks to Mercy's drawing, you see now that we will always succeed."

I glared back at her. "If your definition of success is complete and utter humiliation when I defeat you, then yes, you will succeed."

Her lip curled. "Since the moment of your capture, I've sought to understand you. And I believe I have you figured out at last."

"Oh?"

She smiled. "It's simple. Above all else, you wish to be the hero, the rescuer. And its opposite is your fear, that someone else will charge in at the final moment before certain death, taking the glory and winning the girl."

I stifled a yawn that had been nagging at me since she began her speech. "No, not really. And I should be clear, this is not the girl I would ever hope to win."

"Jaron!" Wilta cried. "How can you say that?"

"No offense, my lady. You are obviously beautiful and intelligent, and you are not without charm. However, there is also a depth of evil within you that should frighten even the devils."

Roden ran closer. "What is the matter with you? She needs your help or she will die in there!"

Confused, Strick stepped back, and Mercy took over once again. He began by giving me a bag to hold the lens and a small carving knife.

"The third lens is likely embedded in the rock but disguised to look like the rock itself. You may need the knife to extract that lens, but do not break it."

"I won't," I said, then quickly added, "I won't break it, because I will not extract it. Instead, I might use this knife to make my escape easier after I cut Wilta's rope."

"Jaron, no!" Wilta's eyes were wide with horror.

"I might." I winked at her. "But you'll be fine."

"Please don't let me fall!" When Wilta's shaking failed to earn my sympathy, she shouted to the crowd, "If he can be so cold, he must be guilty."

"I am guilty of many things, my lady. Of being a fool and a thief, and of a recklessness unfit for a king. But you are guilty too." I turned around and shouted to the crowd, "Bellander women, will you show me the needles in your skirts?"

A confused murmur spread through the audience as women looked around at one another. But no one stepped forward.

That was all I needed to know.

I shouted, "Bellanders, Prozarians . . ." I eyed Mercy. "Snakes. The Monarch stands before you: Wilta, the fraud, the pretender. If you wish to bow, do it quickly."

Before Wilta could respond, I flashed her a grin, and jumped.

· THIRTY-FIVE ·

My weight and my control of Wilta's rope sent her careening over the edge with me. We both dropped more than halfway into the cave, but Wilta was below me, her feet nearly in the water. I had wound her rope around my arm, so although it pulled hard on my shoulder when we finished dropping, both of us were safe.

For now.

"Why did you say that about me?" Wilta cried. "I was forced down here, same as you!"

"No, I don't think so. Someone had to watch me, to be sure that I did find the third lens. The captain wouldn't trust anyone with that task . . . except her own queen."

"Whoever you think I am, you must find the lens, or we'll both drown in here."

"Why are you the Monarch and your mother is not? Did you flip a coin for the title? Or does inheritance skip a generation?"

"Listen to me, Jaron, I've done everything I can to help you."

"And you have," I replied. "You revealed more secrets about

your people than I believe you had intended. So many that I wish our false friendship didn't have to end now."

"The Bellanders have no secrets."

"No, Monarch, they do not."

I twisted enough to get a good grip on my rope, and while keeping the end of Wilta's rope in my hands, I began to climb. It was more difficult than usual, since I had to climb with Wilta screaming at me from below. But that was to be expected, I supposed.

"Jaron, look — the sun!"

I paused as the sun must have descended into the angle they had been waiting for. From the opening above, warm light flooded the cave, brightening the walls, casting them in tints of deep orange and yellow.

I twisted around on my rope, looking everywhere along the walls for any sign of a third lens, but nothing appeared different than any other place.

"You must see something," Wilta said, desperately scanning the walls as well. "Please, Jaron, the water is getting higher!"

Sure enough, when I looked down, her legs were already in the water, and the waves had begun stirring her around, which also pulled at my rope.

"You should probably climb higher," I said, still looking around me.

"But the lens!"

"There, I see something!" I tried swinging toward the cave wall, but a wave grabbed Wilta and thrust her forward, carrying me with her and slamming my shoulder into a different wall. I tried to grab anything solid, but the water receded, pulling me off the wall and sucking Wilta down into its depths. When the next wave entered, I was ready. I angled my body forward so that when I crashed into the cave wall, I grabbed anything I could with both hands. The water pulled at me again, but this time, I kept my hold. From there, I moved sideways along the wall toward my target.

Below me, Wilta climbed higher, choking on water but desperately scanning the nearest wall to her. "The lens isn't up that high," she said.

"If you knew that for sure, you'd have found the lens by now."

The next wave pulled Wilta's grip away from her rope and she fell underwater again. She surfaced long enough to cry for help, but I'd found what I was looking for and was midway through using the knife to pry out a square-shaped rock. It fit neatly into my hand and had every appearance of a carved box with a lid on it of the same size. The third lens would fit perfectly inside.

"You have it?" Wilta climbed higher on her rope again. "Let me see it." Instead, I put the rock inside my bag and began to climb my own rope, but she called, "Wait!"

I stopped climbing and twisted around to see Wilta staring up at me. Something in her expression cut through the danger of this place and pierced my heart. I had already guessed at her true self, but nothing I had imagined about her, nothing I *could* imagine, came close to the realization that she was likely the most dangerous person I had ever known. Her words struck directly at my already wounded heart. "You'd better hope that I am not the Monarch. Because if I am, then once I have that treasure, I will bring you to your knees, begging for mercy, or for your own death. I know who you love most, who you share secrets with and who you don't, and why. All I have to decide is where to begin. With a newfound brother? An adopted brother?" Her eyes narrowed. "Or do I begin with *her*?"

"You will not touch any of them." I'd intended to sound threatening but failed. The truth was that she had rattled me more than I wished to admit.

"I know exactly how to hurt you, and I will, until your hurt becomes your destruction." Her smile turned to ice. "I will do all of that, *if* I am the Monarch."

I could not remain here any longer. Though my heart was pounding and a pit had formed in my gut, I gripped the rope, then used the knife to cut myself free. With the square rock safely in the bag at my side, I began climbing.

Once I climbed higher than the cave opening, Roden's was the first face I saw, and it was nearly on fire with anger.

"You left her down there?"

I wound the rope around my body to hold my place. "Do you trust me, Roden?"

He glared back. "As much as you trust me."

"Then do not pull her up. Wilta is the Monarch."

From below, Wilta shouted, "That's a lie. Please, Jaron, help me! The water is rising!"

"Wilta?" Strick peeked down, then quickly motioned to Lump, her voice rising in a panicked pitch. "Pull her out."

"Wait." Mercy's eyes were fixed on the bag at my side. "You won't let her drown. So give us the lens, and then we will save her."

"Of course she won't drown — I intend to win my wager. But I only win if I refuse to tell you whether I found the lens." I withdrew the square rock from my bag and held it out over the opening. "I don't care whether I save this or not; it's only a rock to me. But you might feel differently. If you want to see what is inside, then let me go free. When you do, I will give this to you to find any treasure you can imagine. And if you want, you can pull your daughter up too."

Strick blinked. "My daughter? Wilta?"

"Is it true what I heard about the Monarch, that she had her own father killed? Your husband? Maybe you don't want her pulled from the cave after all. If you're considering revenge —"

"She's going to drown," Roden cried. "Look below you. She's in the water now."

Ignoring Wilta's pleas for help, I lifted the rock higher. "Give me room to escape, or I will drop this and whatever is inside will be lost forever. Also, your daughter will get really wet."

"Make the trade!" Wilta yelled from below. "He has the lens, you fools!"

I lifted one finger from the rock. "Wilta is running out of time, and this is getting heavy."

Strick's hands were in fists, but she said, "Prozarians, stand aside for Jaron. Let him go." She glared at me. "With an infected leg, you won't get far before we find you again."

With Roden's and Tobias's help, I swung back onto solid

ground, then gave Roden the rock and set off at a sprint along the former riverbed, which was half a stone's throw wide and a knee length lower than the rest of the ground.

Only seconds later, I heard the captain scream, "This is just a rock — get him!"

I reached the rock barrier that held back the pool from the waterfall. Directly in front of the barrier was the same tree I'd rested against yesterday. Lump was halfway to me with a host of other vigils by the time I swung into the tree's lower branches. I leaned over the branch, ready to throw my weight downward against the barrier. Before I did, I shouted to all the people still assembled there, "This barrier will break. Get as far from the overlook as you can!"

Most of the crowd who had assembled began hurrying away down the paths, clearing the area faster than I would have believed possible. Lump urged the vigils to continue forward, while he turned on one heel and began racing back toward Strick, crying, "Get her out of the cave! Hurry!"

As promised, I used my full weight to swing down into the pool, kicking hard against the rocks. I reared up again, doing the same until I felt the first rock shift.

The Prozarians who had remained behind began climbing the wall, though they were helping me more than they realized. Every shift of their weight weakened the wall further.

Finally, I rose up again and said to them, "I'd run if I were you."

Then I slammed back down into the water, thrusting my legs forward so hard that the vibrations echoed through my entire body. The rock gave way, and immediately, water burst forth, creating a mighty flood beyond anything I had expected. In an hour or two, this might settle, but for now, the violence was terrible, the water pulling rocks and layers of mud away from the hills and toward the cave opening, carrying with it everything in its path.

For several seconds, I was overcome by the flow of icy water that forced the air from my lungs. I couldn't breathe, nor could I orient myself. The branch I'd been holding so tightly finally gave way against the rush of water, propelling me into the river. I might have been carried all the way down into the cave opening, except that the branch became lodged against a rock, allowing me to crawl to the water's edge. My injured leg throbbed from hip to toe and was no doubt bleeding again. I rolled southward and collapsed onto the grass, exhausted.

Nearer to the cave opening and on the north side of the restored river, Wilta had been pulled to safety, though the half-cut rope was still tied around her chest. When she saw me, almost directly across from her, she forgot about the rope and instead screamed out my name, adding, "You will not get away with this!"

Ignoring the pleas from the captain that she should rest, Wilta grabbed the sword from Roden's sheath and began running toward the branch, the only bridge from her side of the river to mine.

"Wilta, stop!" Roden ran after her, but her focus was so intent upon me, if she heard him, she didn't care.

I had a different angle and knew how precariously the branch was positioned against the rock. It was not nearly as secure as it looked.

I sat up, waving her away. "Go back, Wilta! It isn't safe."

But Wilta stepped on the branch anyway, taking a moment to check her balance, then walking forward. She wasn't even halfway across before the branch rolled, carrying her into the river and back toward the cave opening.

I ran along the side of the river and dove into the water just in time to catch the rope as she went over the edge. With my other hand, I grabbed a root that had become exposed by the water, but the rope burned my palm as it continued to pull through my hands.

From his side of the river, Roden dove in as well, braced by Lump and a few other vigils, allowing Roden to grab the rope with both hands.

With his help, we began to pull Wilta back toward the surface, but a second branch swept down the river, knocking Roden away from the other Prozarians. He lost his hold on the rope, which pulled me deeper into the river. The branch lodged against the arch and entangled the rope. Half-buried in so much cold, I tugged, but my strength was sapped, and the rope would not give.

"Jaron, pull me up," she begged.

"I can't!"

"You must. I'll do anything you ask."

"Wilta, I can't pull you up!"

"Please do not let go of that rope."

From behind me, Tobias shouted, "We're here, Jaron. We're back. I brought help."

I turned long enough to see Darius wade into the water,

grabbing the rope with one hand and me with the other. On the opposite side of the river, Roden had been working to dislodge the branch, and slowly, we began dragging Wilta up from the cave again.

Finally, Roden reached over and took Wilta by the hand, then pulled her into his arms and dragged her out of the river.

I released the rope and might have fallen over myself except Darius said to someone I couldn't see, "Help him."

Mott reached into the river and pulled me out. "We need to leave while we still can," he said.

"He'll help us." Tobias pointed to Mercy, who was crawling out of our side of the river, coughing on water. Tobias walked to stand directly over him and said, "You lost the wager. Where can we find the princess?"

· THIRTY-SIX ·

I staggered to my feet, casting a glance at Strick and Wilta. With Wilta's bright scarlet hair wet and pulled away from her face, the resemblance was more obvious than before. I wondered if Roden saw it.

He stood beside Wilta, offering support, but he didn't need to. Her anger easily warmed her. We locked eyes, each of us now understanding something dangerous about the other. I could identify her. She could destroy me.

Strick pointed to me, shouting at her people. "Consider that boy our enemy. I will reward anyone who brings him to me. Until he kneels to us, let all of Belland feel our revenge!"

Every Prozarian near her began looking for a way to cross the river — even Roden began looking — but until the flow settled, they wouldn't get far. Rather than care anything for their threats, with Mott's help, I stumbled toward Mercy.

Tobias's hands were in fists and he was speaking through clenched teeth. "Where is she?"

I pulled Tobias back, but in a firm voice, said, "Honor your wager."

Mercy arched his neck. "What you gave us was only a rock. I will not honor that."

"I wagered that you would not know for certain whether I had retrieved the lens. You only know what I gave you, not what I kept for myself."

"Very well." Mercy's eye twitched. "Amarinda is on our flagship. Give me one of your people tonight. I will bring them with me to take her off the ship."

"I'll go," Tobias instantly offered.

I shook my head. "Then they'd have two captives."

"I'm willing to take the risk."

I looked over at Tobias. "I'm not."

Mercy's frown at me was intended for Tobias to see, and he did. "If you refuse my offer, Jaron, I cannot guarantee what will happen to your princess next."

Tobias turned to me in a silent plea to change my mind. But I wouldn't, and he knew it. Finally, he grunted and stomped away.

Mercy waited until he'd left, then his face cracked into a smile. "I did try to fulfil the terms of the wager. What a pity you don't trust me with your friend's safety."

I began to retort, but Mott handed me my jerkin, dripping with water. "Let's go, Jaron."

He gestured across the river. Several of the Prozarians were now halfway across, their weapons out.

I turned to leave with Mott, though I didn't realize how weak and cold I'd become until we were hurrying away. Every step took enormous effort, and at my best, I was still lagging behind with only Mott at my side, urging me to keep going.

Once we made it safely into the hills and rounded the first bend, all of that was forgotten when Imogen darted toward me from behind some trees, where she'd been hiding. She mumbled my name and immediately wrapped her cloak around my shoulders before pulling me into a warm embrace.

"I can't believe you're alive."

I shrugged and glanced back. "Me neither." My gaze fell next on Tobias. "I couldn't allow you to get on that ship."

"If it were Imogen held captive, would you have gone?" He huffed and continued walking.

Imogen kept her arm around me as we fell in beside him. She said, "I was there in the crowd, you know, but I was so far back, I only heard the people talking. Did you really push Wilta into the cave opening?"

"She's the Monarch, Imogen. She's behind everything that is happening here."

"Wilta? Are you sure?"

"It was obvious after I realized that no women there had needles stuck into the bottoms of their skirts."

"So?"

"So Wilta claimed that all Bellander women did that."

Tobias and Imogen exchanged a look. "*That's* your evidence?" Tobias squinted at me, incredulous. "Jaron, that means nothing. Only a few women from Belland were even there."

"What about the scars on her forearm? She implied to Roden that they were from the captain, but they are left from the plague."

"How would you know what a plague scar looks like?" Tobias asked.

I rolled my eyes. "I've received enough scars to know when one is given in anger. Hers were not. And there's more. I knew a Prozarian boy once, back when I lived in the orphanage."

"Edgar?" Tobias glanced over at me. "He stayed at the orphanage in Gelvins for a little while. I knew him too, or at least, I knew who he was."

"Do you recall the way he pronounced the name of Carthya, with a drawn-out sound at the end?"

"No."

"Well, he did. Captain Strick pronounces it the same way. And so does Wilta."

"That means nothing!" Tobias shook his head. "Maybe she learned the name from Captain Strick. Naturally she would pronounce it the same way."

Imogen pressed her brows low. "I'd never risk someone's life on so little evidence."

"Her life never was in danger. She's the Monarch! They were always going to pull her out."

"I hope you're right . . ." Imogen drew in a breath. "And I hope you're wrong. She knows a lot about us."

And she knew how to use that information against me — Wilta made that perfectly clear. My arm tightened protectively around Imogen. Her arm tightened around me too, something I needed.

She continued, "Then to have collapsed the dam! Jaron, what were you thinking?"

"That . . . did not work as expected. If it hadn't been for Darius —"

Darius stopped on the trail and looked back at me. "If Father had been here to see that, he'd have locked you in your room for a year."

"He tried that once. Besides, you were the one who gave me the suggestion, when you reminded me of the time I fell from the parapet. I had to kick the window open to get back inside the castle."

"What?" His brow furrowed. "When I asked if you remembered racing across the parapet, I meant that I had come to help you then and I would come now. Nothing more."

I thought that over. "Oh yes, that does make more sense."

A pause followed, one that neither of us seemed to know how to break. Darius was the first to try. "I see things more clearly now. I'm sorry to have put you through all this."

"We have more to talk about," I added. "But I knew you'd come back for me."

Darius grinned. "You didn't *know* it. You made a lucky guess."

That made me laugh, though it ended with a grunt of pain that only worsened when I tried to take the next step on my own. Imogen's arm wrapped around me again. "Is anything broken?"

"My ankle is swelling in my boot. Kicking at the rocks was a bad idea."

Tobias pointed at my leg. "You tore open the wound again. And you're still shivering — we need to get you warmed up, and fast."

Tobias braced me from one side, and with Imogen on the

other, I began to hobble toward Mott, who had been roaming the area to be sure it was secure.

He said, "Trea told me about an abandoned house higher in the hills. She's waiting there for us. The Prozarians don't seem to know about it."

"I can take us there." Darius sighed as he looked over at me. "Well, Jaron, it seems you've gotten me into trouble once again."

Mott caught up to Darius as he led the way. "Did you ever get used to that, when you two were younger?"

Darius glanced back at me. "Never."

They laughed but I had more serious things on my mind. Thinking back to when I'd first seen Tobias outside the prison house, I asked, "Where is Fink?"

Tobias shook his head. "I don't know. He'd been out looking for water earlier in the day and told me he'd found a place in the north where he could hide. But I don't know if that's true, or if he ever made it there."

"Who's Fink?" Darius asked.

I glanced over at him, curious to how he would respond. "A few things have changed since you left Carthya. You have another younger brother now."

"Named Fink?" Darius chuckled. "It's a good thing he's adopted, or he'd be in line for the throne. Imagine the absurdity of that name, King Fink."

I stopped in place, forcing Tobias and Imogen to stop with me. Darius looked back at me again, still smiling until I said, "Fink is my brother now. He is my brother as much as you are."

"All right, that's not a problem." Darius casually shrugged that away, confirming again that he had no idea of his origins. Imogen squeezed my arm as a silent message of her understanding.

Farther along the trail, Darius asked, "Was he meant to replace me?"

"Never!" I waited for Darius to turn around but this time he didn't, so I continued, "When I left the castle, my whole family was there. When I returned, I was alone. Fink is not your replacement, but try to understand, I needed some sense of family."

"You think I don't understand that? Trea is the kindest person I've ever known, but she'll never be our mother. And all this time, I've thought of Amarinda and how it would be to get back to her, but now your friend, who by the way is holding his sword upside down, has taken my place."

Tobias reversed his grip on the sword. "I didn't replace you either, Darius. She just had to continue on with her life."

His tone sharpened. "I am *King* Darius. Jaron may have allowed you more familiarity, but he's your friend. You and I are not friends."

Tobias's eyes darted. "Jaron is no longer king?"

Darius looked at me to confirm his words, but before I could answer, Mott pointed ahead. "That must be the hut. Trea should already be here. Let's get inside — it looks like it might rain."

Similar to the home where Darius lived, this shelter was also made of rock and mortar. It was small but seemed comfortable. I wondered who had lived here once, and why they no longer did. We crowded inside as Trea welcomed us with dried fruits and meats. "I wish I could offer something warm, or bake some bread, but I don't dare start a fire," she said.

The depth of my hunger was enough that I grabbed a fistful of food before I thanked her and was halfway through a second handful before I was able to slow down. With starvation no longer at the top of my thoughts, I became aware that everyone seemed to have been waiting to speak to me.

Darius began. "You are certain that Wilta is the Monarch?"

"Yes." I wanted to tell them about the threats Wilta had made while in the cave, but I didn't have the strength for it tonight. Maybe I would tomorrow. Maybe I never would.

Darius continued, "Did you find the third lens in the cave?"

"No. I think it is in there, though. Even if you were angry with me, how could you give them the second lens?"

Trea chuckled. "It looked real to you?"

Confused, I turned back to Darius, who said, "We gave them an imitation. It had to look believable. That's one of the reasons I asked the captain to find you — I needed to get her out of Belland long enough that we could forge a new lens." I squinted at him, and he added, "That was one of the reasons. Also, they really did make me wonder if you were responsible for our parents."

"I never was."

"I know that . . . now." He sighed. "They claimed to have proof of it. I understand better now. They always wanted to bring you here. I was just their excuse."

"But why?"

"I don't know. Until we figure that out, we must focus

on what we can learn from the scope." Darius looked up at Trea, who pulled the real second lens from her pocket.

In turn, Imogen reached into her shoulder bag and brought out the satin bag containing the scope and the first lens, which she passed to Darius.

He withdrew the scope and showed me the markings on top. "This is the Carthyan symbol. I don't know why it's there and I don't know the symbol in the center, but I do know this first symbol." This one was a circular arrow with a clear beginning, but no end. "In ancient times, it was applied to all royals, so that if one family needed help from any other family, they could use this symbol to prove their identity. The symbol itself expressed hope that one day, we would all unite under one banner of peace."

I leaned forward to have a better look at the symbols for myself, and when I did, my face brightened with excitement. I looked around the group and said, "I know the scope's message!"

THIRTY SEVEN

The group gathered even closer around me as I held the scope near candlelight to explain. "The first symbol represents unity. If it were a number —"

"One," Imogen said.

"The second symbol is Mendenwal's pride, claiming to be superior to all other countries."

Tobias smiled. "Greater than all others."

"And the last symbol is Carthyan, representing equality among the original rulers."

"Among *three* rulers," Darius said.

"One is greater than three." I smiled. "That's the message."

"Yes, but what does that mean?" Mott asked.

I shrugged. "Well, I don't know *that* . . . yet. If we had the third lens, it might make more sense."

"At least we have two lenses, though I've never seen them together." Darius slipped both lenses into place and handed me the scope. "With some luck, that will lead us to the third." He aimed it toward the candlelight, and his shoulders fell. "That can't be right. It's exactly what the Prozarians thought."

He gave me the scope, and when I did the same, I saw what he meant. Where the first lens clearly showed the cave of Belland, the second lens added the position of the sun, falling in the western sky so that its beams would aim directly into the upper opening of the cave.

I passed the scope to Tobias, who began laughing to himself as he rotated the tube until it was upside down. He continued laughing until Darius finally threatened him.

A smug grin was still on Tobias's face when he lowered the scope. Looking around at each of us, he said, "When Jaron was in the cave earlier, I overheard Mercy speaking to one of the vigils. He claimed the markings on this scope indicated there was only a thirty-hour window in which the third lens could be found, then it would close for ten years." Now he focused on Darius. "The lens that you gave to Captain Strick was missing something, correct? Stars."

Something sparked in Darius's eyes, almost a hint of respect. Then his eyes widened. "A grand moon is in the skies tonight!"

"I read a book about this last year. Once every ten years, the moon aligns differently with the stars." Tobias smiled at Darius, and to my amazement, got a smile in return. "As it will tonight, and tomorrow night."

Darius took the scope back, then lowered it, clearly frustrated. "The moon is too high now. We've missed it for tonight."

"Then we will try again tomorrow," I said, relieved at having some time to recover. As we'd talked, my body had begun to thaw from the cold water. I felt the aches in my leg and my foot, and every part of my body that had taken a hit, a punch, or a scrape over the past few days was complaining just as loudly.

"You don't look well." Trea pointed to a small cot on the other end of the room. "Rest awhile."

Imogen helped me limp over to the cot, and I fell asleep before she finished pulling a blanket over me. I might not have even rolled over once before I awoke again. When I did, morning light was coming through the window, but she was exactly where I last remembered her. No one else appeared to be in the hut.

I sat up on one elbow, stiff and with my eyes still heavy. If I listened carefully, I could hear voices outside, though they were too low to identify who was speaking. I looked around. "Where is everyone?"

"You slept late. Darius and Trea are outside talking. Mott and Tobias went to continue searching for Fink. How do you feel?"

"Like a brick." I forced myself to a seated position. "What did you think of Darius?"

"He seems to have a good heart, though in all other ways he's very different from you." I waited for more, and finally she said, "You want so much to have him back as your brother. Have you considered whether Carthya should have him as its king?"

"That's not my decision."

"But it must be. Today, you are Carthya's king. Will your people do better tomorrow with Darius?" Several beats of silence passed, then she added, "Can you be sure that Darius's throne will not soon become the Prozarian throne?"

My jaw clenched. In truth, I could not be sure of anything regarding how Darius would rule. But I was not so arrogant as to believe I was doing any better.

Imogen touched my arm, drawing my attention back to her. "I know you love Darius and that in your memories, he's become almost perfect, but he's not."

"Nor am I!" I didn't want this to turn into a fight, but Darius was my brother, and I would defend him. "When he's king, I'll do everything I can to stop him from making any other agreements with the Prozarians, but he will be king."

"When will you convince him to change? Before or after the Prozarians execute you? Because that is still their plan!"

"I've come this close to death before, and I've found a way out of it."

"That's because you fought it before. Why aren't you fighting now?"

"You think I'm not?" My muscles began to tighten. "How many more bruises are necessary before you'll accept that I am fighting?"

"There are other fights, Jaron, those that come from a strong heart and a will that cannot be broken. I know it's in you because I've seen it over and over again. Why aren't you fighting for the throne?"

"What more would you have me do? My mind is full; my heart is broken. But no matter what I do, this story ends the very same way — Darius has claim to the throne! Would you have me keep it by destroying my brother? Or should I be the reason for civil war in Carthya?"

For the first time, Imogen raised her voice. "I would have you live, Jaron. I would have you fight for your title, for your life, not hand it over to your brother and his controllers!"

"But it *is* my life, Imogen! My life, my decisions! No one else's."

Her expression stiffened. "I thought it was *our* lives now." Her voice was nearly a whisper, which hit me hardest of all.

I looked away. My mind was racing for what I could say to fix this. I'd immediately regretted my words, but it was too late — they still hung heavy in the air, and I could not pull them back.

Imogen stood and brushed her hands against her skirts. "Do what you will, Jaron, as you always do. Maybe I cannot stop you, but I do not have to be here to watch it. I urge you to consider this one last thought: If your brother requires your life so that he can take the throne, is he really your brother? Or is he simply another name on your list of enemies?"

Before I could answer, she walked out of the room.

And just like that, the inevitable happened. Imogen had finally given up on me.

· THIRTY-EIGHT ·

As sore as I was, and with a swollen foot, it took me twice as long as it should have to follow Imogen out of the hut. By the time I did, she was nowhere to be seen. I called her name, but received no answer.

"She said not to follow her." Darius pointed to a basket of dried biscuits. "Hungry?"

I ignored the food. "She shouldn't be out there on her own."

"She's not alone. Trea is with her. They'll be safe."

I stared off in the direction in which Imogen had gone, or in which I thought she had gone, then finally limped over to a rock to rest.

Darius was staring at me from behind; I felt the weight of his eyes, the intensity of his gaze. Finally, he said, "Is there any place on your body that hasn't been injured since coming here?"

"I've had worse."

"Once I'm king, you won't have to fight these battles anymore. We won't have to fight them at all."

I turned to him, curious. And worried. Imogen's warnings still rang in my ears.

Darius crossed so that he stood in front of me. "Every instinct you have is to fight. That's the trait of a great warrior, and you shall be great, as captain of my guard. But the mark of a great leader is refusing to fight. During all of Father's reign, he never had to fight a single war. Better than any of the kings before him, Father knew how to keep the peace."

I disagreed. "During Father's reign, Carthya was being sectioned away like slices of a pie. Father ruled in a permanent state of surrender."

"He was a great king, Jaron!"

"He was a great man, in many ways. I loved him too. But he was not a great king."

Darius drew back, folding his arms. "And you think you were?"

"I've never claimed to be anything great." I stood again to look for Imogen. I wasn't even sure that I was a particularly good person. If I were, I'd never have said the things to her that I did.

Seeing my concern for Imogen, Darius's tone softened. "You were never trained to become a king, not like I was. So it is understandable that you are feeling your way blindly through the many responsibilities you have. But they are my responsibilities now."

I finally took a biscuit, though I had little appetite for it. "If you become king, I cannot be your captain of the guard."

"Why not? You're the most logical choice."

"Only in theory. In life, we are too different. Even if we both wanted the same thing, I would make choices as your captain that you would disagree with. I fear you would never trust me to —" I stopped, choking on my own words. Suddenly, everything that Roden had been trying to tell me for the past few days, even for the past several weeks, made perfect sense. "You would never trust me to do the job the way I would want to do it. And without that trust, I am nothing but your puppet."

Darius nodded, though I doubted he understood the full meaning of my words. But I understood now. I owed Roden better than he had received from me thus far.

Something must have caught Darius's eye because he walked to a different overlook. Though we were quite far away, the spot offered a good view of the village below and a corner of the beach. Rows of Bellanders, pirates, and Prozarians were working together to carry heavy crates off the *Shadow Tide* and toward the five other Prozarian ships in the harbor.

"What are they doing?" he asked.

I followed him over and drew in a deep sigh. This was hardly the first time I'd had to offer a difficult, and usually humiliating, explanation to my brother. However, this sank to an entirely new level.

I scratched my head with one hand and gestured with the other. "Well, you see, those weapons were intended for Carthya. It appears they are currently being transferred to the Prozarians."

Darius turned to me, dumbfounded. "*Our* weapons are in the hands of the enemy? Those five crates probably represent the bulk of —"

"Of the weapons supplies we desperately need, yes. I agree, this looks bad."

"It *is* bad, Jaron! You accuse me of weakness, of giving in to Prozarian demands, and then you let *this* happen! No wonder you cannot claim to have been a good king — this is beyond your usual level of foolishness."

"We didn't give them the weapons. They were taken when our ship was captured."

"How did you guard and protect these weapons at sea?"

"There was no guard. We were on an Avenian pirate ship."

"Which made it easy to attack you!" He threw out his hands. "Since when does the king of Carthya travel in the company of pirates?"

I sighed. "Since he became a pirate." I pulled up my right sleeve, revealing the branding they'd given me months ago. "Roden is too. He's been my captain."

"Roden, who is now in service to our enemy?"

"No more than you've been in their service."

Darius's face continued to redden. "The two of you, the two most powerful people in the kingdom, belong to the pirates, also our enemies. This is treason, Jaron."

"Things have changed since you were home. The pirates are only our enemies sometimes."

Darius pushed his hand through his hair, all the while shaking his head in disbelief. "This is why Father sent you away so many years ago. You act without thinking, and the way you think makes no sense. This was bad enough when you were a prince, but you are not fit to be a king."

"I know I've made mistakes, but —"

"These are not mistakes, these are disasters! Nothing has

changed since the day Father sent you away, and it's all too clear why he did. You are an embarrassment to the throne!"

A horrible silence followed, one in which I could not speak. His words hit me harder than the worst of any punishment I'd ever taken, and I felt it nearly the same, as if the words stripped me of my last breath.

I looked down and bit my lip, and after a moment, more gently, Darius said, "I'm sorry, Jaron. I didn't mean that."

I nodded, but said nothing. I knew that Darius hadn't intended to be unkind, but he had opened a wound that still ached inside, confirming every doubt about myself that I'd ever had.

"You know that I never wanted you to leave the castle. And after the pirate attack, once you were found, I begged Father to let you come home again."

"Did you ever see me?" I asked. "When you and our parents would ride through the streets, did you ever see me standing there?"

A horrible pause followed before he answered, "Every time." A corner of his mouth turned up. "It was impossible not to see you — everyone else bowed." Then he became somber again. "Father's instructions were clear, that if we saw you, we should distract Mother. She never knew you were still alive, though I almost told her several times."

I hardly dared to ask the next question. "Did Mother ever . . . talk about me?"

"Your highnesses?"

We turned to see Roden behind us, flanked by two Prozarian vigils. He looked unnaturally stiff, and his eyes darted between me and Darius, as if he wasn't sure who was in charge here. I wasn't sure of that either.

Yet I was still reeling from what Darius had said, so he was the first to respond. "What do you want?"

"The Monarch would like to speak with you . . . both of you." Roden shifted his weight. "Immediately."

"Why?"

"Last night, the Monarch said she would take out her revenge on the people of Belland. It's already begun. That's how we knew where you were — she forced them to tell her about this place. She has already arrested several Bellanders suspected of violating their oaths of loyalty. She intends to burn their homes and destroy the resources of this land. When she finishes, nothing will remain of Belland."

"The people here have nothing to do with this!" Darius snarled. "They are innocent!"

Roden's face betrayed his worried emotions, though he was trying not to let the vigils see. "That is why the Monarch chose them."

"Give us a moment to talk," I said. Roden dipped his head and stepped back while Darius and I reentered the hut.

Once we were inside, I turned to Darius and whispered, "I have a plan, but it's not ready yet. For now, we must stay here."

He pushed his hand through his hair. "Your plan to save these people is to wait here while they take the punishment that should have been yours. And after that?"

"When Imogen comes back . . ."

"She won't. Not after the way she stormed out of here. Even

if she does, we need to help the people now. You made promises to the Bellanders! You cannot give them hope and *then* abandon them. Why did you promise them freedom anyway? If anyone were to make that promise, it should have been me."

He stopped there, almost reeling back at his own words. "It should have been me," he mumbled again, this time to himself.

Darius looked up again. "Back home, I was separated from the people by castle walls, or I waved at them from a carriage as they stood at the sides of the road. But here, I work with these people, take meals with them, and learn from them every day, so much more than I ever learned from the castle tutors. These are my people, more than Carthyans have ever been." He turned to me. "You gave them hope, Jaron. We must help them now."

He was right. But to do so meant separating myself from a plan Imogen and I had discussed while on the fishing boat. If that plan failed, all else here was lost.

Darius grabbed his sword and sheathed it at his waist. "Will you join me or not?" I hesitated and he added, "Your king orders you to join him."

"That is a trap down there. Trust me, I've walked into enough traps, I can usually recognize them."

"That's why I need you with me." He grinned. "Protect the king."

"With what? I have no sword."

Now his smile vanished. "Where is it?"

"I dropped it into the sea."

Darius closed his eyes and whispered something under his

breath. I only caught the words "devils" and "cursed." Whenever I heard those words together, they were almost always about me.

Finally, he said, "Well, I have mine. We'll start with that."

"Let me go alone. We shouldn't approach Wilta together."

"I'm not afraid of her." He put his hand on my shoulder. "Jaron, I know now that you were right about this, about them. I was weak, and I was wrong. For the last month, I've given these invaders everything they wanted, watched dozens of my people go to their deaths because I failed to defend them. They have looked to me for answers and I've turned away. How many times did I protect you when we were younger? I am going down there. Please come, and not because I'm your king, but because we are brothers again."

"We are brothers again," I echoed, and I genuinely loved the sound of those words.

With little else available in the area, I grabbed Tobias's medical bag. Darius tilted his head, curious, but by way of explanation I simply added, "You've seen how often I get hurt. Let's go."

· THIRTY-NINE ·

I left the home first, informing Roden, "We will follow you at a distance. There is no need to escort us down."

"We need to talk."

"No," Darius said, following me. "We have been invited to speak to the Monarch. You will not bring us there like prisoners."

Roden's eyes locked with mine and when I wouldn't give in to his request, he finally said, "Very well. But if you fail to appear, the Monarch wanted me to remind you of your conversation while in the cave."

"What conversation?" Darius asked.

Before I could answer, Roden added, "We'll go on ahead."

Once we had started on the trail, far enough from Roden and the two vigils that they were no longer in sight, Darius grabbed my arm, forcing me to stop walking. "What conversation?"

My eyes darted as my heart began to race. It wasn't only *what* Wilta had said, it was the controlled rage in her eyes as the threats had poured from her mouth. I opened my mouth to explain, but the words wouldn't come, and not because I thought he couldn't hear them. I just couldn't speak them. So I began walking again, answering, "There's a plan. If we follow it, everything should be all right."

"What if the plan fails?"

"What if it does? Failure isn't the end of a plan. Just keep pushing back until all that's left is to win."

For some reason, that made him chuckle. "I've always envied you."

"Me?" Certain I had heard wrong, I turned to look at him. "I'm the embarrassment, remember?"

"That's because you try. You stand at the base of a mountain that cannot be climbed, or should not be, and you start to climb anyway. No, it doesn't work every time, that's why it can be seen as an embarrassment. But when it works, it's a victory." He lowered his eyes, as if in shame. "I don't even try the climb, because I know that I might fall. That is a far greater embarrassment."

"Well, your embarrassment comes with fewer bruises."

"I see the Prozarians better now, for who they are, for what they would do if I allowed them into Carthya. I'm determined to be bolder. I promise that when I am king, I will do better than I have done here. I will do better for *you*, Jaron." He threw an arm over my shoulder as we walked. "I am the elder son, but I need you by my side. Will you trust me with the throne?"

I considered my answer carefully. "Carthyans must see a peaceful transfer of power from me to you. It shouldn't be done here in Belland."

Darius bit his lip. "Do you think there's any chance Amarinda might . . . still consider herself betrothed to me?"

"I don't know. She loves Tobias now."

"But she did love me. She'll have a choice to make, now that she knows I'm alive. Me or him."

I didn't know who she would choose, but if Tobias's intense behavior over the past few days was any indication, I did know he wouldn't give up easily on her.

Darius added, "You should know that Tobias will have no place in the castle when I'm king. Nor Roden."

I turned to him. "Do you know what Roden is risking to help us?"

"He's not doing anything for us. He clearly likes Wilta — their monarch! He is in her service now."

"He won't betray me," I insisted. "He's loyal to the throne."

"I am the throne now," Darius reminded me. "It will take time for us both to get used to that, but from now on, I make these decisions, and trusting Roden is not one of them."

My jaw clenched, and I turned my attention back to our path ahead. Just as Roden had promised, smoke was beginning to rise from the areas where the people lived. With a growing urgency in my mind, I asked, "What is your plan once we get down to the beach?"

"We can't attack. I've seen you fight, Jaron, and you're good, frighteningly good actually, but you're also limping on one leg and you have no sword. I'm out of practice, and even at my best, the two of us could not take on all the Prozarians."

"Now you know one of the reasons why I grabbed that medical bag."

We were still high on the trail, still well hidden by thick brush alongside our path, when Darius casually asked, "*One* of the reasons? What's the other?"

"This." I grabbed Darius's arm with one hand, and as he turned, I pulled his sword from its sheath.

"What are you doing?"

"Protecting the king."

He glanced down, unimpressed. "This is absurd. You won't kill me."

"No, but I have a lot of bandages if I cut you." I pulled out those same bandages. "Put your hands behind you." He hesitated, and I added, "Do it, Darius, I'm serious."

He obeyed, but said, "By definition, this is an act of treason."

"You're not king yet. Thus far, this is only the act of a terrible brother." I bound the knot on his hands, then said, "This is a five-minute knot. It shouldn't take you any longer to undo it. If it does, that's really more your fault for not being better with knots."

"Don't do this, Jaron."

"It's done." I replaced his sword, then hurried along down the trail. He wouldn't call after me; he'd hardly want to draw attention to either of us if he did that, but I felt the heat of his glare on my back, one powerful enough that it continued to burn long after I'd rounded the next corner.

It had to be this way. For all his good intentions, Darius would have been defeated on that beach within the same minute of entering it.

My leg was protesting the entire time I hurried down to the beach. I darted off the trail when I was getting close enough to be within earshot of the activities there.

And in doing so, I ran straight into Roden, who had clearly been waiting for me, though without the two Prozarians who had been with him earlier. He was leaning against a tree, using his sword to draw lines in the sand. I couldn't tell by his expression whether he was disappointed to see me, or proud of himself for having figured me out.

"You knew I'd leave the trail?" I asked.

He nodded, but added, "You should have known this was where I'd be."

"Maybe I did."

He cocked his head, confused, then said, "No matter what I do or don't do, you will never —"

I stared at him, being sure to look him directly in the eye. "I trust you, Roden."

His face brightened a moment before it fell again. "Thank you, but I still have to take you to Wilta."

"I know."

Without protest, I followed him up the beach, passing the trail leading to a cluster of homes, several of which were already burning. Prozarian vigils stood doing nothing while families rushed to put out the fires.

"You're letting that happen?" I asked Roden.

He lowered his head. "All I can do is help you, with hopes that you can stop all of this." Now he stopped walking and turned to me. "Can you?"

"I don't know." Words that haunted me even as they fell from my lips.

We continued forward toward a shelter that had been hastily built of logs and brush, nothing fancy, but enough to provide shade for a handful of people. Wilta sat on a platform in a padded and finely gilded chair that could only have come off one of the boats.

She was dressed the part of a queen now, in a long green satin gown with white trim, her hair piled high on her head, far grander than any other woman here. She carried herself with a confidence I had not once seen before, though for the first time, I knew I was seeing the true Wilta. The Monarch. The actress.

She was in a conversation with a few of her vigils, the same people who had treated her as a prisoner only a day ago and now knelt at her feet. When she saw us coming, she called for them to grab me, but Roden said, "That isn't necessary. He'll cooperate."

I glared over at him, making sure he understood. I had said I trusted him. I never said I would cooperate.

When we were closer, Wilta said, "Bow to me."

Roden did, as he'd have to do. I only straightened up taller. She clearly noticed but moved on, addressing me. "I will not thank you for saving my life yesterday. Roden saved me. My mother saved me. You nearly got me killed."

"And who are you again?" I tilted my head and suddenly

smiled. "Now I know! Were you not in the theater recently? In that performance about the girl who pretended to be something other than what she truly was?" Now my smile fell. "I think you lack talent."

She smiled back. "Were you not in that same performance yourself once? Or did you think no one but you could play that role?"

"I played it better," I said. "You were found out."

"It was only a good guess on your part. If you think you got information from me, I got just as much from you." She leaned in closer and whispered, "If you want to live now, you will give me everything else."

I glanced back at Roden, who did and said nothing to help me. I understood why. He had asked for my trust. He had never guaranteed my life.

FORTY

You're out of options." Wilta smiled over at Roden. "Thanks to him."

I glanced away. I had better things to look at than either of them. Such as the nearest patch of mud.

Roden eyed me with suspicion. "Unless he wanted me to bring him here. One of the few things I have learned from Jaron is how to be hard to predict."

"Have you?" I asked. "Because honestly, I had predicted you would do the obvious and search me for weapons before bringing me so close to your monarch."

Roden grunted and reached for my sword, only to realize it was not there. He raised one brow, obviously confused. "You came all this way without a weapon?"

"Would you consider that . . . unpredictable?" I lifted Tobias's bag. "Yet I am not defenseless. He has a roll of bandages in here. If I throw them, they might hit you in the eye."

"We can't risk that." Wilta stepped down from her perch and took the bag to begin searching it herself. "Where is Darius? I specifically asked for both of you."

He should have been here by now. Maybe he was worse at knots than I had expected.

I made my smile match hers. "Planning something worthy of a king. I'm only the distraction."

She blinked hard, clearly irritated. "We'll make sure you become a fine distraction. You're going to give me everything I ask."

I snorted. "Absolutely I will, *if* you are asking for a humiliating defeat."

Roden's search of me was thorough. In checking other pockets, he removed two knives, some nuts I had hoped to eat as a midday meal, and the petals of a flower I thought Imogen might like.

Wilta said, "Last night when we were in the cave, I think you saw something."

"Other than you crying like a helpless infant?"

Her mouth pressed into a thin line. She returned to her seat and motioned again to the vigils behind her. "Bring my mother here."

While we waited, I turned to Roden. "You claimed you can predict my plans. What do you think is about to happen?"

He glanced sideways at me. "You're going to fake an injury, expecting me to force you back to your feet, in which case you'll start a fight and hope to give Darius time for whatever he's about to do."

I grinned. "Obviously that is not my plan . . . anymore."

"But it will all be a distraction for a larger plan involving help from your friends."

My grin widened. "Trust me, you will love that part of the plan."

Wilta said, "Whatever the plan was, it's over now. We have your brother."

Confused, I turned to glare at her. "Darius?"

Roden leaned in to me. In a quieter voice, he said, "Fink."

As quickly as he had spoken, my blood ran cold. "Where did you find him?"

"I tried to tell you before." Roden frowned. "We followed Imogen and Trea when they left that hut. Imogen led us directly to everyone else, right before I came to get you. Tobias was the only one to escape, but he'll soon be found too."

I cursed under my breath, then asked Wilta, "Who do you have?"

Wilta's smile was probably the first true sign of happiness I'd seen from her, which worried me. "Other than Tobias, we have everyone. But Imogen threatened a revolt, so we've now separated them across all of our ships. You will not know who is on which ship, and if you attempt a rescue of one, the others will be sacrificed."

My eyes lit with anger. "You only wanted me. They are not supposed to be part of this!"

"They have carried out attacks on my people, stolen from us, defied our rules of order and obedience, and caused unrest here on Belland. All of them deserve their fates."

Scarcely able to breathe, I looked at Roden again, who nodded his confirmation at me, adding, "Fink was forced to tell them where he hid the stolen items. The captain sent a group of Prozarians to search for them."

"My lady!" Lump was running up the beach behind us, pushing between Bellanders doing assigned labor.

Wilta stood, clenched her teeth, and said as she began walking away, "The two of you will wait here."

Roden dipped his head at her. I turned to study the Prozarian ships, wondering which of my friends was on which ship, and whether they were safe for now. If they were, it wouldn't be for long.

Keeping his head down, Roden mumbled, "Do you remember in the crow's nest when you said in the end, I'd have to lose?"

"Yes."

"It's just the opposite. I need you to lose."

"After what I just heard?" My jaw clenched. "That is not how this works."

"Then you do not trust me."

We locked eyes, fury in mine, pleading in his, and I did not care why.

Having spoken to Lump, Wilta turned and addressed Roden directly. "Our finest warriors are gone to search for those stolen items, and now the pirates have left their ship. They weren't happy to see Jaron down here alone. You're one of the pirates. Can you stop this?"

Roden glanced over at me. "Jaron is the pirate king." He withdrew his sword. "Order them to return to their ship."

"No." I stared back at him. "I will not *lose* . . . them to the ship. Nor will I *lose* . . . their trust in me."

Seconds later, grumbling sounds began from farther down the beach, growing louder as my former crew of pirates marched around the cave, weapons in hand, and with shouts of anger.

With Lump at her side, Wilta faced them. "I am the Monarch, and you will stop now or face death."

Lump charged toward the first pirate to reach them, only to be knocked flat on his back by three others, one who put a boot on Lump's chest. Another two pirates grabbed Wilta.

"Stop this!" Roden cried, pushing them away. "You gave pledges of loyalty!"

"We are loyal first to our king," Teagut said. "To Jaron."

"If you are loyal to your king, then your loyalties belong to me." Roden turned my way, raising his sword. "Jaron, I challenge you."

I arched a brow. "Seriously?"

Roden took a swing at me. I ducked, but if I hadn't, he might have done real damage.

When I rose up again, I squinted back at him, only getting another raised brow in return.

In a quieter voice, Roden murmured, "You said you trusted me."

Now I understood, and I grinned back at him. "I accept your challenge."

So began our battle. It started with me running away as fast as I could. Without a weapon, what other choice did I have?

I passed the same fallen tree that had tripped me before, stopping only to wrench a branch loose, just in time to hold it up and clash with Roden's sword. He hit hard enough that I fell back to the beach, but I grabbed a handful of sand and threw it in his face.

Admittedly, that wasn't my finest moment. But it gave me a second's advantage.

I rolled back to my feet and continued running, only to be tackled by Roden, who punched my side. I grimaced and went still for a few seconds, until he whispered, "Is it your leg? Are you hurt?"

"Hardly." I threw Roden's weight off me, and in the same moment, one of the pirates surrounding us tossed his sword at my feet.

I looked over and saw Teagut motioning for me to pick it up, calling out, "You can pay for it later!" I nodded and grabbed the sword, swinging it in a wide circle, forcing Roden back.

When Roden fought strangers, he was always difficult to beat, for he was as fierce and talented an opponent as nearly anyone a warrior might encounter.

But it was different when he fought someone who knew him. Because Roden always followed the same pattern of attack, like a dance he'd learned once and rehearsed with every new battle.

Roden was fighting me precisely according to that dance.

Which meant I knew where he'd be next, and how he'd get there. I waited for him with every new step, every turn and strike and rotation. And when I could move fast enough, I worked in a swipe ahead of his movements. Nothing that would leave any glaring scars, but enough that I knew I could win.

But I would not.

The pirates had gathered in a circle around us, many of them shouting my name. But there were shouts for Roden as well, and those were the calls that echoed loudest in my ears.

He needed me to lose.

I clashed with Roden's sword again. "How far into the grave will I have to trust you?"

"Further than this." With a frown, he blocked my sword with his, then twisted around, aiming for my leg.

"Again?" I shouted.

He moved to kick the wound, but before he did, I stepped back and dropped my sword, then raised my hands.

"Do you surrender?" Roden asked, keeping his sword raised.

I sharpened my glare at him, forcing words from my mouth that went against every instinct within me. "I suppose I have . . . lost."

"Will you go to your knees?"

"No."

"Fair enough." Roden turned to the pirates. "I am your king now, and we will honor our oaths to the Monarch. If you cannot do that, then until I am able to deal with you, you are banished to the north side of Belland."

Someone from the back called out, "The uninhabited region? Nothing is there but rocks and water."

Teagut stepped directly in front of Roden. "I'd rather be there for a lifetime than serve a Prozarian for an hour. Or you." Teagut frowned at me next, clearly disappointed that I had lost the duel. He retrieved his sword and followed the rest of the pirates down the beach, the lot of them grumbling and cursing the entire way.

When the last of them had gone, Wilta smiled admiringly at Roden. "That was impressive."

I rolled my eyes. That had not been at all impressive.

"I know that —" Roden stopped midsentence. I turned to see him standing taller, his eyes widened. "Darius, don't do this."

"Step away from my brother." Darius entered the beach from behind a clump of trees where he must have been hidden. His sword was against Roden's back and his tone was as commanding as I'd ever heard it. In a louder voice, he said to Wilta, "I have a proposal for you."

My shoulders slumped. Darius meant well, but whatever Roden's plan had been, Darius had just ruined it. And now he was ruining this as well. I gritted my teeth at him. "We are not bargaining with them."

"Yes, we are." Darius turned his attention to Wilta. "Jaron made you an offer earlier, and I suggest you accept it. Surrender now and you may leave in peace. Any delay will cost you dearly."

Wilta didn't even blink. "Have you considered what you could lose right now?"

I followed her gaze toward the harbor, where Captain Strick was standing beside Amarinda on the beach. Amarinda's hands were bound and her hair hung loose around her shoulders, and even from here I could see that she was shaking with fear.

The time had come for them to use their strongest weapon

against Darius, and it was clearly working. He immediately lowered his sword. Without his notice, Roden took it from his hands, pausing in front of me long enough to whisper, "My idea would have worked."

"I know that," I replied.

"Give me a reason to save her life," Wilta said. "And it had better be good."

Darius eyed me. "Sorry, Jaron, but I can't put her at risk."

I knew that too. Still, a knot formed in my gut as he reached into a pocket of his long coat and withdrew the satin bag containing the Devil's Scope. With his gaze still locked on Amarinda, he said, "Let me speak to her."

Wilta took the scope and pressed it against her chest. "We hoped you would say that."

· FORTY-ONE ·

The distance between where we had fought and where Amarinda stood on the beach wasn't far, but the walk there seemed to take hours, the gap between us remaining as wide apart as ever until suddenly it wasn't and we stood facing one another. Captain Strick and Amarinda were on one side. I was on the other side with Darius, Roden, and Wilta.

Amarinda looked tired and worn, but she didn't appear to be injured, and in fact, her eyes brightened considerably once she saw Darius. I couldn't read her expression as she stared at him, though I was sure I recognized disbelief, shyness, and maybe some sadness too. I wondered if love was there as well. That was all I saw in Darius.

They stopped short of being able to touch each other, but continued to stare until Amarinda said, "I thought you were —"

"I'm not." Darius licked his lips, clearly nervous. "I've thought about you every day since I left."

She lowered her eyes. "This isn't the time for that, Darius."

"Perhaps not, but I wanted you to know."

He stepped forward, but Wilta extended her sword between

them, forcing Darius back. She said, "Now that we're all together, I see that there's a problem. Or rather, three problems. You three represent the royalty of Carthya. If the Prozarians are going to destroy Carthya — and we will destroy it now — then all of you must die."

Darius crossed to the point of her sword. "None of that is necessary. We made agreements before —"

"And we will never do so again." I refused to look at Darius as I spoke. "Your time is running out, Wilta. Surrender now, while you can."

Under his breath, I heard Darius mutter my name, followed by his whispered, "Stop."

Wilta turned her sword to me. "You will be the last to die, after watching every person you love go to their deaths, after watching your country fall in flames."

"Ignore my brother." Darius put himself between me and the sword. "Mine is the only death that will matter. If there must be a punishment, take me. I am Carthya's king."

Strick laughed, a cruel, biting laugh. She locked eyes with Darius to be sure he heard every word.

"You still think you are the king?" she sneered. "My sweet boy, you are not even a prince. You are the child of a nursemaid, son of a traitor. There is not a drop of royal blood in your veins."

"That's not true." He shook his head, but tension filled his voice. "You're only saying that because you don't want me on the throne."

Her smile grew cold. "On the contrary, until you chose sides with Jaron, we wanted you on the throne very much. Not because you were easy to bend, but because when the time came, we knew how we'd break you."

Darius looked over at me, a thousand questions in his eyes. He wanted to deny everything Strick had said, but it seemed that something deep inside wouldn't allow it. As the reality of her words set in, I could almost see his heart shredding. I could only stare back at him with a slight nod to confirm what he could not ask.

Wilta said to Roden, "Take the princess to the prison. I have further business with these two . . . brothers."

"Let me stay." Amarinda turned to Wilta. "If I must die with them, I should remain here with them."

Though he wouldn't look at her, Darius said, "You'll be safer in the prison. Please go with Roden."

Unable to meet Darius's eyes, Amarinda looked at me, and I gestured with my head that she should leave. She nodded sadly and left, with Roden at her side.

When they had gone, Wilta's attention shifted to Darius. "Now that we have the scope, let's discuss the second lens."

"I gave it to you, as we agreed," Darius protested.

"Did you?" At a signal from Captain Strick, both Lump and Mercy came forward, with Mercy holding the second lens that Darius had given them last night. He held it up to the light. "I admit, this is a good forgery." He snapped the lens in half, then hurled it into the sea. "So good that when we find the Bellander who made it, we'll see that they never make glass again."

Wilta turned to Darius. "Give me the real lens."

"I don't have it." He spoke convincingly, but I knew him

well enough to know when he was lying. Darius had brought the scope with him, so I knew he had the lens here with him too.

Wilta absolutely could not get the second lens. No matter the cost to . . . My gut twisted as I made my decision. No matter the cost to me, I knew what I had to do.

With my heart pounding, I said, "I have the lens. But it's hidden."

"Where?" Mercy asked.

I rolled my eyes. "If I told you that, what would have been the purpose in hiding it? Honestly, you're supposed to be smart and *that's* your question?"

He and Lump advanced on me and I turned to run, hoping to draw them away from Darius and give him time to escape. But after my fight with Roden, I was slower than usual, and Lump easily reached me, kicking me from behind and forcing me to my knees.

The captain caught up to us and loomed over me. "You've wondered what I want from you, Jaron? Well, this is it. *You* on your knees before me."

My hands balled into fists, which I pressed into the sand to force myself back to my feet. "That is not what you ever wanted from me, nor is this about the lens, or the trial. I am here for one reason only: revenge for what happened to Edgar."

Strick drew in a sharp breath. "How do you know that name?"

"Edgar was in the orphanage with me, the only Prozarian boy I ever knew. Was he your son?"

"Do not say his name! You know nothing about him!"

"I was drawn to him because he looked so much like

Darius. There were differences, of course, but nothing that Conner couldn't remedy with some hair dyes, the right clothing. The effects of death would take care of any other details. He disappeared from the orphanage a couple of weeks before Conner came to take me as well." I drew in a deep breath, aware of how devastating my words might be. "I think he must have been the boy who was chosen to take Darius's place in death, so that Darius could be sent here."

Strick's eyes moistened. "We followed Edgar's trail as far as the orphanage. The keeper there, Mrs. Turbeldy, told me that Conner took him."

"Why was Edgar so far from home?"

In contrast to her mother's obvious sadness, Wilta's voice lacked any hint of emotion. "Once we had the first lens, my father and Edgar immediately began a search for the second lens. Father found it in Avenia, but he had become corrupted by greed and envy. One night he told Edgar that they only had to wait until the plague took Mother and me, and then they could return and claim the scope and first lens for themselves, along with all of my power. Edgar immediately sent me a letter, detailing the betrayal. He hoped I'd offer forgiveness, but he'd given me no choice. I ended my traitorous father's life."

Strick picked up the story. "Edgar still had the second lens and was afraid Wilta would do the same to him, so he entered the orphanage to hide." She sniffed and looked away briefly. For the first time since we'd met, I didn't see a ship's captain, or a warrior. I simply saw a mother mourning her child.

Gently, I said, "When Conner took Edgar, he probably

never expected to find that lens. Edgar must have told him about the first lens too, and about Belland, which is why Conner sent Darius here." I let that sink in, then added, "He never deserved such a fate."

Strick straightened her spine. "No, he did not. But someone must pay the price. After some effort, we were able to trace the second lens here. Darius was our first target, but as we talked, we realized you must have worked with Conner to obtain the throne, so you also became the focus of my revenge."

"Edgar was my friend, Captain."

"And he was my son! Who unwillingly gave his life for Carthya; therefore, Carthya must sacrifice itself for him."

Wilta stepped forward. "Once we have all three lenses, the scope will lead us to the greatest of all treasures, and once again, the Prozarians will become a nation of unlimited power. We will crush Carthya beneath our boots."

"*Those* boots?" I angled my head. "Your boots do not worry us."

"They should." And by the tone of her voice, I knew her threat was real. The corner of her lip twitched before she added, "Where is that second lens?"

Darius had been standing nearby, watching us. He said, "Let's give it to them, Jaron. They'll get it anyway."

My eyes misted as my pulse began to race. I wasn't hiding my fears nearly as well as I wanted. But I managed to whisper, "Never."

At a glance from Wilta, Mercy picked up the same branch I had used earlier to fight Roden. He made a slow circle around me, stopping behind me to swat the branch against my legs. I gasped with the sudden sting and fell to all fours.

Strick leaned over me. "Where is the second lens? Maybe your brother will tell us."

I gritted my teeth and stood. "Ask me instead."

"All right. Will you give us the second lens?"

"Never."

Immediately, I was hit again and fell back to the ground.

"I will tell you!" Darius shouted.

But I shook my head. "He doesn't know where I hid it. Ask me again."

"Will you give us —"

"Never."

I had no sooner returned to my feet before I was hit again from behind. I withstood that blow, but it only meant Mercy's next hit came at me harder, sending me to my knees.

"He does not have the lens!" Darius said.

"But he knows where it is." Wilta crossed in front of me as I stood. "Tell us, Jaron."

I braced myself, though it wasn't enough to remain on my feet when the next hit came.

"Ask me again."

This time, my legs shook when I tried to stand. I'd just lifted one knee before the next hit came, hard enough that I fell completely flat on the ground.

"Where is the lens?" she yelled.

I rolled to my side, pushing myself into a sitting position. "I will never tell you."

"Enough of this." Darius met my eyes. Hoping to stop him, I mouthed his name, but he frowned back at me and reached into his coat pocket. "The lens is here."

My heart sank. Darius could not have known how high the price would be for saving me now.

"How easily you crumble," Wilta said with a cold smile. She snatched the lens from him, then slid it into the second position on the scope.

"Take them to the prison cell," Strick ordered Lump. "Let the people know there will be a triple execution at midnight. We want everyone there to see this."

Darius helped me stand and braced my weight as Roden led us back toward the prison cell. I knew they were both trying to speak to me, but I barely heard any of it. The only thought passing through my mind was that Wilta was one step closer to her quest.

And we were only one step away from execution.

· FORTY-TWO ·

Back in the prison cell, Amarinda tended to my injuries as best she could, but Darius sat slumped in one corner. She had been steadily watching him all afternoon, but he hadn't seemed to notice.

"He's not all right," she whispered to me.

"I know." But I had no idea what to do about it.

Even with Amarinda here, the life seemed to have gone out of Darius. As we had raced toward the beach before, a fire had lit in his eyes. It was the fire of purpose, of freedom, the fire of a king in defense of his people. That spark was diminished now. No, it was worse. That fire was gone.

I bore some of the blame for that. Although I'd sworn to keep Trea's secret, this was not the way he ever should have found out.

Part of me wanted to ask what he was thinking. Was he angry with Conner for sending him here? Or with my parents for lying to him all his life? Or angry with me? He had every right to be. Did he still consider us brothers?

That question was the reason I didn't ask, because the other part of me didn't know if I could bear to hear the answer.

"Is it true that they've captured everyone else?" Amarinda asked.

Though it deepened the ache in my heart, I nodded. I understood Imogen's reasons for leaving Trea's hut the way she had. I knew she had her own plans, and maybe a few secrets of her own. But I was terrified that everything might fall apart before tonight. Time was passing far too quickly in this cell.

It was evening before Wilta and Lump entered the prison. Both Darius and Amarinda stood to greet them, and by the time they were at the bottom of the stairs, I had managed to stand, though I was leaning on the bars of our cell for support.

Wilta looked over the three of us, but her eyes rested on me as she said, "With the correct lenses, we now know the time to enter the cave. You've already climbed it, Jaron, so you know those walls, and you will climb them again tonight. If you bring me back that third lens, I will release your friends."

I stared back at her. "Soon after we met, I promised that I would set the people of Belland free. I still have to fulfill that promise. Your offer to save my friends is pointless, because not one of them will face the executioner. Before this night is over, any Prozarians who are still alive will be racing away from this place."

Her expression hardened. "Let's try this negotiation differently. What if I bring your friends to the executioner right now . . . unless you come with me?"

I rolled my eyes. "Can't you negotiate with anything but lives saved or lost? Honestly, where's your imagination? If you want my help, I want one thing only." My gaze shifted to Lump. "Tell me his name."

Wilta's nose wrinkled. "Him? His name is Rosewater."

"Rosewater?" My grin widened as Lump's face turned to shades of purple. He held up a pair of chains, obviously for me. "Let's go to that cave."

Lump grabbed me from the cell, chained my wrists, then roughly pushed me ahead of him up the stairs, though I stopped plenty of times to make him run into me. I never tired of this game.

"I'm wagering every coin I have that you will die inside that cave tonight," he said.

"I'll take that wager . . . Rosewater. Prepare yourself to lose every coin you have."

Unlike yesterday, there were no great crowds gathered here tonight, only Mercy and Captain Strick and a few other Prozarians. From this height, I could not see the village below, nor see the smoke rising from any homes still on fire, but I smelled the ash in the air.

Mercy drew in a breath of it too and smiled. I loathed him.

Surrounded by Lump and two other vigils, I was led to the cave opening, close enough to the river's edge that if I tripped, I would instantly be carried into the seawater below. With a bright moon already beginning to rise, it was easy to see inside the cave. The tide was lower than before, but still too high to walk in through the beach, and the riverfall only increased the turbulence of the water below.

Mercy widened his arms to welcome me. "For my people's sake, I hope you return with the third lens. For myself, I would be equally happy to see you washed out to sea."

"My happiness will come in watching you crumble in defeat tonight." My eyes narrowed. "I'm looking forward to it."

He only smiled, something that genuinely made him look frightening. "Why is that?"

"When I declare victory over the Prozarians tonight, I will preserve as many lives as I can . . . except yours. Do not get in my way tonight because I have no interest in saving you."

By then, Captain Strick and Wilta had arrived at the overlook. Folding her arms, the captain said to me, "I understand you better now. You are a curiosity of opposites, leaving me to wonder if you are a brilliant mind or a great fool. If you are a servant or a dictator. If you are the greatest of friends or the worst."

"I am no curiosity," I replied. "I am simply a person with whom you never should have started a fight."

"And why is that? Do you fear losing? No, I don't think so. Are you so arrogant that to lose would damage your pride? Again, I don't believe that." She smiled, coming to her conclusion. "Is it death that you fear?"

My body tensed. "If understanding my mind is the point of sending me after the third lens, I will not go."

"You will go," Wilta said. "But not alone." The red-haired

man who'd disposed of Erick's body, and who had fought me outside Darius's home, stepped forward from the group. "Phillip is an expert diver. Maybe you will find the third lens, or maybe he will find it, but we will not be tricked again."

I tightened my jaw and said nothing. Admittedly, this was a problem.

Phillip knelt before Wilta. "Monarch, if I cannot return with the third lens, I will not return."

"I like his plan." I patted his shoulder. "Go ahead with it, Phillip."

Wilta frowned at me. "Why do you keep resisting? Don't you think it's time you admitted defeat?"

I widened my arms as far as the chains would allow. "Does this look like defeat?" I shrugged. "I mean, I know this *looks like* defeat, but things are not always what they appear." To demonstrate, I stuck my pin inside the chain and released one, then the other, dropping the chains to the ground.

Wilta was clearly unimpressed, which only meant she had never attempted to pick the lock of a chain before. She said, "Do you think that simple trick changes anything? We have played a much better trick on you."

Roden stepped forward, tears thick in his eyes. I'd never seen him looking so upset before, and when he began to speak, I understood why. "I failed you, Jaron. I'm sorry, I'm so sorry."

My fingers curled into fists. "Are you on my side, or hers?"

"He's on yours, and that was his mistake." Wilta curled one hand over his shoulder. "Ever since his capture, we let him lie about his true loyalties, knowing eventually he would do something truly harmful to you."

I looked directly at Roden. "What did you do?"

Roden took a deep breath to get control of his emotions, but still struggled to choke out, "I caught Tobias trying to free Amarinda from the jail. I had to deal with him."

I rushed forward as if to strike him, but Mercy pulled me back. "*Deal* with him? Where's Tobias?"

"He escaped, but Roden left him injured," Wilta said. "We will find him again soon."

"Why would you have done this, Roden?"

"If I didn't help them, they'd throw us both into the opening!"

My expression hardened. "That should have been your choice! You asked me to trust you and *this* is what I get for it?"

"He's weak," Wilta explained. To demonstrate, she pushed on Roden's shoulder and he immediately crumpled lower, tears still rolling down his cheeks. "Once we understand a person's weakness, we can bring them down to nothing, and then we take control. That's why my mother has sought to understand you, because we will do the same to you."

"I understand him perfectly now." Strick turned to me again, her lips thinning as a smile spread across her face. "You do fear death, Jaron. That is the curse you constantly bear upon your shoulders, haunting your every step. But it is not your own death that keeps you awake at night. It is the deaths of those you love."

She had hit closer to me than anyone ever had, which

unnerved me more than I dared to let show. Instead, I looked from her over to the cave entrance and muttered, "I am about to be the curse upon your shoulders. Before morning comes, you will kneel to me."

Before she could answer, I saluted her as I had done once before, then jumped back into the cave.

· FORTY-THREE ·

I had tried to prepare myself for the icy cold that would greet me, but the instinct to suck in choked me almost immediately and I arose from the pit coughing on water and already shivering. The cave was much colder tonight, or maybe my strength was finally failing. I needed to get out of the water, if I could.

Phillip had followed me into the water, though the tide had carried him some distance away before he surfaced inside the cave. "You cannot escape me!" he shouted. "We will find the lens together."

Ignoring him, I swam out from beneath the waterfall to the same wall that I had climbed before. By this time, I knew the holds well, though because of the river now running into the cave, the wall was wet and the holds were slippery.

I shouted up to Strick, who was leaning over the opening, "You are wrong about me. The greatest of my fears is not death. It is that one day I will be faced with a challenge that I cannot overcome. Today is not that day. You will never see the third lens!"

I doubted she could hear me, but that wasn't the point. Nor

was it even meant to be my response to Phillip, though from his side of the cave, he was glowering at me. I had only said those words because I needed to hear them.

I didn't know where I should be on the wall to see the third lens, only that once the moon rose into the proper location, I needed to be high enough to see the entire cave clearly. With that thought, I began to climb.

The first attempt lasted less than a minute before I lost my grip on the slippery wet walls and fell, splashing into the frigid pool and sinking almost to the very bottom. The incoming tide was little threat to me, but the pull of the water to take me out to sea was almost more than I could fight. I finally righted myself, only to be caught by a wave, which sent me crashing into the side of the cave wall. I tried again from there, just to take hold of any place where I might breathe, but I fell again almost immediately. I climbed higher on my third attempt, looking across the cave to see Phillip on the wall across from me, shaking his head.

"You are wasting your strength," he said. "This is not about the climb."

"It's always about the climb!" I shouted back, though the distraction cost me my balance and only made my fall harder than before.

This time, the cold surface slapped against my body like I'd landed on rock. I also landed heavily on my injured leg, and it screamed at me when I tried using it to kick toward the cliff wall again. That same leg shook as I relied on it to lift me out of the water, but I had no other choice. I started to climb again.

Thoughts entered my mind, telling me that this was not a fight I could win, and I pushed them away. What I had said before was the absolute truth. Every risk I ever took, every leap of faith, every step into the darkness, was to prove to myself that I could overcome any challenge that came my way. No matter how small I often felt, I needed to know that I could face the hard thing ahead because I'd already done harder things before.

But I had rarely faced anything like this. If I only had to find the lens, or only had to climb these walls, it would be difficult enough. But this was proving to be impossible.

And the impossibility of it was how the cold was affecting me internally. My teeth were chattering beyond my control and the tips of my fingers were numb. But I was already experiencing something worse: Thinking was becoming difficult. I couldn't even remember how to think.

I recalled my conversation with Imogen from early this morning, that I had come close to death before and always found a way out of it. She had said that was only because I had fought death before.

So I would again. Gritting my teeth together, I found a hold for my fingers and climbed.

I had been here before. I had done this before, though it was different tonight. The riverfall was back now, as it had once been. As Tobias had suggested, a grand moon was rising, sending a sliver of light through the opening. But tonight, that light reflected off the riverfall to the water below. There, strange lights suddenly appeared, not in the turbulent water coming in from the sea, but below it. The lights came from within the pit.

"There it is!" Phillip said. "The lights will lead us to the lens!"

I'd paid little attention to the pit the first time I'd seen it. It had appeared to be nothing more than a tube created by the volcanoes that formed this land, and maybe it was. But Phillip was correct — this was the pathway to the third lens.

I studied the strange lights a moment longer, wondering about their glow in shades of blue, purple, and pink, darkening in tone as they descended deeper into the pit.

Again, the devils must have been laughing at my expense. To obtain the third lens, I'd have to dive into a deep pit and survive a water-filled tube that might continue forever underground. Whoever designed this clearly did not want the lens to ever be found. I gritted my teeth and began to climb again. My leg ached horribly. Every part of me hurt by now.

"Still wasting your strength." From a position far below me, Phillip angled his body away from the wall. "I will get the lens first. I will get the glory."

He dove toward the pit, and should have made it, except at the same moment, a new wave crashed into the cave. Had he been higher, the greater speed of his body might have pushed him downward, but now the wave thrust him against the opposite wall. He crashed hard against the rock and was knocked unconscious, then the same wave carried him back out to sea. Just like that, he was gone.

I cursed under my breath, then cursed again until nothing was left but to attempt the same dive from higher up on the wall. Maybe it wouldn't matter. The very same thing could easily happen to me. Inhaling deeply, I let go of the cave walls and dove directly into the pit.

The speed of my dive and flow of the water carried me deeper into the pit than I would have expected to go in only a few seconds. Soon, I was being pushed through a dark lava tube with my only light being what must have been a form of glowing algae.

Once the tunnel flattened out, I began to swim, though my body was already begging to breathe. Finally, when I could stand it no longer, I rolled to my back and exhaled. To my surprise, there were no bubbles. This was air.

I opened my eyes and realized I was floating past a thin layer of air, created by a pocket in the tube that was higher than the level of the water. I drew in a new breath just in time for the tube to narrow again, and I continued swimming. I pushed one finger upward against the lava tube. As soon as it widened, I rolled and took a new breath, then returned to swimming, never knowing how long it would be until I found more air. Never knowing if I *would* find more air. I just swam.

Ahead of me, the tube seemed to split. To my left, almost impossibly, I saw sunlight, which was surely my chance for escape. But the glow that had carried me this far through the tunnel flowed to the right, into total darkness. Death.

That was the direction I had to go. Not to fight against my fate, as Imogen wanted, but to accept it. I hoped that one day she would forgive me.

I took what might be the last breath I ever drew, and swam to the right. By the time I realized the truth about the choice I had made, it was too late. I was carried headfirst over an underground waterfall with no idea of what lay below me.

I splashed deep into an icy pool of water and fought my way upward with lungs about to burst. The river ran onward, continuing deeper underground and into total darkness, but there was land to the side of me. The air in here was as cold as the water, but at least it was air.

I rolled out of the pool onto the patch of damp ground and looked up to find myself in a small room carved out of the lava rock. I could easily touch opposite walls with both arms spread apart, but the ceiling became lost in the darkness overhead.

I attempted to climb the rock, but my injured leg failed me, and I fell back to the ground. I had no strength to escape this place. I didn't know if an escape was possible, even if I did make the climb.

Less than a minute later, that question was answered. The moon reached an angle where it shone down directly into the room, bathing it in light. A glint of metal caught my eye. Curious, I stood and limped to the far wall, toward a sword balanced on two hooks that were embedded in the wall. The sword's workmanship was the finest I'd ever before seen, artwork as much as it was weaponry. I doubted the best craftsmen in Carthya were capable of producing such a sword.

Both edges of the beveled blade were sharp, and the metal lacked any nicks or scratches. The hilt was ornate and made of curled steel with similar carvings on it as I had seen on the scope. I almost didn't dare to touch it.

Almost.

My eyes lifted. Directly above the sword was the third lens, also embedded in the wall. I brushed a finger over it. There was writing on the glass that I could not read. I tried to pry it from the wall, but my fingers were shaking too much to be of any use, and the lens was in too deep anyway.

I reached for the pin lodged in my belt, then cursed under my breath. It was no longer there. So I cursed louder.

My gaze returned to the sword. It seemed like a crime to use such a fine weapon to pry glass out of rock, but I had no other choice.

I lifted the sword, already amazed at how light it was for its size, how perfect its balance and grip. Breathing an apology to the craftsman who made it, I inserted the tip of the sword into the rock and carefully wedged it against the third lens. This was far more difficult than I had expected, and I worried about breaking the glass.

Finally, I had my first hint that the lens was coming loose, though it was anything but good news. Water began leaking from inside the rock, and not a small amount of it. Just loosening the lens had started a chain reaction of cracking sounds throughout the entire room, spurts of water coming through seams in the walls, and a realization that my feet were now standing in water flowing up from below.

A realization that I was about to die.

I pried the lens free in the same instant water burst through the hole I had just created. It came at me with so much pressure that I splashed onto the ground. Where was all this water coming from?

A splitting sound ahead of me turned to a deafening crash and the lava wall opened, rocks flying at me in a sudden flood of water. I was slammed to the far wall, finding myself rapidly being carried upward by the water. I tried to avoid the rocks swirling around me, but to no avail. One finally hit me, and water filled my lungs.

· FORTY-FOUR ·

I awoke on dry ground, coughing out water. Someone was kneeling behind me, propping me up. The moon was lower in the sky, suggesting morning wasn't far away, but it was still a cold night, one that worsened my shaking after I drew in air again.

"He's all right, he'll live," Tobias said from behind me. I looked up at him and just managed to nod. I still couldn't speak.

"We can see he's going to live," Teagut said, crouching in front of me. "What kind of a physician are you, telling us what we can plainly see for ourselves?"

"How do you feel?" Tobias asked me.

"Horrible." I took a few more deep breaths, each one sending fresh pain to my lungs. "It's not only the water; I'm sick."

A few of the pirates around me chuckled, and when I looked back at Tobias, he held up the bottle of medicine he had created to fake an illness. "A heavy dose will cause nausea. I hoped it would be bad enough to make you spit out all that water."

I lay back on the ground, still shivering. "I don't know whether to thank you first, or to curse you."

"I saved your life, Jaron. So did they."

For the first time, I realized it wasn't just Teagut around me, but all the pirates who had been expelled by Roden after I lost the fight to him.

Teagut shrugged. "This is where Fink has been hiding. After he was caught, he told Roden about this place with a lava tube so far underground he couldn't see the bottom of it."

"Ever since last night in Trea's hut, I knew the second lens would send you underground," Tobias said. "I studied the geography of the land while I was in hiding, and Roden asked the Prozarians a lot of questions about their search of Belland, and —"

"Summarize, Tobias."

He sighed. "Roden and I figured you'd be the one chosen to go after the third lens, and that if you came back to the surface again, this was probably where you'd be. He claimed to have caught me trying to free Amarinda from the prison, giving me this reason to escape and wait for you here."

I'd known very little of what Tobias was doing, but Roden's part in this plan was no surprise. Back when he'd put me in the crow's nest, Roden and I had agreed that he would make the Prozarians believe that he was giving them what they wanted. Even when he was crying in front of Wilta about having failed me, he was leading the Prozarians in the direction he knew I would want.

I said, "Roden claimed he injured you."

"Oh, he did, and it might be serious." Tobias turned his

head to show a tiny cut mark on his cheek, barely more than a paper cut. "Don't laugh. It really hurts." He added, "Roden also banished the pirates here, so that they'd be waiting to pull you out if you appeared. Which you did."

"With your face down in the water and unconscious and somehow still gripping that sword," Teagut said. "It would have drowned you if the water wasn't pushing you upward so fast."

My attention fell to the sword. I hadn't realized it was still in my hand. If I had to say goodbye to my old sword, I couldn't imagine a finer replacement.

Suddenly, I sat up, patting wildly at my pockets. "Where is it?" I mumbled.

"Where is what?" Tobias asked.

"The lens? Did you lose the lens?" Teagut leaned over the water hole behind me and peered in. When he saw nothing, he rocked back on his heels to glare at me. "You cannot have been this foolish!"

I continued searching through my pockets until ending at the one in the right leg of my trousers. With my brows pressed low, I looked from Teagut to Tobias. "The lens should be here."

"There?" Teagut snarled. "You should have known it would fall out!"

"Well, I didn't exactly have time to plan my escape!" I gestured toward the water hole. "But if you want to swim back down and search for it, go ahead!"

One of the pirates behind Teagut lunged at me, swiping me across my jaw. "Search him!"

Three other pirates followed his lead, digging through my pockets until Teagut and Tobias pushed them off me. Tobias shouted, "You won't harm your king!"

"Roden won the duel," said the man who had hit me.

With Tobias's help, I stood, massaging my jaw. "If you want treasure, then take it from the Prozarians who brought you here." The grumbling stopped . . . or at least, quieted a bit. "Return with me now, and if you get me back to the cave before sunrise, I promise that you will be rewarded."

The pirates continued moaning over a treasure that now would never be theirs, but several of them did hurry ahead. Tobias kept his arm around my shoulders to help me walk and Teagut joined him on the other side. But we had only taken a few steps before Teagut said, "Without the lens, you have nothing to bargain with after we return."

My brow pressed low with sincere concern. "I know."

Tobias frowned over at me. "Then let's hope nothing else goes wrong."

Teagut sighed. "We know you, Jaron. Something always goes wrong."

Yes, it did.

At Tobias's urgings, the pirates pushed me along the trail faster than I wanted to go. At first, I tried explaining that I'd fought a duel with Roden, taken a beating along the backs of my legs, swum through an ice water tunnel, and had a rock crash into me, knocking me unconscious, only to be recovered by a medicine that would've made me lose my last meal, if I'd had one.

"Sounds like an ordinary day for you." Tobias didn't let up on his pace for an instant.

My next strategy was to dig my feet into the ground and slow everyone down, but Teagut only laughed and pushed me onward, with a few of the pirates threatening to carry me like an old woman if I couldn't keep up.

Since I'd have rather been beaten again than carried, my third strategy was to keep up. And as I did, I slowly warmed up, and the effects of Tobias's medicine faded.

By the time the cave was in view, I was sore and exhausted, and my temper was stirring. In other words, I felt almost normal.

Dawn had begun hinting at the horizon, a reminder that if Tobias had not forced us to move so quickly, it would have been too late. On the north side of the river, Darius, Amarinda, and Roden stood with their hands bound behind them, each of them surrounded by Prozarian vigils, eighteen in total. None of my other friends were here.

Wilta was the first to see us coming and immediately alerted her mother. From her shocked reaction, she might not have expected me to return by land with an army of banished pirates. In truth, I hadn't expected this either.

Strick rushed to the edge of the overlook, wildly waving her arms to get the attention of those down on the beach. "All Prozarians, come to the defense of your monarch!"

I said to Teagut, "Send everyone down to stop them. No one gets up here."

Teagut turned and called to the rest of the pirates, "We've been itching for a proper battle. Follow me!"

With eager shouts, they raised swords and scattered, filling the trails down to the beach. Tobias remained at my side, a knife in his hands. I still had the sword from the caves, which I held ready as I crossed onto the overlook.

Captain Strick and Wilta walked forward to greet me, with Lump and Mercy trailing behind them, their weapons out.

Wilta looked past me. "Where's Phillip?"

When I shook my head at her, she nodded with understanding. "In truth, we didn't expect to see either of you again, not after all this time."

"I'm sorry to disappoint you."

"On the contrary, I'm relieved to see you here." She held out her hand. "I assume you have the third lens. I am willing to keep my promise and allow your friends to go free."

I shook my head. "It's time to keep my promise to free Belland. Consider this the beginning of our negotiations. But I warn you now, I'm terrible at negotiations. This will be easier if you give me what I want."

"And what do you want?"

Our eyes met. I didn't blink once when I said, "I want to finish this. Now."

· FORTY-FIVE ·

Wilta withdrew her hand. Her expression was tight and her temper was already warming. "We are not leaving Belland without the third lens."

From this height, I saw the ships emptying out as Prozarians ran to the beach to fight the pirates. I grinned. "You are leaving, though not on that ship."

She turned to see which ship I was talking about. As she did, I lifted my hand high into the air and quickly lowered it.

But nothing happened.

Which was rather embarrassing.

Nothing happened for long enough that the captain finally sighed. "Enough talk, Wilta. End this."

Wilta gestured for Lump and Mercy to advance on me, but neither one had taken a single step before a loud explosion out in the harbor shook the ground.

Pieces of wood scattered high into the air. A few men who must have still been on board one of the Prozarian ships jumped into the sea as the vessel angled sideways, taking on water from below.

While the others ducked and covered their heads, I rocked back on my heels. It was impolite to boast at a moment like this, but the explosion had been grander than I'd expected. Absolutely worth the extra few seconds of waiting.

Captain Strick's eyes widened into saucers and her hand covered her mouth. Wilta's cry of horror still lingered in something between a gasp and a slow exhale.

"I didn't like that boat anyway," I said. "Now, release my brother and my friends, then send your fighters to the beach to surrender to the pirates."

Wilta merely glared toward the sea with clenched teeth. That was a mistake. I shrugged, then raised and lowered my arm once more. "You should have believed me when I said I'm not good at negotiations."

I'd anticipated the delay this time, and so within seconds of my speaking, an explosion rocked the second ship, rolling it sideways to lean against the third ship. As before, any crewman on that ship quickly jumped into the water.

"Did you see that?" I asked.

She had. Panicked, Wilta motioned to Lump. "Untie the prisoners. The rest of you, leave this overlook."

Quickly, the Prozarians left, except Lump, who was untying Amarinda, and Mercy, whose face looked as if he too might explode.

He freed Roden, who grabbed Tobias's arm. "Let's help the pirates."

Tobias stepped back. "How?" Maybe Tobias didn't want to fight the Prozarians. Maybe he didn't want to leave Amarinda up here with Darius. Either way, he protested the entire time that Roden pushed him along the trail.

Wilta asked me, "How are you doing that? I will agree to nothing more until you explain."

"It must be those crates of weapons," her mother said. "We transferred one crate onto each ship. Roden warned they may have some gunpowder on them."

"They had gunpowder *in* them," I said. "You willingly carried to each ship the method of your own destruction."

"We can end this now." Wilta held out her hand. "Give me the third lens and we'll leave Belland."

"I have no lens to give you. It was only from thin luck that I even made it out alive."

"You lost the lens?" The sudden rage in her eyes was alarming. "I'll make you wish you hadn't made it out alive."

I glanced over at Darius and Amarinda, stunned at Wilta's boldness. "They're still threatening me? Will one of you remind them that I am currently *exploding their only escape from this island*?"

Amarinda said, "Please do as Jaron asks. Vengeance will cost far more than you have already lost. Learn that lesson now, and go home, in peace."

Strick shook her head. "If we leave now, it will not be in peace."

I said, "You've worked hard to understand me, but I think I understand you too. You are a coward, Captain Strick. Like all cowards, you attack because you feel weak. You gain respect through fear and threats because nothing else works for you. I pity that."

Darius added, "There will never again be any agreements

between us. Long after your time has passed, the true king of Carthya will continue to reign."

"We do not fear you." Strick's eyes turned as cold as I still felt. "We will come for you, Darius, after you have become fat and comfortable on your throne."

At her side, Wilta turned and raised her arm to signal to the Prozarians below. "It's the weapons crates," she called. "Find them and —"

"Don't lower that hand!" I reached around her back in an attempt to stop her, but she pushed me away, barely casting a glance at me. Instead, her eyes flew toward the harbor when the third ship exploded.

I clicked my tongue. "I did warn you. Now, you and all your people will abandon Belland with a vow never to return again, nor to make any further demands on these people."

"Belland is ours!"

"No, I don't think so. Listen to the name of the people who live here: Bellanders. Did you hear how their name sounds like their country?" I pulled my hand from my pocket and raised my arm high. "I assume that you come from somewhere that sounds like your name. Where is that? Prozaria? Prozar? Prozariamalaria?"

"Never!"

"That is another mistake." At my signal, the fourth ship exploded, this one so violently that the ship actually seemed to have momentarily leapt from the water.

Two ships now remained in the harbor: their flagship and the *Shadow Tide.*

"We'll leave Belland," Wilta agreed. "Stop destroying our ships!"

"You will never step foot in Carthya, nor in any of the countries with whom we have treaties."

"How will we know which countries are forbidden to us?"

"Should we repeat the lesson on countries that sound like your name? Stay inside your own borders. To replace the pirate's ship you sank, the *Shadow Tide* is mine now, which leaves you only one ship. Give me your answer, or you will swim away from here."

Wilta's shoulders slumped as she turned to her mother. "Call our people back to the ship. We surrender."

Captain Strick glared at me unflinchingly, even as she sent Lump to the beach with orders for an immediate departure. I hardly cared. I was good at glaring too.

"There's one more thing," I said.

Strick sighed. "What?"

"I want every Prozarian weapon. In exchange for the weapons you stole from me."

"No, Wilta," her mother warned.

"What other choice do we have?" Wilta snapped. She walked to the edge of the overlook, held out her arms for the attention of everyone on the beach, and shouted down, "My people, surrender your weapons!"

She bent to her knees, then released her sword and a long knife that had been at her waist, letting them clang to the ground far below. Her mother followed her example, then the two of them left the overlook, arm in arm. Wilta's head was bowed in defeat. Her mother's head was not.

The Prozarians on the beach must have followed their example, because that was when, for the first time, I heard the voices I had been almost desperate for. From the beach, Roden's voice rose up first. "Pirates, collect those weapons. They will serve as payment for our time here."

I cocked my head. We could negotiate that later, along with who would keep the title of pirate king.

"Mott, have you seen Darius?" That was Trea's voice, arriving on the beach.

"Where is Jaron?" I grinned, relieved to hear Imogen's voice. Equally relieved that she was asking about me.

I started toward the overlook, only to hear Mercy cry, "Curse you for this, Jaron!"

I turned and saw him racing toward me, a knife in his hands. I raised my sword but wasn't fast enough to lift it to the proper angle. Before he reached me, Darius attacked him from behind. Mercy attempted to twist around and stab Darius instead, but when he rolled away, his legs fell into the river. Mercy continued squirming, throwing his weight away from Darius. He wormed free, only realizing too late that the current was carrying him toward the cave opening. He clutched at some grasses on the shore, but his grip was slipping.

"You are the son of a traitor!" Mercy growled. "How dare you challenge us?"

"I am a king." Darius held out his hand to drag Mercy out of the water. "Swear to never harm my brother again."

Mercy only spat at the proffered hand, and in the same

moment, the clump of grass broke off in his fist. Seconds later, we heard his body splash into the water far below.

Darius crouched low, resting his arms on his legs, head bowed until Amarinda touched his shoulder. He smiled up at her, but immediately turned back to me, meeting my eyes with an expression of relief.

"Thank you," I whispered.

He nodded back. "You already saved me. I owed you this."

Unaware of what had just happened, Fink called up, "Jaron, are you up there? You need to see this!"

I took a slow breath, then Amarinda joined me on one side and Darius on the other, and together we walked to the edge of the overlook, where Wilta and her mother had just knelt in defeat. There, I caught my breath in my throat. The Prozarians on the beach were on their knees in surrender. Pirates stood among them with the collected swords and knives in their arms.

From below, the Bellanders must have joined the pirates in the fight, and they were the first to see me. Someone pointed up and shouted, "Hail to the Giver of Freedom, and brother of our king."

"Brother to a king," I murmured. I smiled over at Darius and genuinely meant it. I had my brother back. That would always be enough.

· FORTY-SIX ·

I was alone on the cave overlook for some time, warmed by the rising sun. I remained there long after the Prozarians had begun their evacuation, after the pirates had loaded the *Shadow Tide* with the weapons Roden had allotted to them, and long after the Bellanders had returned to their homes in peace.

I stood at the edge of the opening into the cave, staring down at the rising tide, waves crashing against the walls before flowing back out to sea. The Prozarians were leaving, but with icy hearts and bitter threats about when they would see me again. I was not foolish enough to doubt them. The consequences for what had happened here would be severe. To me. To Darius. To all of Carthya, and perhaps even beyond our borders. I would have to be ready.

Teagut soon arrived at the overlook, carrying a large bag of coins in his arms. "There's a man on the beach who says he goes by the name of Lump now. He owes you payment for his lost wager."

Teagut dropped the bag on the ground, but I said, "Everything you can carry in one hand is payment for the sword you lent me. Take the rest, for equal distribution among the pirates."

"What about payment for pulling you out of that lava tube?"

"Equal shares, Teagut."

"But I . . . very well." Teagut hesitated again. "Earlier this afternoon when Roden challenged you to become pirate king, he didn't truly win. Jaron, you are our king. When you're ready, we'll be waiting to carry you back home."

After he left, I sat on the edge of the overlook, facing the sea. The ships that I had exploded were in various stages of sinking, tilting, and falling apart. The pirates were salvaging from them as well. The Prozarians would return home with almost nothing other than the clothes on their backs, and most seemed relieved to even have that much.

I had never wanted to bring so much devastation upon them. I wished they would have listened sooner than they did.

"Jaron?"

I looked behind me and started to my feet, but Imogen was quicker to sit at my side. Her wet hair was neatly combed and rebraided, and I couldn't imagine her any more beautiful than she was right now. I still didn't know if I had lost her, or even if I had any chance with her.

When we had last seen each other at the hut, I knew my words had hurt her. Half my time on this cliff had been spent trying to figure out a way to repair things between us. I had come up with nothing other than to conclude that on my best day, I still did not deserve her. I worried that she had finally figured that out too, or maybe she had known it all along.

I quickly said, "It is my life, Imogen." She turned away, but I took her hand in mine, adding, "There is a part of us that is only my life. It is full of flaws and mistakes and stupidity, nothing that would ever describe you." She lowered her head, and I knew she was listening now. I folded my fingers between hers. "Another part of us is *our* life, and it is beautiful because of you. Imogen, you are my purpose, the reason I open my eyes each morning. I close my eyes each night only in hopes of dreaming of you. Every day that my heart still beats, it is because of you." For the first time, I looked at her and saw tears rimming her eyes.

The first tear spilled onto her cheek. "You really do say the worst possible things at the worst possible times . . . but not always. Sometimes you know what to say to make me love you more than I did before."

I cocked my head, an excuse to get closer to her. "Please tell me this is one of those occasions."

She reached for me and leaned in for a kiss, one that was too quickly interrupted by Fink, who had come up behind us. "Really? You're doing that here? The whole beach can see you."

"Go tell them to look somewhere else," I said.

Fink folded his arms and sat beside Imogen. "You're only saying that to get rid of me."

"On the contrary, I've never been happier to see you." He was the one I'd worried about most since reaching Belland. "You were never meant to cause one of those explosions."

Fink smiled proudly. "I told Imogen I could do it, and I did."

I squeezed her hand. I may have loaded the gunpowder in the cargo hold with Fink, but while on the fishing boat, Imogen was the one who figured out how to make it work.

It began with an understanding that everyone would need a way onto the ships. That was why Tobias had gathered them in a place where they'd easily be found, and why Imogen had threatened an uprising to ensure they were separated onto the various ships. Once the ships were emptied to fight the pirates, the rest was easy. They watched for my signal, lit a fuse, and escaped the ship before the flame reached the gunpowder crate.

I glanced over at Imogen. "You really are brilliant, you know."

She beamed back at me. "It may take a lifetime for you to fully appreciate that."

I leaned toward her again, only to catch Mott and Trea in my side vision as they came around the bend, hand in hand.

"Will you sit with us awhile?" Imogen asked. I groaned. I wanted to kiss Imogen properly, and I was tired of interruptions.

It appeared Mott and Trea didn't want to sit with us either, and perhaps for similar reasons. After glancing at Mott, Trea said, "That's very kind, but it's been so long since Mott and I were together, we'd like the time alone. Maybe for dancing."

I preferred that they were alone too. I'd never seen Mott in love and had no interest in watching him dance. I couldn't even comprehend what that would look like.

"I have a request," he added. "I would like to remain here on Belland for a while. Trea wants to help these people rebuild, and I want to help her. The work will be good for me, Jaron. It'll strengthen the old injuries, from the war."

"I agree."

He continued, "Besides, I don't need your permission. I'm simply telling you my plans."

I smiled warmly at him. "Yes, Mott. Stay for as long as you are needed here. But I hope you will return to Carthya soon, for you are needed there as well." To Trea, I added, "And you are wanted there. I know Darius will have every hope of bringing you with him."

"We'd better be leaving soon ourselves," Roden said as he walked up to join us. "We don't want the Bellanders to get the idea that we're taking the Prozarians' place, and the pirates are beginning to take the Bellanders' things."

"How much have they stolen so far?"

"Plenty."

"Tell them to give it all back. These people have lost far too much already."

"I will tell them," Roden said. "I am their king." He eyed me. "Yes?"

"Don't be absurd. I only lost as a favor to you."

"You think you did me a favor? That was my plan to save your life."

"Or your plan to get a kiss from Wilta. Saving my life was only an extra benefit."

Roden sighed. "I really did like her. Just my luck that she turned out to be the monarch of our enemy."

"And a soulless villain."

"Yeah, that too. Do you think maybe one day —"

"No, I don't."

"Well . . . maybe."

"How long until the repairs are completed on the *Shadow Tide*?"

He shrugged. "The pirates will finish them today, if they hurry. You left quite a mark on that ship."

"He leaves his mark everywhere." Tobias arrived with his medical bag in hand. "Where do you feel the worst?"

"Everywhere. I'm cold, but I'll be all right."

"You're still shivering. I'll stop complaining about spending a night in the crow's nest. This is much worse."

"Do you think so?"

Imogen gave me a cloak, which Tobias wrapped around my shoulders, then he looked down at my leg. "I heard it's infected."

I smiled over at him. "My leg is fine. If Wilta expected less of me because she thought it was infected, that was just an unfortunate misunderstanding."

Tobias still reached for another bandage. While he worked, I looked down at my thigh and said, "*This* was not my plan, though."

"Nor mine. I truly am sorry." Roden quickly added, "Though you gave me no other choice."

"Maybe not, but I am cutting your pay as captain, if you will be captain again. I'll make things easier on you this time."

A corner of his mouth turned up. "Then there are things you're sorry for too?"

"There must be."

Roden groaned. "Can't you tell me you're sorry? Just two little words: 'I'm sorry.'" I only grinned back at him, so he said, "Perhaps your apology will come in the form of a reward."

I arched a brow. "Such as?"

"The greatest of all treasures? Between the few of us here, is it true what you told the pirates? The lens is gone?"

My grin faded as quickly as it had come. "When did you last see the Devil's Scope?"

He shrugged. "When Darius gave it to Wilta on the beach, in exchange for Amarinda." I continued to stare at him, and with a long sigh, he finally said, "I suppose it's good the lens is gone. We cannot take any risks of her getting it."

"Agreed."

Another beat passed, then he seemed to cheer up. "Perhaps you'll reward me with a new title? Something more than just captain of the guard."

I was ready with an answer. "I'm glad you asked, because I have been waiting a long time to give you this title."

His eyes narrowed. "What is it?"

"The one I offered to you earlier: minister of oats."

"No, Jaron!"

"It's too late. I've decreed it!"

"It's not yours to decree," Tobias pointed out. "That's for the king to do." His eyes softened. "That's for Darius now."

"Jaron clearly is confused about who is the true king here." We all turned, startled to see Darius approaching us. He eyed me. "You forget who you are, Jaron, and who I am. Let's settle this."

FORTY-SEVEN

I stood to greet Darius, feeling strangely anxious about speaking to him. I did understand who he was, who he would be now, and I'd accepted it, but that wouldn't make this conversation any easier. Perhaps because I no longer had a sense of who I was.

Notably, Amarinda was not with him. His only explanation was, "Don't worry. She's safe."

Darius next gave his attention to Tobias, who looked terrified. Tobias reached for a weapon at his side, then realized he had no weapon there. So he squared his body to Darius's and stared back at him, respectfully, but with courage.

"Do you really love her?" Darius asked Tobias.

Tobias rarely looked directly at anyone, but he did this time with Darius. "She'll choose who she will choose. But for my part, I love Amarinda more than my life."

Darius kicked at the ground for several seconds. "She and I have talked. Take care of her." Tobias began to say something, but Darius finally glanced up. "It's her choice, not mine. We're not friends, Tobias."

I stepped between them, then pulled the king's ring off my finger and held it out for Darius. "I believe this is yours."

He only stared at it, gave a sad smile, then turned to me. "Can we talk?"

All of us were standing now, in deference to Darius's title. I looked around. "Shall we talk here, or alone?"

"It doesn't matter. Everyone will know the truth about me eventually. How long have you known it?"

"Only since coming to Belland. But I don't care, and neither should you. We are brothers, Darius, as we've always been."

He smiled and turned to Fink, at my side. "And is this our brother too?"

Darius offered his hand to Fink, who pushed it aside to close Darius in an embrace. Surprised, Darius widened his arms at first, then finally closed them across Fink's back.

The instant Fink pulled away, he began speaking, so quickly it was clear he never intended to take a breath. "I suppose you'll want your old room back, but Jaron gave it to me and I've changed a few things. Or maybe you'll want the king's room, that makes more sense. Jaron hasn't used it yet. He's still in his old room, which I can't understand because the king's room is much bigger, but maybe that's for the best because it's yours now."

The instant he was forced to draw a breath, I grabbed him and pulled him away from Darius, then said, "Leave him alone, or he'll never want to come back."

Darius turned to Trea. "Is it true? My father was Bevin Conner?"

Trea's eyes filled with tears. "The only father that should ever matter is the one who raised you and loved you as his own, King Eckbert."

"If Eckbert was anyone but a king, that would be enough." Now Darius turned back to me and Imogen. "Will you both walk with me?"

I put the ring in my pocket, then took Imogen by the hand, saying nothing as we followed Darius away from the cliff and farther up the hillside. Against the rising sun, we saw the sole surviving Prozarian ship pull away from the docks of Belland, hopefully for good.

"The people are free again," Darius said. "Thanks to you."

"Thanks to us."

"No." Darius shook his head. "Thanks to *you*. We both know that, and yet the people here have asked me to be their king. They are rewarding me for a gift I did not give."

"They chose to honor you for two years of reasons," I said. "And if it were possible for you to accept their offer, I know you would be great here."

Darius patted my arm, then turned to Imogen. "What I have to say is for you, and I hope you will pass this message to Jaron when he is able to hear it, and that you will make him understand that these are my wishes."

I stepped back. Obviously he knew I was here. Why should he address Imogen as if I weren't?

He took Imogen's hands in his. "Yesterday, I said something cruel to Jaron, calling him an embarrassment to our family. Those words have haunted me since. You see, I am embarrassed for myself, that I did not understand what he understands, that I did not see what was so clear to him. That for so long, I failed to follow, even when he led with such clarity."

Imogen shook her head. "Please say this to Jaron, not me."

"I can't. We both know that he is also stubborn beyond reason and that even now, he is biting his tongue to keep from arguing back against everything he is hearing."

He was wrong about that. Even so, I loosened the pressure of my tongue against my teeth and forced myself to unclench my fists.

Darius said, "There has been a great deal of talk these past few days about a true king. In Carthya, that is Jaron."

I couldn't stop myself any longer. "Darius, come back with me —"

"The throne belongs to him, by rights of birth, and more importantly, because he has earned it." Finally, Darius released Imogen's hands and turned to me. "When you were in the river trying to rescue Wilta, there was a point when your shirt rode high on your back. I saw scars there that a king should never bear. I see the cuts on your hands and wrists now, the slight limp to favor your right leg, and I know you will leave here with new scars. Jaron, I may one day earn the throne the Bellanders have offered me, but there is only one true king of Carthya. And it is you."

"You must come back." Tears filled my eyes. "You're my brother, Darius."

"I am your brother, always. But we are brothers who will

rule from opposite sides of a sea. For now, Belland needs my help here, to rebuild, to regain all that we have lost over the last month."

Imogen touched my arm, and in her hand I saw Conner's journal, pulled from her shoulder bag.

I passed it to Darius, who took it with curious eyes. "Read this, and understand who this man was," I said. "Learn what was good about him, and be warned for where he destroyed himself. In this book, Conner requested that all his possessions be passed to his heir. That's you, Darius. Other than a portion reserved for Mott, it's a significant inheritance."

A smile widened across his face, the smile I remembered so well from when we were boys at play on the castle grounds. "Send everything that you can. That is how I will rebuild this place, make Belland greater than it ever was."

"I am relieved to do that," I said. "Because I promised the regents that I would return with a trading agreement. Tell me what you need, and I will provide it."

"All I ever needed was my brother back in my life." Now Darius's smile fell on me, though it could not match the happiness I already felt. "When you return, bring our brother, Fink, along too."

Darius offered me his hand, and just as Fink had done, I folded him into a warm embrace. I would always miss my parents and mourn their loss, but for the first time since hearing the news of their deaths, I felt something begin to heal.

When I pulled away, I said to Darius, "I will try to be as good a king there as I know you will be here."

He swatted me lightly against one arm. "Wherever Father and Mother rest with the saints, I know they are already proud of you. Now go back and make Carthya into the country we always believed it could be."

I embraced him again, then he excused himself to begin addressing the needs of the Bellanders, *his* people now.

And I took Imogen's hand again to walk back down the slope.

"What do you think?" she asked. "How does Carthya become the country you wished it would be?"

"For now, I need to sleep," I said. "After that, it begins with you and I talking through our ideas together. That must always be part of *our* life."

"I have only one more request," Darius called back to me. "Tonight there will be an official ceremony to make me king of Belland. Will you be there?"

"Of course." In that moment, I believed that nothing would ever make me prouder.

I was wrong.

· FORTY-EIGHT ·

That evening, a large fire was built on the beach. The platform that Wilta had used for her own glory had been expanded and raised high enough for all those who had assembled to see their new king. Imogen and I were given a place in the front of rows of hundreds of people, who all arrived while singing what appeared to be an anthem for Belland.

Imogen slipped her hand into mine. "How do you feel about this?"

"Darius will be a great king here," I replied. "But I will miss him."

"He's alive, Jaron." Imogen kissed my cheek. "And somehow, so are you."

With the setting of the sun, another moon would rise. It would be smaller than last night's moon, at a degree's difference in angle, and it would no longer be a reason to hold any people in captivity. Tonight, it would simply be something beautiful.

As soon as the sun dipped below the horizon, Trea stepped onto the platform. In words that sounded well practiced, she said, "Darius Hadranius Eckbert has lived among you for almost two years. He has worked at your side, fought at your side, and most recently, triumphed at your side. Welcome him now."

Enthusiastic applause thundered around us as Darius climbed the steps to the platform. A long purple robe hung from his shoulders, trailing behind him as he entered the platform stage. He smiled and waved at the people, earning himself even more applause.

His sword was at his waist, and Trea said, "By authority given to me —"

"Stop!" With a kind smile, Darius leaned forward and whispered something in her ear. She immediately set down the crown and pillow, then exited down the back of the stage.

"What's wrong?" Imogen asked.

I didn't know. He didn't look upset or uncertain, but he clearly was waiting for something.

A moment later, Trea touched my shoulder. "He wants it to be you."

I stared at her, sure I could not have heard her correctly. "Me?"

I looked up at Darius, who had his eye on me. He smiled and motioned with his head that I should join him on the platform.

"Hurry, everyone's waiting!" Imogen pushed me along with Trea, who walked me around the rear of the platform.

"It should be you." Trea spoke as proudly as any mother would in such a moment. "Go and make your brother a king."

I walked up the platform, unsure of how to greet a people who were not my own. I didn't know if they'd respect anything

I said up here, or if they'd even listen. It seemed more fitting to have another Bellander do this.

I stood beside Darius and the crowd went silent. I looked first to Imogen, silently vowing yet again to one day fully deserve her. From here, I scanned the crowd, seeing rows of faces that had been through far too much over the past month, faces that had lost hope once and then had it returned to them again. Faces that had a future now, and Darius to lead them.

"People of the great country of Belland," I said, hoping my voice would carry to the farthest rows, "this is a glorious day for us all! Today you celebrate your freedom, and a new beginning. For these new ambitions, you have a king who will serve you, and make possible what you had only dreamed of in the past."

I glanced at Darius. "But this new king is also my older brother. He was always the one to pick me up when I fell, to warn me of dangers I had not yet discovered, to teach me the wisdom I had yet to learn for myself. All my life, I thought if I could only be more like him, then I would somehow find the best in myself. All my life I have fallen short of that goal, and yet he believed in me anyway, and gave me hope of being a better person tomorrow. He will do the same for you. Tomorrow will come, and when it does, Belland will always have a friend in Carthya across the sea."

I paused to look at my brother. "Kneel, Darius."

He did and lowered his head. Using his sword, I tapped him on the right shoulder, then the left. "Darius Hadranius Eckbert, you were born to be a prince, but you will live forevermore as a king." I held his sword flat on my hands to return it to him, and once he took it, I picked up the crown from its pillow and placed it on Darius's bowed head, then announced, "Rise, Darius, king of Belland."

Darius stood to even more enthusiastic applause than before. He smiled and waved to his people as they fell to their knees. Then he lifted his arms, inviting them to stand again and to be silent.

I stepped back. These would be his first words to Belland as their king, and I had no interest in being in his way. So I lowered my head, as he had done before, and stepped to the far corner of the platform as he spoke.

"We have just come through a difficult time," he said. "And perhaps other hard times will come, but we will greet them with new eyes. For we have learned so much . . ." His voice seemed to choke. ". . . *I* have learned so much in these past few days. If we have any hope for a future, if there is a tomorrow and we greet it as a free people, then it is only for one reason. My people, I am your king, but today, I ask you to kneel to my brother, my hero, and to *my* king. Hail Jaron Artolius Eckbert, the Ascendant King of Carthya. Hail his new title in our lands, Giver of Freedom."

Darius turned back to me with his hand outstretched, inviting me forward. I shook my head at him, but he gestured again for me to join him at the front of the platform.

As I did, he went to one knee, something I barely could comprehend. One by one, each row of onlookers followed his lead. Their heads were not bowed, as they had been for Darius. Instead, they looked up at me with smiling faces, hopeful faces. From somewhere in the crowd, someone began to sing. Soon, every person as far as I could see was singing.

Darius stood again and slung an arm over my shoulder. "You know this song."

I did. Carthya's anthem had not been sung since our parents were alive. In their absence, I had never wanted to hear it. But I did now. I'd forgotten how beautiful the song was.

I turned to Darius with a broad smile. "It's time for me to go home."

He embraced me and whispered into my ear. "If you should ever need me —"

"I always will need you," I replied.

He pulled back, his entire face lit with happiness. "Then I will come."

"And I will never be far away."

I gave him one last embrace and offered a final wave to the people. With Imogen at my side, we boarded the *Shadow Tide*, the last ship in the harbor.

Teagut was waiting for me on the main deck. I shook his hand, and he gestured toward the captain's office. "The pirate king should get that room."

With a mischievous grin, Roden tried to push past me. "Hear that? I'm taking the captain's quarters."

I raised my new sword, blocking the doorway long enough to glance back at him. "Not a chance. Let me know when we're home. Until then, I'll be asleep."

Yet, even as exhausted as I was, I barely slept that night. I could not sleep, not for the emotions swirling within me. Finally, I had no choice but to get up and return to the captain's desk. I opened the lower drawer and pulled out a black satin bag, then set it on the desktop.

I stared at it for several minutes before finally withdrawing the Devil's Scope. The last time Roden had seen it was on the beach when Darius sacrificed it for Amarinda's life. But Wilta had still had it in a pocket of her long coat after I returned to the overlook with the pirates. When I tried to stop her from lowering her arm, my other hand easily transferred the scope from her pocket into mine. She must have forgotten it was there after I began exploding her ships.

The first two lenses were still in their slots, but without the third lens, the scope was useless.

I reached behind me to my belt, where the metal pin used to be. The third lens had easily fit into that gap, though it had nearly gotten me killed to put it in there rather than try to swim away from the rock walls of the lava tube. I still wondered if it was a mistake to have saved it.

By now, surely Wilta and her mother had realized the Devil's Scope was gone. If they were coming back to look for it, we'd have seen them already.

But they hadn't come back.

They would go forward, likely for revenge. For utter destruction.

They were on their way to Carthya.

With that in mind, I inserted the third lens into its slot, raised it to my eye, and aimed it toward the candlelight.

And couldn't help but smile.

· ACKNOWLEDGMENTS ·

*When fans of the Ascendance series asked whether I'd
ever do a fourth book, my answer was, "Yes, if Sage
ever returns to my imagination." Then one day, he did,
letting me know, as only Sage could, that he was bored
and ready for more trouble. I loved diving
back into his world and his mind, and to associate
again with the people he loves most.*

*But that would never have been possible without the
incredible support of several people around me. When
I presented sample chapters to my agent, Ammi-Joan
Paquette, after so many years since the third book of
the series, I genuinely had no idea what she would
think. Her response was immediate and enthusiastic,
greater than I had hoped for.*

Scholastic was equally enthusiastic, especially my editor,
Lisa Sandell, who has been wonderful beyond measure.
I am forever indebted to these two women.

I am always grateful to my family for their love and
encouragement, especially my husband and best friend,
Jeff. I could not do any of this without them.

And more than with any other book I've written,
I have the fans to thank. For every letter, email, or
personal contact expressing love for the series and a
wish for it to continue, you kept Sage fresh in my
mind until the day he was ready to return. This
book exists because of you.

· ABOUT THE AUTHOR ·

JENNIFER A. NIELSEN is the critically acclaimed author of the *New York Times* and *USA Today* bestselling Ascendance Series: *The False Prince*, *The Runaway King*, *The Shadow Throne*, and *The Captive Kingdom*. She also wrote the *New York Times* bestseller *The Traitor's Game* and its sequels, *The Deceiver's Heart* and *The Warrior's Curse*; the *New York Times* bestselling Mark of the Thief trilogy: *Mark of the Thief*, *Rise of the Wolf*, and *Wrath of the Storm*; the stand-alone fantasy *The Scourge*; and the critically acclaimed historical novels *Resistance*, *Words on Fire*, and *A Night Divided*.

Jennifer collects old books, loves good theater, and thinks that a quiet afternoon in the mountains makes for a nearly perfect moment. She lives in northern Utah with her family. You can visit her online at jennielsen.com or follow her on Twitter at @nielsenwriter.